＊KILLING GILDA＊

Killing Gilda
Copyright © 2024 by Yahya Gharagozlou

All rights reserved under the Pan-American and International Copyright Conventions. This book may not be reproduced in whole or in part, except for brief quotations embodied in critical articles or reviews, in any form or by any means, electronic or mechanical, including photocopying, recording, or by any information storage and retrieval system now known or hereinafter invented, without written permission of the publisher.

Library of Congress Control Number: 2024944077

ISBN (paperback): 978-1-963271-40-9
ISBN (ebook): 978-1-963271-39-3

Armin Lear Press, Inc.
215 W Riverside Drive, #4362
Estes Park, CO 80517

KILLING GILDA

Yahya Gharagozlou

ARMINLEAR

To My Wife, Two Daughters, and Brother.

I also want to thank Maryanne Karinch my publisher for her full support and guidance, Judith Bailey my editor for her subtle corrections, and all the discerning readers especially Ali Rahnema, Parinaz Eleish, Taghi Gharagozlou, Soad Koushehi, Nicole Fegan, and Nader Ahari.

CONTENTS

PRELIMINARIES	3
SUBRISIO SALTAT—SMILE OF THE ACROBAT	5
1. 2023: What Was the Name of the Nursing Home	7
2. 1965: Assassins Up the Wazoo – The Lede	13
3. 1979-2023: Second-Life First	15
WHO KILLED MADEMOISELLE G.?	21
1. 1975: A Date with a Beautiful Body	23
2. 2023: I Fume Without a Cigarette	33
QUIETUS RELEASE FROM LIFE	37
1. 1971: The Teenage Beauty Makes Her Entrance	39
2. 2023: Daughter Speaks	43
3. 1947: Mum Powders Herself	47
THE JESTER	51
1. 1965: We Slide Up the Slippery Slope with Fair Winds at Our Back	53
2. 1965: Details of Thirty-Four Bullets	57
3. 1965: Choose Your King and Lie with Him	61
4. 1969: Junk Gets Reported	65
FIRST THINGS FIRST	73
1. 1975: Listen! I Hear the Court Jester's Cap and Bells. The King is Coming!	75
2. 1975: I Exchange My Motley for a Deerstalker Hat	79

Life Unfolds 83

    1. 1949: School Bends to a Kid's Will   85
    2. 1949: Tennis Under a Glaring Sun   89
    3. 1953: Uncle Fits a Snaffle Bit and Takes Over My Bridle   93
    4. 1975: Spiro Agnew Sings *That's Life*   97
    5. 1963: Compromised Youth   103

Did you Read This in a Newspaper? 111

    1. 2023: It Was Like This, Mrs. Lambton of Framingham   113
    2. 1965 On-the-Job Training   121

Clueless 127

    1. 1975: Amateur Hour with a Breast-Biter   129
    2. 1975: The Bad Guy Makes an Entrance   133

Nless, Opium, and Gifts 137

    1. 1972: Prince Pimp and the Blinking Swiss   139
    2. 1972: The Bad Guy with an Opium Outlook   147
    3. 1972: Success with the Swiss and Miss Lehmann with Two Ns   153

It Begins 157

    1. 1973: A Guide to Bedrooms   159
    2. 1973: Walk in the Palace Gardens with Friends   167

In June, Ice Melts in Paris 173

    1. 1973: The Lambton Affair   175
    2. 1973: A Thawing Doesn't Melt the Steel Edge   181
    3. 1973: The Paris of Madame Claude   187

Sight, Seeing, the Queen of Senses 193
    1. 1973: Plastic Germany 195
    2. 1973: Hospitals at the Beck and Call of the Rich 199
    3. 1973: Performance by the Narrator with a
        Recuperating Dulcinea 201
    4. 1973: Cigarettes, Regrets, and Deafness to Reality . . . 211
    5. 1973: The Nose Gets Tweaked 215

The Reckoning 219
    1. 1975: An Islamist Marxist Has My Daughter 221
    2. 1975: Sam & Belle Reach an Agreement 225
    3. 1975: It's Her 229
    4. 2023: Questions of Choice 231

The Short Goodbye 235
    1. 1973: The Lèse-Majesté of a Mistress 237
    2. 1973: The Smooth Transition 241

Bad Deeds Go Unpunished 243
    1. 1975: The Ripe Empire Requires an Amateur Detective 245
    2. 1975: An Opium Addict Needs No Torture 255

Earning an Ending 265
    1. 1987: The Beginning of the End 267
    2. 1978: Lost a Mother, Gained a Daughter 271
    3. 1980 The End is Near 277

Afterward 1943: An Embarrassing Nakedness
. . . . 285
An Author's Note J'adoube 289
About the Author 315

"I recall a story of an old actor asked to portray an old man, who said with dismay, 'But I've never played an old man!' That was professionalism."

Iris Murdoch, Novelist and Philosopher

PRELIMINARIES

"Many stories require confusion in the reader, and the most effective way to achieve it is to use an observer who is himself confused."

Wayne C. Booth, Literary Critic

Not all the names, characters, businesses, places, events, and incidents in this book are the product of the author's imagination. Any resemblance to actual persons, living or dead, or events is not coincidental but vague. The impurity of coincidence gives me latitude.

The central character in the book, G., exists. I use Gee with a dot (always pronounced in my head as "Gilda") not to introduce mystery or discreet chivalry, an old novelistic practice, but as a convenience to separate the protagonist of my story and the woman who appears in the epilogue. My G. and the Gilda of the Court of Mohammad Reza Shah Pahlavi, who was known as Tala (Gold) for her blonde hair, share traces. Small changes early in our journey end their voyages in different destinations.

I didn't know the Gilda who walked on Earth except through a few articles with a bold 72-point agenda. Fiction writers relish the lack of information. G. and Gilda each became mistress to their respective Shah - the Shah who walked the Earth from 1919 to 1980 and the one I imagined.

SUBRISIO SALTAT—SMILE OF THE ACROBAT

1. 2023: What Was the Name of the Nursing Home

"Who killed G.?" I wake up with a start at 4:00 a.m. from the press of the bullet, bed straight-backed, supported by half a dozen pillows—another lousy night. My melted buttocks aggravate the problem. My eyes open calmly, unsleepy, alert. I give the impression I never sleep. A streak of red crosses my window like an artist's paintbrush. It's the sun's early work. I hear the drone of Route 9, far off, as though through acoustic binoculars.

Pain has an upside: It comes with short-term lucidity. It works like a pencil sharpener. Whets the brain. I start the touristic hopscotch. Memory and perception intermingle. Not an older man's failings yet, though I admit I can no longer control my recall at will. The magical butterfly that once flew from flower to flower, gathering the good things in life and reporting back its findings, now flies with clipped wings. Now, it's more like flower to no flower.

I know the stages of dementia. My doctor tells me I have graduated from the onset of dementia to early dementia. In early dementia, a few pieces of the puzzle might not fit, but you can still make out the complete picture. I will graduate to full dementia when I forget I have it. I don't expect the approach of the all-engulfing blank for some time. I don't sit in a prison where the executioner comes early; I don't have to write this all down in one night.

I see myself in bed, the unshaved white stubble of my face reflected in the square mirror like a hotel room TV. It is not a vanity mirror but set to a government-sanctioned height for wheelchair use. Above it, to the right, is the cyclops of a TV, which stares down from the tri-corner of the two walls and ceiling. "How a man of eighty feels is not a topic for conversation," said Freud. I look like an overripe banana: dark yellow with black blotches. The mirror reminds me to keep my mouth shut to hide an older man's hollow black gape, a permanent mid-yawn. It presages the end, an aesthetic shared in retirement homes. We suffer the indignity of vanity until our last breath. Daudet looked at a mirror and wrote, "What emaciation! I've suddenly turned into a funny little old man." I have turned into an old man who used to be funny.

I inherited my skin's smooth, *chocolate au lait* color from Birjand, on the eastern front of Persia. My nose does not possess the aquiline curve of Arabia but the spread of Africa. At eighty, my *jolie-laide* looks fit unquestionably on the far-right side of the hyphen.

I am a decade past the worn look that settles contentedly on the face. Its purpose is to astonish friends at a reunion. But here there are no witnesses to compare the past. A painful, static present repeats itself daily. As good as unconscious, we slip into a discernable future. I am bored with wasting away.

I scribble with intensity as if my ancestors hover over my shoulder. They do not. Between one dip of a pen and the next, time passes, said Petrarch. I dip into a dark pool. I scribble on Post-it notes and ignore what I don't recognize in my distinct handwriting. Here-and-now loses continuity. Continuity has lost continuity. Questions have to wait. Answers will come in their own time.

I once accused Laurel and Hardy, my caretakers, of planting the Post-it notes to play with me. Their faces were so outraged, I instantly knew who the culprit is. In a way, I enjoy the unannounced descent of these mini parachutes of random thought. It takes me from one neighborhood of my thoughts to another.

I sit in my high-tech bed, for which I paid $4,000 plus $500 for installation in my room. I can articulate my position in space like a weightless astronaut. The manufacturers tout the five degrees of freedom the bed offers. I understand these terms; I wrote technical manuals for thirty years.

Patients pass my room with an air of who-does-he-think-he is. I am about to tell them. The Post-it note is a marvelous innovation with its re-adherable glue strip, which resembles a neat line of never-dry drool. You can pick up half a column and do an analog paste into the middle of another. I use dated Post-it notes to leave myself breadcrumbs of memory as they occur. I build a monument of Post-it notes.

Despite how often the doctors spell out the ravages of Alzheimer's—with far too much detail if you ask me—I find that my rickety memories still exist. It's the just-in-time retrieval mechanism that fails and foils me. To help with this, I write. As I write, memory grows; thoughts thaw. It's less of a problem to remember the old times. Memories rush at me like snowflakes attaching to the windshield of my brain. I grab a flake, and before it melts, I write it down. Whatever comes up randomly, I note and date.

I use Pilot Hi-Tec-C 0.3 inch micro fine, razor point, gel ink pens. If there is any deterioration in the nib, I throw out the pen I've used. If I won the lottery, I would insist on three luxuries at the start of each day: a new Pilot pen, a new stack of Post-it notes, and each morning, my valet must fit a new Gillette Fusion5 razor blade to my happily abuzz and atremble, battery-operated Gillette SkinGuard. I get this luxury once a week when my daughter, Marie, visits. I am *this* close to a rich man's life.

At the start of each day, I arrange the columns of Post-it notes. I have all the colors and sizes. My daughter gave me a faux cherry box with silk velvet cutouts like an assorted tea box. My laptop sits unused. The aged PC needs a new battery, which you can buy on eBay. If I plugged it into the wall, I could use it. I don't.

Didn't mid-twentieth-century writers use index cards to write their books? By the time I drop the end of this knotty yarn, I promise to give it a few hard tugs to make the thread taut. I will put this colorful chain of Post-it notes in order so you can read them. The plot of my life lives in different parts of my head. Details emerge when the thief of my engine connects the red and black wires underneath the dashboard and randomly sparks a thought. The big bang of an idea becomes the gusher. Once I write a header, it works like a memory palace. A strong mnemonic spring, like the tap of a reflex hammer, starts the flow and the anecdote follows until it drips dry. Then I wait again. How could I have missed randomness until this late in life? Connectedness unreeled—the opposite of conspiracy theories.

Each morning, I wait for Laurel or Hardy to Ku Ku me awake. People forget they—the comedian duo Laurel and Hardy—made their name with the Ku Ku song. One of their (I now refer to my keepers) heads pops in halfway down the edge of the steel-lined door like a corporeal puppet show, with stock phrases like "Are we decent? Are we naked?"

"Like the moon in a bowl of piss," I want to reply. Infantile wake-up calls like "wakey, wakey, sleepy head" for us, the old, have a long, disrespectful history. The metal door of my room would have served better as a meat-packing refrigerator. Did they think we would use our wheelchairs to break out of this heavenly place?

My Laurel and Hardy, black men in their thirties, share the physical traits of their doubles, with a few exceptions, one of which I have given away. My Stan Laurel doppelgänger, Malik, has a sizeable rectangular chin with a bend that puts enough pressure on his mouth to make it a prim affair. His eyebrows fight gravity upwards and his pupils cover the upper half of his orbitals. He's prissy to get his duties done but can turn emotional on a dime. He becomes at his Laurelest when he confronts death. "Oh, Mr. Sam, Mrs. Underwood died last night," he will say, tears gathering at the corner of his black eyelids. The entire face moves upwards, like a stretch of an extremity after a long sleep. For Malik, everybody dies comfortably in bed like a gentle breeze putting out a candle. He forgets we hear the stertorous breaths, the rattle of death throes, as medical people call it, on average, twenty-three hours before someone dies. I understand why we have the heavy metallic doors fitted in each room. It keeps the muffled death noises out. Write, and you discover.

Elijah is not as similar to Oliver Hardy as Malik is to Stan. We have to correct for inflation to compare the weights. The actor Hardy would look reedy next to Elijah. Elijah, a symbolic Oliver, walks with a twist of his middle. He could throw a child against the wall were it caught in his tornado of a twist. He walks with a face-wide smile. I imagine he doesn't lose the smile even when asleep. This wallpaper of a smile delights us. If I make him laugh, he loses the smile, covers his mouth with a palm, and titters with curiously feminine delicacy. "Oh, Mr. Sam, you are sumpthin else."

I am sumpthin else. I am a rational man who understands the practicalities of life. I don't need prescription glasses to stare down reality. It's not far off from my endpoint. My king used to call me Le Philosophe Manqué. He had derision and disdain down pat. Mockery no longer interested him. I am also a calculating man. That should conjure up sly, cunning, devious. Conjure away with precision. I wasn't born sly.

Did I mention that, in the early years, His Imperial Majesty loved to watch Laurel and Hardy films and Charlie Chaplin and Jerry Lewis? He and Her Majesty the Queen watched the movies in the basement of the downtown Ekhtessassi Palace, a cramped building. It forced us to move palaces uptown in the late sixties as the four children made their triannual appearances during that happy decade.

Before I forget, they named this assisted living home the bright, optimistic name The Rising Sun. Seriously. It accompanies the even stupider mantra plastered on walls: Eighty is the new sixty. "Old age is the most unexpected of all the things that happen to a man." No shit, Tolstoy.

2. 1965: Assassins Up the Wazoo – The Lede

I buried the lede. A bullet near the opening above my ischium, lodged in the obturator membrane, has kept me company for 20,000 lousy nights since it made its way there on the 10th of April 1965. Let me not be bashful. The bullet I took up my ass was for my king and not my country. The blooming, clover-shaped shell, a frozen smoke ring on the X-ray film, shows four spread petals. Each steel petal ensconced itself in the flesh surrounded by nerve. It made me walk with a slight bent forward like I never climbed the last step on the evolutionary ladder.

Bullets travel a calculated path. They cause incalculable damage. Take the non-fatal shot two years before mine. It entered its target on the 22nd of November, 1963. The Carcano Fucile di Fanteria bullet fired from the sixth floor of the Texas School Book Depository whistled through fifteen layers of clothing, seven layers of epithelium, and a foot of muscle tissue, merrily unknotted a necktie, removed four inches of rib, shattered a radius bone, and didn't come to a stop well buried in a thigh—if you believe in the single bullet theory. The other bullet, Kennedy's headshot, produced what we recognize as a worldwide tragedy.

Eighteen months later, a different bullet, one among many, was fired by a soldier who ran amok with a machine gun in the Marble Palace to assassinate His Imperial Majesty, HIM. It ricocheted from the marble wall in front of the palace to enter my posterior—writ in gaudy, florescent colors: a local comedy to delight the courtiers for years. Reza Shamsabadi, the guard, killed two of his colleagues with the intention of doing away with the monarchy for good. One of the injured guards, who died later during surgery, shot six bullets back. The assassin succumbed to his injuries.

HIM worked from his office on the first floor, first door on the left, for the rest of the day; his work ethic self-evident. That Monday in the afternoon, HIM drove his convertible around the capital for an hour and a half. He commented that no one gets assassinated twice in one day—he forgot Archduke Franz Ferdinand. People recognized him and clapped with enthusiasm. Few had heard of the attempt. He was popular.

The well-known fool, Golet, warned William of Normandy and saved him from would-be assassins. He saw the start of an empire. I took a bullet for my king up the ass and got a jester's seat, the best seat, to watch the fall of the Persian Empire. That is a personal comedy.

3. 1979-2023: Second-Life First

My baba named me Samsam, a traditional family name of the roaming Khans of the plains. My mother descended from the eighth century's Kazem bin Khoseymeh, the general dispatched by Al Mansour, the second Abbasid Caliph, to the province of Khorasan to quell one of the metronomic revolts. The family stayed for a thousand years.

My paternal uncle, a movie buff and an opium addict, shortened it and called me Sam after Dooley Wilson, the piano player in *Casablanca*. The pronunciation resembles "Sum" as in "some" as in give me "some" of your money. My fingers on the piano keyboard surpass my skin's smoothness. I play far better than Dooley. In real life, Dooley played the drums; he fake-played the piano in the movie.

My felicity with the piano comes from my mother, who had little in common with my father. A ferocious man, he distrusted and rejected culture, femininity, softness, modernity, democracy, large cities, and urban people. He disliked the piano, books, electricity, phones, and me, not necessarily in this order. In all his taciturn moodiness, my father could not hide his recoil when he saw me. I don't recall a sustained conversation between my father and me—the presence of servants disguised the embarrassing inattention.

In photos, one finds my father's leathery, sun-beaten face and luxuriously thick, unkempt, peppery facial hair belonged to earlier

Asiatic tribesmen. He lived a simple life as a landowner. Most of the land belonged to my mother.

History sliced my life into a two-chapter book—the older man watches the younger warily but not without sympathy. A revolution works like a director's cut. In my first forty years, I grew up in my benighted country in a cocoon of privilege. In the second forty, I grew old in the land of all possibilities where I am now mothballed—a smell I can attribute to my assisted living home. Two lives lived by two different people. It sounds downright biblical. The older man tells a love story. Words will not come close to what the younger man experienced. A felon commits felonies—there's no word for someone who commits misdemeanors. I am not practicing the confessional genre, yet my life had moments of can't-look-in-the-mirror shame and sleep-in-a-bed-of-thistles of guilt. From the ammonia-smelling haze of my surroundings, I reflect and can, with no effort, forgive the jejune and prankish deeds of my first forty years. Compared to today's standards, I am a committer of serial misdemeanors.

Betrayal, though, does not fall within a legal purview. No amount of bleach can cleanse my traitor's heart. Someone said "old age" is a sentence for a crime you haven't committed. Inaccurate: It only refers to physical deterioration. Regret, the Easter egg of old age, hatches and metes out exquisite punishments for a life led as a coat-changing exercise.

In my second life, I lived a quiet, middle-class American existence, observing a world in transition. I spent my forties with an immigrant's fou energy: At nights, I bartended, piano-played, and schooled. The days I spent dazed with my daughter while my wife worked. Then came my anxious fifties: wife, daughter, financial worries, office work as a technical writer. Happy sixties: more wife, more daughter, more manuals. Flinty, hard seventies: My wife died. Stealthy arthritis crept in and crippled me. I will not survive far into my eighties.

What makes a revolution a revolution is the odd bedfellows. I escaped it by tiny coincidences. It was 1979. The brother-in-law of a tennis ball boy at the Imperial Club heard a rumor that my family name had been entered onto a list. The ball boy, recipient of negligible generosities, sat in the lobby of my apartment for hours to warn me that the authorities, who were not yet authorities, would descend on our apartment in hours. The Swiss Embassy helped to transport my wife, a Swiss national, and our family with a few hours to spare.

Fresh off a 747, with my unkempt tail between my legs, we arrived jetlagged on a cold, misty morning at the space-age, ring-shaped Charles de Gaulle airport. In her soigne accent, the womanly voice over the loudspeaker softly beckoned passengers toward their gates. I loved that voice. The Charles de Gaulle airport is the closest we will get to Kubrick's vision of 2001, which came and went without a stone of knowledge on the horizon.

The glass tunnels from one floor to another had five-year-old Marie agog. She ate her first warm croissant in the arms of my mother, who lived in Paris and came to pick us up. My mother, now thin like her mother, had the makeup of someone not ready for her close-up. Clouds with an eggshell smoothness filled the sky outside. It looked like a permanent Paris fixture. My mother, not calibrated to her financial reality, hired a car to take us—all anxious about living together after so many years—to 16 Avenue Paul Doumer, her two-bedroom once *pied-à-terre* now refugee apartment. Mamdou, the East African servant, slept in the alcove with the stacked washer and dryer machines next to the kitchen. Sixty-year-old Marte, with the complete fetishistic frilly getup of a French maid, lived in the attached *chambre de bonne* across on the roof.

I showed more energy during those months in Paris than most exiled colleagues. Younger than most, I also had a wife and daughter. I wrote my CV on both sides of the smooth, thick, cream-colored paper—English on one side, French on the other. Nice classy touch, I thought. I used bullets, semicolons, and colons to connect or disconnect my skill set. I sought ceremonial ministerial positions in Middle Eastern or African dictatorships. A few months in, I obligingly relaxed my high standards for the burgeoning oligarch class. I described my experience as understanding complex, courtly etiquette with nothing-beneath-me service, including the smooth, legal delivery of human flesh. Semicolon. I double-lined and underscored legal age. Semicolon. I advertised myself as a gentleman's pimp, which is technically what I was.

I further underscored my ability to design ingenious intrigues to further my employer's interests while exposing all treacherous plots against my employer. Colon. Bullet. Adept at burying the handle deep in any back, yet top-down loyal. Bullet. Adaptable to all styles, I can give smooth, undetectable praise designed to boost the ego without a shade of condescension. Semicolon. Or tell harsh truths but never, I mean *never*, forget my place. I will move anywhere in the world save for failed states. Bold, centered.

The lack of opportunities suited to my credentials should have warned me of the approaching barbaric times. There were fewer and fewer powerful royals left, and those with pretensions ruled failed states. Russian oligarchs and Chinese billionaires didn't yet exist in the late seventies. Arab Sheikhs showed little respect for tradition or *savoir-faire*. They didn't know they didn't know.

The state of the world made me search for a particular autocrat who looks oh-so reasonable today. Let me even say agreeable: agreeable to deal with and agreeable to live with. Someone with whom I shared at least some values. Even if the ends might not have justified the means, that kind of relationship followed a Western philosophy that demanded rationality of purpose.

Today, I concede my father's cousin, the court minister, had been right. We lacked the *je ne sais quoi* of ruthlessness. Akhmatova commented under Khrushchev that power had become vegetarian. We were sober vegans.

What am I getting at? Now we live in ruthless times where the means have no end in sight or imagination. Ruthlessness used to be a practice to teach a lesson to others. We have turned ruthlessness into a tradition or a way of living—ruthlessness for the sake of ruthlessness. Our wave of Eastern philosophy ricocheted from the walls of ignorance to flood and short-circuit my beloved age of enlightenment. Le Philosophe Manqué pontificates.

We arrived in Boston a month into my forties. Boston because a year in Paris saw me leave our savings on the tables of Fouquet's, Deux Maggot, and other hangouts for the exiled rich. Because I skolled and downed one too many pear schnapps glasses to our delusional reunion in Tehran: *À bientôt!* Because I spent a year looking for jobs with an unwanted resume. Because my mother lacked funds and died in Paris, leaving me the last month's rent to pay. Boston because my Swiss wife found a job at the Swiss consulate. Because we wanted our daughter to grow up in what we still referred to it as the New World. But most of all, because only after the deaths of my mother, the Court Minister, and HIM did my lived life surface for my serious consideration.

I want to reconcile my intricate toils in a Persian Empire court with 2500 years of history with my transformation into a technical manual writer for small tech companies that dot the borders of Route 128. To write manuals, I needed a singular focus. I freelanced without a compromised soul.

My love story does not spill into my second life. I don't confuse my love for my late wife and living daughter with my all-surface love for *her*. As this second person, I carry an embalmed, mummified memory. I am unwrapping it into thin strips of hieroglyphic-filled linen to put it to rest before I go to mine.

WHO KILLED MADEMOISELLE G.?

1. 1975: A Date with a Beautiful Body

I wake up to a call from General Nassiri, head of SAVAK, the Iranian intelligence agency. I switch on the light to look at the clock: 3:00 a.m. "You remember the discussion I had with your uncle last week?" he says like we have been conversing for the past ten minutes.

I croak that I remember, my thoughts sputtering with the purling imprecision of a dullard. My wife Annabelle lifts and twists her head to inquire about the interlocutor. I cover the handset and mouth Nassiri's name.

"Well, it solved itself," Nassiri says. I must have sent an invisible question mark through the hiss of the imperfect 1975 telephone lines. "I can't talk on the phone." He reads me an address in Dezashib near the Tajreesh district where I live. "Drive discreetly to the street. Ring the bell three times." I hang up. Annabelle groans about the horrible man on the phone, makes a sign of vomit, and promptly returns to sleep.

The address belongs to G.'s house, bought for her by General Khatami, the Imperial Iranian Air Force commander. He died in a kite accident a few months before at the Dez Dam. The Court worked hard to stamp out the gossip of foul play. I remember the lunch. The two doctors, Ayadi and Professor Adl, left the lunch table. They returned to let HIM know Khatami instantly died when he crashed his glider into the rocks. HIM went chalk white. You can't act chalk white.

As instructed, I ring the F.F. door's plastic answering panel three times. I blow into my fists and stamp my feet as I wait in the unexpectedly teeth-chattering cold of a November night. An oatmeal-colored cloud sits like tonsure on top of the city, a red open sky around its periphery. The door buzzes out of spite. The lock clicks the door open. I walk in through the small metal door, inset in the corner of the larger garage door. I climb the stairs next to a white parked car into a plateau of a backyard with a dark pool in the center: a typical middle-class home, a run-of-the-mill two-story Tehran villa built with Travertine stone tiles. Darkness cloaks the house except for the second-story corner room, which shines a square of enthusiastic light onto the yard. On the other side of the pool, two bulky men with flashlights walk about like shadows around what looks like masonry material under a burlap fabric. A third man approaches me and places his index finger vertically to his nose, in the universal sign to let me know he wants me quiet. I know him since my time at SAVAK. Captain Nader Yasin worked with me in intelligence gathering. We give each other a friendly smile. I follow him up to the second floor.

In the living room—with its clean, modern look of an American apartment and contemporary light furniture—I find Nassiri. He sits in a curved armchair. I know him well. I set his weekly appointment with HIM. For thirty minutes, he reports the latest intelligence.

He has hooded eyes and a weak mouth. His underlip hides beneath his upper lip. He suits the role. When he wears his light grey military uniform, he looks like a French collaborator in the

Vichy government. He resembles the famous comic French actor Bourvil without the humorous eyes. He attended military school with the then Crown Prince. So many of them did.

He wears a somber pinstriped suit with a grey tie; the long collar of his shirt hides the knot. The trousers look baggy on him. Did we all wear those loose-legged trousers that broke like a theater curtain on our shoes?

He watches me patiently, the crescent under his eyes faint purple, as if on the mend from a week-old boxing match. His head rests on the palm of his hand, the elbow on the curved blonde wood of the chair, a modern rocker chair. Like a kid, he enjoys his hobby horse. Nader stands by the stairs.

"Do you know where you are?" he asks. I shrug in vague ignorance. Never admit, never deny, avoid verbal responses: an Intelligence rule. "You sit in Mutmuzell G.'s living room." He pronounces mademoiselle with a Persian accent to sound sarcastic. "You passed her remains downstairs, under the bag."

I ask, "Who killed Mademoiselle G.?" I emphasize the French accent.

He watches me with a tired, now impatient stare. "Who said killed? But irrelevant," he says. "My men have kept watch since your uncle informed us of her activities. The two fellows downstairs have hung around for the last week. They are from the operational side of the Intelligence. Let me call one of them up here to report." He makes a signal to Nader. Nader doesn't call his colleague. He walks silently downstairs.

"What are we so quiet about?" I ask.

"A neighbor heard her scream. We rushed in to quiet her down. She might eavesdrop. In another hour, the judiciary will take over. I wanted to give you time to get control of the situation. If we don't handle this just so, it will blow up in our faces."

I understand. The end of the string lies downstairs, tied to G.'s body. You pull on it, and General Khatami rises from the dead. You pull on him, and the Court wakes up. You ferret in the Court, and people will remember her name from a couple of years back. The country gets interested. The Shah gets implicated. In this way, day in and day out, I understand why I exist on Earth.

The sun makes its presence known but is not yet visible. A dull light shows in the east. It filters through the window in the back of us. You can see Mount Damavand, with its perennial white bodice and grey skirt, our North Star, when lost in Tehran's streets. I hear dogs bark in the distance. General Nassiri rocks the chair with a small boy's insistence. In walks a man with a brutalist face of about forty, with smooth, cleanly shaven dark skin. We Persians have good skin. He wears bellbottom jeans, no belt, and a black sports shirt tucked in. The collar competes with an elephant's ears. The upper, crimson-red rectangle of a packet of Dunhill's shows from the waist of the tight jeans. He wears large dark red glasses with an orange tint. The windows behind reflect on the lenses in small, shaky squares of white light. I cannot make out his eyes. He's dressed a tad young for forty but could pass anywhere in Tehran—well disguised.

"Captain, please repeat your report." The Captain looks uncomfortable, reluctant to reveal information to a private individual. He introduces himself as Yazdani in section two. Nassiri points at me. "He is one of us, or was one of us," he says. I take this as an insult. The SAVAK of the early sixties had nothing in common with Nassiri's SAVAK. Yazdani speaks fluently with no verbal ticks. He drops English words like "operational section" and "Information Research Department" with a perfect accent.

"Last week, on orders from the General, we established three groups from the operational section to conduct a twenty-four-hour watch on this villa and its occupant. We saw little activity. The occupant received a family member four nights ago for dinner." Nassiri turns to me. "You see, I jumped immediately after your uncle asked me to investigate." He points to me again. "Mr. Sam works in the Darbar."

"How do you know it was family?" I ask the Captain.

"I know General A., the lady's father, by sight," the Captain says. "Otherwise, the occupant stays to herself. She drinks alcohol after five, never before. She smokes opium and hashish daily. She also uses cocaine." The Captain points to his right at the glass dining room, where a small peak with an uncanny resemblance to our Damavand vista sits ready for consumption.

"To her neighbor's dismay, she blasts music in the middle of the night. A few hours ago, she walked drunkenly on the balcony. She lifted her drink." The Captain looks awkward and sheepish. "She drank to our health." I raise an eyebrow. "She recognized our presence. She drank three times and saluted us. She shouted, 'Be Salamati, to the health of the Shah and SAVAK.' We didn't deem a drink to HIM's health a crime. We backed off to watch the house less obtrusively."

He looks at his shoes with even more hesitation and embarrassment. "One hour later, at 12:54 a.m., we heard a quick scream followed by a thud." The Captain hollows one hand and claps to produce a convincing imitation of a body striking the tiles near the pool. "As we approached the house cautiously, Captain Bokhara," he refers to his colleague with a nod to the outside, "saw the neighbor turn the lights on. He rang the bell of the neighbor's house while I picked the lock on this house and ran in."

"Fast thinking," the General approves. The Captain doesn't acknowledge the compliment. He continues, "Bokhara introduces himself as an official and asks the neighbor to return to her house. He promises to be back to get their information in the morning. The neighbor wants to lodge an official complaint." My eyebrows make another diacritic circumflex. He explains, "The neighbor thought Bokhara, I mean Captain Bokhara, investigated previous complaints against the Miss making a racket at night." He smiles. "I tend to the body right away and try to resuscitate her. She died on impact—a massive head injury." He rubs the back of his head circularly.

I ask the General for a tour of the house. My old colleague, now Nassiri's adjutant, looks at his watch. "It's late. The cook arrives at 6:30, the maid at 7:30." Nassiri agrees to a quick tour. I search the desk and the shelves. In the bedroom, Nader and I look under the mattress. He lifts with a heave. I see parallel boards making the frame of the bed. He tells me he has searched, but we do it again. He does it without a complaint. I open her closet. The smell of her perfume knocks me over. Downstairs, the kitchen has a small square hole in the wall and a heavy corrugated glass door to the back. I ask where this goes. The Captain says he has not yet investigated. I open the door and enter an even smaller courtyard than the kitchen. Another narrow door stands at the back with access to an alley. I open the door and, without stepping out, look left and right. The alley is narrow. The joub, the gutter, runs through the middle with trickles of water. "Captain," I say, "you realize the alley runs parallel to the main front street with no other cross-alley connecting this one to the main street?"

Nassiri stands behind us. He understands my import, as does Captain Yasin. The surveillance was a joke. People could come and go at will. "Please take us to the girl," I say.

"I have seen the body," Nassiri says. "I will go upstairs. I saw a Johnnie Walker bottle." He trudges off. Nader takes me outside. The clouds have moved to the east. The light has a white stone quality now. He takes the burlap off with respect. She lies on her side, the blood under her head already clotted dark brown. Otherwise, she sleeps, one arm across the other. The light petrifies her for eternity. I think, *What better way to preserve beauty? To die young, not go through the humiliation of aging.* Then I think, *What a stupid thought.*

"I know her. I mean, I knew her," I say. "Give me a moment alone."

I kneel next to her. She wears a light blue summer dress all scrunched up above her knee. I straighten it. She also wears the ring. I gently take it off. I stroke her face, cold and resistant to a caress. I feel under her chin the small scar of her surgery. Here lies a young girl who sat on the fence in the Niavaran Palace two years ago. She sucked on a sour bonbon and made childlike grimaces while she dangled her sandal-shod left foot back and forth.

Her lips have an unnatural green hue. I can see some traces of white powder on her left nostril, but a trickle of clotted blood has mixed with any other trace. I wipe with my pinky a couple of grains of white powder from the right side where her upper lip curves on her lower lip. I put my small finger in my mouth. I spit it out. I know the bitter taste of cocaine. This powder tastes sweet;

it isn't cocaine. *And how can there be any trace of a powder on her lips if the Captain performed first aid resuscitation?* I walk back to the living room.

A red semicircle of the sun graces us with its presence. The room looks like a furnace. The objects melt into shapeless geometries. Nassiri has a drink in hand. His scotch looks like a red sherbet. He offers me a glass. I pass. I come down on him. "General, we have a disaster on our hands."

"Don't exaggerate, my boy," he says. "We can take care of all this."

"General, the surveillance was amateurish. A drunk twenty-two-year-old recognizes your agents, screams, and drinks to the Shah and your institution's health. Worse, unaware the back door opens to an alley, your agents did a week of surveillance while people could go in and out. Any foul play will be impossible to determine."

"Teenage girls commit suicide daily in this town. What foul play?"

"General, you claim no foul play. Will the papers, will the Court think so? You understand, don't you? I saw the corpse. The white powder on her lips and the green color of the lips point to possible foul play. We can't have rumors."

"My guys tell me she did cocaine even during the daytime," he says.

I educate him. "Cocaine would ring her nostrils, not her lips, and it doesn't taste sweet." I pause. "Did you find any connection to HIM?"

"Nothing," he says.

I show him the ring. "I need to take this back." He nods.

"Here is what we need to do. Her death will come out. There will be a one-inch column in the paper. Give me a few hours to do my work. Do your bit. Please don't overuse your propaganda. Less is more here. Caesar's wife must be above suspicion, but no need to publicize her virginity." I look up at Nader. He nods. "Can I ask you to have a third party inform the family she committed suicide? No one from the Court or SAVAK. Don't fret about the family. I know them. They understand consequences."

The General, with three kids, shakes his head. "What father does this to his daughter?" A rhetorical from the head of SAVAK. I am in no mood for irony. I let it pass.

"Please make sure the family understands there is to be no fanfare with the mourning. Write your report to the Shah first thing in the morning. No need to mention any discrepancies. In a few hours, I will talk to HIM and my uncle. I will mention the bare facts." He lifts the glass to me as a token of appreciation. "She gets buried following Islamic precepts. Have the family bury her in the next 24 hours."

Captain Yasin's head appears above the stair railings. "You gentlemen can no longer be here. I have invited a friend from the local police station to take over." We descend the stairs. As we leave the house, the Captain lifts the burlap again. G.'s body reconstitutes the scene in its original, undisturbed arrangement. I am sure one of the captains will remember to clean the General's whiskey glass. She looks like a broken mannequin with hands and arms at strange angles. We descend the stairs. Nassiri steps out into the street. His silly mafia suit billows. His trousers flap as he walks. I follow. We walk to the end of the road where his car awaits him, away from curious eyes. Nader takes a moment to hang behind as the General strides toward the car. He whispers, "Call me." I nod my head.

I see Nassiri from my bed in Massachusetts. I remember him days after the fall of the Shah. He talks to a kangaroo tribunal in 1979. He wears a bandaged head like he wears a hat made of gauze. The Islamic Republic shoots him without due process, and there is no one to intercede.

He is no longer in the shadows. They photograph his body and print it in newspapers for the world to see. He dies a less painful death than General Rahimi, lying next to him in the official photos. When he hears the name of the Shah, right before his execution, Rahimi, deputy commander of the Imperial Guard, gives a worthy, stiff military salute. They cut his arm off for the salute and then shoot him dead.

Today, in downtown Tehran, stands the Ebrat Museum—the Edification Museum, though a better translation would be the Judgment Museum. You can see Nassiri's statue. It sits in a limousine surrounded by his alleged victims—a poignant propaganda piece. The General would have approved.

2. 2023: I Fume Without a Cigarette

I sit in bed and fume. Sheets of hard rain wash my widow. Dissatisfied with the results, they repeat the washing throughout the day. I scratch my scalp with a commitment akin to monkeys grooming each other for lice. It itches, like ants running all over my head, from an intermittent thyroid problem. My thoughts are viscous and thick, in need of a good rinse. I fume at the victory of ignorance and superstition. I fume at the population. I fume at the exaggerated hypocritical foreign press coverage we battled daily. I once had an interview with an American reporter. The self-righteous son of a conglomerate CEO wrote about the luxury of the Niavaran Palace, completed a few years after I joined the Court. I asked him to add a picture to his column. He asked why. I told him people would recognize it as a modest home in Hollywood. The Western press damaged us irreparably. They denounced our lives of luxury when many in the country lived in poverty. It reeked of double standards. I lie in bed here at this third-rate assisted living home in Massachusetts. I still cannot fathom why a man-made geographical border exempts rich people from moral responsibility.

I fume as I watch coverage of Trump's stolen documents. The reporter stands in front of the Mar-a-Lago Club, built a hundred years ago and now a hideous, tasteless, gold-leafed 124-room golf club. Trump added an extra skin of gold leaf vulgarity for $7 million. The press smirks at the poor taste. You never get the camera cut to a hungry Appalachian community. We dealt with unconnected cuts daily.

I am being unfair. I should revise my rating of the Rising Sun, my assisted living home in Framingham, Massachusetts. Let's call it a second-rate nursing home. If you compare it to nursing homes in other states of the country, it could even have pretensions of creeping up to the bottom of the first-rate list. Nursing homes are always in danger of relegation, similar to the Premier League. I watch both diligently. Yesterday I plugged in my battery-dead portable with difficulty and emailed the management a few paragraphs of our agreement when they announced we must pay for the sports channels.

I chose assisted living after my diagnosis. I did a fair due diligence on the Rising Sun. I reverse-mortgaged my home on advice from Tom Selleck, a joke. Adding my Social Security, 401K, and modest savings, I came out even. I ignored marketing nonsense like bistro-style meals in the Reverie Café, a hole in the wall subcontracted to a large woman from Revere with a mouth on her that would make Joe Pesci blush. She serves mostly cheese melts and coffee she buys from Dunkin' in the morning. We all support the tai chi instructor, a pre-med college girl. We cover for her fleeting presence.

I checked one promotional bullet thoroughly: It said each suite offered individual temperature control. Before I moved in, my daughter Marie and I walked into the room with the salesperson. Weeks before, on first contact, he had informed us he had hyperhidrosis, an excellent admission by a professional salesman; it explains why he sweated. I suffer from Raynaud's disease. It narrows the arteries. My fingers and toes feel numb and cold even in the summer. Like two alien cultures, our environmental comfort zone differed by a hundred degrees. I dialed the thermostat to 85 degrees Fahrenheit. We sat for thirty minutes. I thawed my extremities, and he cleaned his brow repeatedly with his large towel-like handkerchief, looking like he had just played a five-set tennis game on a sweltering summer day. The suite worked as advertised.

No abuse so far by the caretakers, but then I still have my marbles. I gladly put up with the loud-speak, the efficient disregard for our likes and dislikes, and the consistency of average food. The friendliness and concern advertised on the brochure come off like an Indian software support person from Comcast.

I now look forward to Tuesday or Thursday afternoons when my beautiful daughter walks in like a Brazilian mannequin; she inherited my dark, soft skin and nothing else other than the quick flick of the wordy tongue. At fifty, she could stop the crowd on Newbury Street. How did she get so much taller than me? Like a proper resident of Cambridge, she has a streak of white hair, like a braid. It parts her curly black hair but skews to the left. She teaches freshman writing at Boston University on the other side of the river. To my wife's utter fury, I never denied my Marie anything. Voluntary imprisonment is the exception; I refused her pleas to live with her.

She married an Iranian engineering professor while she did her Ph.D. in literature at Northeastern University, down one street from Mass. Ave. on Boylston Street. The marriage only lasted two years. He got tenure at Michigan Tech. She refused to leave with him. Good riddance. If he were forty years younger, he would have joined the Confederation of Iranian Students, the blighted, leftist organization of well-to-do and not-well-to-do students with governmental grants in the seventies. He dared to defend the indefensible: 9/11.

Laurel and Hardy always await her arrival, both smitten and deathly frightened by her advocacy for my care. One look at me and the room and inquiries pour out of her, questioning the stubble on my face, the yellow water damage on the ceiling tiles, the food stain on the remote. She misses nothing. "Go easy on them," I protest mildly. It fires her up to a more sustained barrage, to my utter satisfaction. After she leaves, both are relieved. They ask with sham indifference when she will return. "She's sumpthin else."

QUIETUS RELEASE FROM LIFE

1. 1971: The Teenage Beauty Makes Her Entrance

She must have been fifteen or sixteen the first time I saw her— in the summer of 1971. I sat at the Imperial Club, dining next to the pool with Shojaedeen Shafa, the deputy minister for the Court, who we called Agha Shoja. The dry, warm nights of Tehran could support your weight. How light I felt. The pool had reconfigured itself from a rich kid's urinal in the daytime into an imperial blue in the evening. The gentle light undulated under a slight desert breeze.

Agha Shoja took my education into his hands when I joined the Court. A well-read man with distorted ideas about the end of Western Civilization; he kept a copy of *The Decline of the West* by Spengler beside his pillow, just as a Seventh-day Adventist keeps his Bible. Agha Shoja believed in the second advent of Persian pre-Islamic imperial grandeur with the same zeal as Shiites believe in the second coming of Imam Zaman, the Lord of Time. We had developed an anti-Western veneer, which I now realize was also a Western mode of thought.

I saw Agha Shoja as an ally with his feet in both the King's and Queen's camps. The Queen had the intellectuals. To HIM's delight, I coined the word an-tellectual as a play of words. "An" in Persian vernacular translates to excrement, to shit. He repeated this, far from a *bon mots*, often. I never took credit. I also kept a foot in each camp to curry favor wherever I could. No burning bridges for this sly fool.

We sat at the club bemoaning the Western media bashing our bash of all bashes, the celebration of the 2500th anniversary of the Persian Empire. Still a few months out, we worked at a furious pace to plan it. I had returned from Oberriet, Switzerland to inspect the finished tents to house royals, presidents, and prime ministers next to Persepolis in Shiraz.

Agha Shoja got up. He downed his drink, then quoted some writer while shaking his head in faux melancholy. "'Closing time in the gardens of the West,'" he said. "See you bright and early." Then he walked out. I sat drinking a Cognac. I remained a skeptic. Not until 1973, when the oil money gushed our way and Vietnam and Watergate became an anchor to the West, did I convince myself Agha Shoja had it right.

"If it isn't Sam!" a familiar voice exclaimed behind me. Prince Davallou Qajar, a charming courtier, approached the table. He has a special place in my heart. Through him, I met my wife, Annabelle. Through his stupidity, I made my name in Court. He had a *mot unjuste* for any courtier not in hearing range. (I will resist the temptation to wander; I am on a roll. My Post-it note, like an Achaemenid tablet, has inscribed at the top: 1971 Teenage Beauty. We need to get back to her.)

"Come to my table and bring your drink," he said. I got up and walked with him. His table stood back from the pool—the dark spread like an awning over the table and chairs. A jittery candle danced and lit the three people around the table. At the table sat a bourgeois family. They clearly didn't belong. I could see the man's face. He watched me approach. Mustachioed, the meaty face of a grocer. A military carriage, with hair sprouting out of the edges of his white, short-sleeved shirt. The wife coiffed with a can of hair spray, visible like a net. Mousy but ferrety eyes, the pupils of which moved left and right. Not fearful, but watchful. The daughter wore a pink sweater, *à l'américaine* of the fifties.

"General, let me introduce my good friend, Sam. We work together at Court," said Davallou. He white-lied. He had no portfolio. His type was well-defined from time immemorial in all royal courts: a sycophant, a toady, a hanger-on. I shook hands with the General and sat beside the girl on my right. We faced her parents. Davallou sat on my left. He ordered caviar from his stash at the club. We knew him as the King of Caviar. He talked. He could talk. An opium eater's vomit: voluminous, steady, and not uncomfortable at all. The girl said nothing. I assumed she was a teenager and didn't glance with any interest. The mother cooed at every mention of HIM.

"I saw His Majesty once at the parades. He..." the General began. Before he could relate his majestic experience, Davallou's voice flooded over him. It drowned him without offense. "But my dear General," he interrupted, and on he went—His Majesty this, His Majesty that.

She said out of nowhere—I mean the girl, not the mother, "He is just a human after all, no?" Silence fell on the table. I could hear the tables around us talking and laughing. Far in the background, I listened to a few jackals. I turned to look at her: fifteen, sixteen, the voice of a mature woman, mannish in its timbre. The woman hovered a layer beneath the teenager, not yet out. She had beautiful, blonde, green eyes and applied nothing artificial to her face or hair. Her looks struck me as extraordinary.

I watched the parents who looked horrified at her comment. I looked at them to grasp how nature had assembled this girl from a blend of the two coarse people who sat on the other side of the table. A hospital mistake or a paternity question lurked there somewhere. (Then again, how could my daughter be mine and look so beautiful? I often asked my wife the same question. She'd laugh and say, "Have you seen your forehead?")

"It will charm His Majesty to hear you describe him as all too human," Davallou said, smooth as ever. I looked at him. He grinned at me with his canary-loving cat's eyes. His look said, "You fool, can you now see why I sit here with these people?" He was hard at work.

"G., maybe you can one day meet His Majesty," the father said. "He is no ordinary man."

"We can arrange it," Davallou said. He said it too quickly. He shot me a glance.

"Can we?" the mother said. She threw wide open the curtain of her yearnings. They all looked at me.

"In a few years. His Majesty doesn't have time for girlish crushes," I said. I spoke the truth. His tastes didn't tend toward the prepubescent.

"But I…" she began, outraged.

"Well, my dear, have some of the excellent caviar," Davallou interrupted while the authoritarian father looked at her.

I should not give the impression I had scruples about introducing a sixteen-year-old going on twenty; I simply knew HIM's tastes. Later, I gave Davallou a piece of my mind. He smiled, probably hazy from the opium he had digested, and said, "She called you monkey face." Later, I returned the favor. I gave her the moniker of Tala, or Gold.

2. 2023: Daughter Speaks

On Thursday, I wait for Marie. I sit in my wheelchair. I watch the news. The orange ape, Trump, trumpets his victimhood like the angel Israfil, warning us of consequences. He, I mean Israfil, calls all creatures to assemble in Jerusalem for the day of judgment. The day of judgment won't require any trumpeter. Trump gives me a reason to live. Like an unfinished action movie, we all, I mean us Americans, want to see a happy ending and justice done. I bet a happy ending for this writ-large reality show will see him handcuffed on his way to jail. I doubt if I will live long enough. Even if I do, when the assured conclusion is at hand, my brain will not connect the import of handcuffs to justice.

My daughter comes in head high, high heels loud, nostrils faintly flared. She smiles. My addled brain smiles wide in response. We no longer wear Covid masks. I couldn't see her for eighteen months, and we lost twenty percent of our population at the Rising Sun. It is hard to tell if the death rate would have differed without the COVID-19 infection. The rest of us, the survivors, act more presumptuously. Deep down, we, the elders who still stand, *a façon de parler*, suspect our genetic makeup is a superior stock of humanity.

A small minivan with a mechanical elevator blast repeated ear-piercing warnings. It transfers four volunteers for a half-day outing. After Covid, our nursing staff, more skeletal than the residents, cannot cope with the additional work. They require chaperones. My daughter will follow us to the Natick Mall. A slight shuffle of wheelchairs to get ahead of the line ensues. I won't humiliate myself. A cold, bright winter day cuts me to the bone as the van elevator lifts the three octogenarian residents upward ahead of me.

We enter the mall through the basement parking and go up the elevator. Malls really should pump oxygen as Vegas casinos do. Aside from the air, I enjoy these cathedrals of luxury. My wheelchair makes cheerful squeaks on the faux marble floors as Marie pushes me through the Nordstrom department store. To my right are stands of glass displaying sparkling jewelry, and on my left are women's shoes of colorful variety. She guides me to the coffee shop attached to Nordstrom. I can see false, thin birch trees. They line the middle of the mall perpendicular to our path.

At a round table sits a familiar thirty-something woman. Head shaved to a fine blonde stubble, she carries enough pierced metalwork in her ears, nose, and lips to excite any MRI machine. Marianna, my daughter's partner of five years, smiles a horizontal crescent of a smile. She shows her perfect pearly teeth. A slip of a girl, she looks like a teenager unless you get close to see the mature parentheses around her mouth and eyes. One arm in a sleeve of tattoos contrasts against her white skin. Her hair is dyed black as a crow. I don't know anyone whiter than her. I love Marianna. I kiss her cheeks. I caress the stubble of her head with the intimacy of an uncle; she lets me, like an orphan starved for parental love. I feel so tender toward her. My eyes bulge with tears. Her Colorado parents reject her lifestyle. Who knew Colorado nestled Russian Adventists in the nooks and Rockies? It is all about lifestyle.

We drink permutations of coffee. I down a three-shot espresso like in the old days. I will tremble well into the night like a greyhound before a race. I bask in their intimacy: my daughter's womanly affection, and Marianna's boyish enthusiasm. Marianna's upper lip carries a thin line of foam. Marie signals. Marianna brings her face forward, willing, like a child. My daughter removes the foam with her manicured pinkie. She licks her pinkie and uses a tissue to dry it. Both teach at BU, where they met. Both married once in their early twenties. They share an apartment in Cambridge. We talk aimlessly until Marianna says, "Tell him."

"Tell him what?" I ask. I hitch a ride on Marianna's excitement.

"Dad, I wanted to tell you last week, but I didn't get a chance." She looks flustered.

"What is it? You know you can tell me anything," I say.

"We want to get married," she says.

"Wonderful," I say.

She then says, "Marianna and I have applied to adopt a baby girl."

I go mum. I now know I have to tell my story straight without distortions, without entreaties for sympathy that I can so well fabricate.

3. 1947: Mum Powders Herself

I woke at 3:00 to the tune of *Marā bebus* (Kiss Me) playing in my mind. The singer is Golnaraghi, the one-song-wonder who dealt only in antiques.

Pretty girl
I am your guest tonight
I will stay with you
To press your lips against mine

How does a demented brain wake me by singing the most melancholy song the world has ever heard, tears falling down my stubbly cheeks? Music, I am told, clings with stubborn stamina against dementia before it also slips away in silky sulkiness. When I play the piano, my hands remember tunes with little difficulty. I read somewhere that the Octopus's tentacles host parts of its brain.

I have peed myself overnight. Little indignities become more important than my health. I thank Dignity, my adult diapers, for their ability to soak 10% more moisture than other brands. I should thank my lucky stars. I only require the PM type. During the day, I use a walker to service myself with dignity. The indignity of the smell accompanies us all. It permeates the halls. No amount of Resolve, the Urine Destroyer in its ironic plastic yellow spray bottle, can remove the odor from my nostrils. It just mixes it with an industrial fragrance. I know the scent of Carbolic or Eau de Javel doesn't exist in this third decade of the 21st century in a nursing home in a well-to-do suburb. I don't smell a modern disinfectant. Something is wrong. Gravity has sidled up to my thoughts. It weighs them down. I can't tell if they are driven by a random parade of memories or fed by nature's relentless presentation of continuity to my senses. The misfolded protein amyloids form fibrous plaques sprinkled on my brain's floor. They cause intermittent shorts.

Yesterday, like a clarion call in a dream, I heard the elongated duet *quelle surprise* of my mother and French grandmother. I could pick up only the string end of their vocal breadcrumb. I saw my maternal grandmother a few times before she died in the late fifties. I recall a desiccated Parisian with proper turkey wattles like theater curtains about to open. Her icy blue eyes had grey-white rings at the edge of the cornea.

Her spindly legs could not support stockings. They wrinkled at her ankles horizontal to her wattles. A gentle woman, she never referred to me without the sobriquet *mon pauvre petit garçon* and, as I got older, *mon pauvre garçon*. Then, *mon pauvre Sam*. A look of deep pity would come into her Basset Hound eyes, even when she handed me a *grand cadeau* — a large gift box wrapped in beautiful paper.

I saw my mother sitting at her *table de toilette*, spreading dull, pink powder on her face while she sipped a pale, watery whiskey and soda. I sat on the floor between the wall and the table in my pajamas with gift boxes imprinted on them. Over them, I wore an uncomfortable, thick dressing gown. I was recounting a movie plot in detail, including a dramatic musical soundtrack (da-da-da-da-da-type noises). With my pusillanimous fists, I mimicked the hero. He punched his way out of the swinging doors of a saloon, the door so like the two wings of a butterfly.

In the background, a more polished soundtrack played. My mother stacked six 45 rpm vinyl records on the notched, thin spindle meant to play 33 rpm vinyl records continuously. "The songs I want," she'd say. A star-like, three-pronged, snap-in plastic converter fitted each 45 record. It changed the unseemly, gaping center hole of a 45 into the elegant, spaghetti-sized hole of a 33 record. This stacked pile, the equivalent of a modern playlist, gave her control of the mood she wanted to create. It timed her *toilette*. "No woman should sit in front of a mirror for over twenty minutes," she would say. "Or she risks going out like an overdone gigot." She found life in the eastern borders of Iran uncivilized, crass, and beneath human tolerance. Sometime in my late teens, she moved first to Tehran and then to Paris, permanently separating from my father.

 The flat fall of each record on top of the previously played track increased my anxiety about the evening's end. As the last 45 traced its last grooves, the crazed stylus skated freely back and forth in the ice-smooth last concentric circle. The music turned to an amplified scratch. I reached the apogee of my misery. My mother stood up abruptly, ready to go to some official dinner. She flicked the soft powder brush a few times against my face, kissed the tip of my nose, rubbed her face against my face, murmured, "Mmm, soft," and left the house.

THE JESTER

1. 1965: We Slide Up the Slippery Slope with Fair Winds at Our Back

It is Monday morning. In Massachusetts, the sun shines 200 days per year. Outside my window, water drips from the icicles on the side of the gutters. Snow covers the hard ground. My PC sits on the square table. The table sits in the small alcove, an offshoot of my room, with a small, deep brown refrigerator and a sofa. The sofa resembles an armchair, giving the alcove the look of an Embassy Suites hotel. Management charges my account $15/month for the fridge. I prefer the bed as my office.

You may be wondering: How does a young man of a good family, with land and money to spare, turn into an arrant pimp? How did James Hamilton, 2nd Duke of Abercorn, become the King's ass-wiper, the Groom of the Stool? Proximity to power smells like flowers, even if you're only wiping or licking an ass. I recall my self-importance and the vitality it offered. I don't need to give my job a sheen of respectability.

I don't recall a moral slippery slope. I saw a metaphorical escalator. We stepped on, and it, with hydraulic smoothness, took us up and up. An escalator with rails, like a zipper, closed behind us. We never looked for or wanted an exit or an off-ramp. There was nothing to question; we served the royal loyally, to the best of our abilities.

"The difference between a king and a dictator," my uncle, the court minister, would say, "is that the king and the country are the same sides of a coin. God appoints a king. The dictator appoints the dictator." I add that kings have no choice. They suffer compulsory pre-birth impressment. Edward VII defied the genetic compulsion, and look what we think of him. Kings are disappointed sons. Their fathers, by definition, can never witness their feats.

Today, a monarchist might look foolish, but not then. We never doubted his legitimacy; his father had won the crown. You buy in, or you don't. It was just a style of government, a tradition not to be messed with. The Shah, His Imperial Majesty (HIM), developed late—a slow progression. You can't pinpoint how he accumulated so much power.

The courtiers had a markedly different lens from our fathers and HIM. In the second half of the twentieth century, the West went through its whirlpool of a cultural revolution none of us could escape. The West educated us. Those in power attended colleges and high schools in the US, France, Switzerland, and England. We fought the battle for Westernization without apologies. At Court, we lived a Western lifestyle. We didn't live the life of Muslims because nobody brought us up as Muslims—simple stuff. The truth about our generation: Our grandfathers prayed daily. Our fathers pretended to pray. We didn't know the words. And you know what? It felt better. Much, much better.

I am always irritable on Mondays. I write a few paragraphs with my razor-thin Pilot pen. I reread them. I crumple the five Post-it notes filled with my tiny squiggles. I attempt to throw the bundle into the basket next to my bed. They resist their destruction with all the might of their sticky band, facing all the angles of crumpledness. The pink rock sticks to the side of my bed tray. The impurity of my memories irritates me.

I rescue the five Post-it notes and flatten them with a fair warning. Today, forty-four years after the dynasty's fall, I blame HIM. Not for all the silly interviews he gave in the late seventies. Not for spending an enormous amount on military hardware. Not for his rash, large projects that turned the economy inflationary. I don't even blame HIM for SAVAK's overreach in the seventies; the war was real, but the mission was as wrong-headed as the actions of the CIA, MI6, or SDECE. Not even for his bouquet of Court sycophants, of which I am a poster child—a small price to pay.

He who let the worms of Qom develop into the dragons of today needs to carry the responsibility. And early in his reign, the Shah let them back in. Our young king was the Trojan Horse who brought them back amidst us. He believed. Superstitiously. All beliefs are superstitious. He believed Abbas, a Shi'i saint, had once broken his fall from a horse; the saint had placed his hand between his head and the stone. During a walk in the royal palace, he believed he saw a vision of the Imam Zaman. The redeemer passed him by, weighed by his saintly halo. He believed Ali, the prophet's son-in-law, sat on his heels on the floor and offered him a liquid to drink; it cured his typhoid.

I am familiar with how a small child builds an emotional fortress. The child with layers of concrete protection then grows into an adult, maintaining the beliefs the superstitious mother and household servants lodged—not those instilled by the father.

Of all of us, I count HIM as the naïve one. We understood the stakes. We, the irreligious, fought a lifestyle war against the religious. I never fooled myself. I never thought my actions didn't have unfair consequences. I never pretended to twist unfairness into fairness. We pushed all the chips into the middle of the table. We played enthusiastically. *"Les jeux sont fait rien ne va plus,"* cried the croupier in 1941. These are the dangers of a Monday morning.

2. 1965: Details of Thirty-Four Bullets

What did we do in those days before the fall? I can't will my copious memories to move in any linear fashion. Reminiscences fly around detached. I quickly capture them on paper before they sluice through the grey holes of my brain, each larger than a thought—the holes created by the plaques. They lie on the muddy floor of my brain.

Right after the assassination, the confused press didn't know how to tackle the story. The papers and the weekly magazine reported the incident, but not even as the major headline. In a larger font, the headlines announced a Jordanian airline's crash into a mountain with 54 passengers dead. The assassination news was squeezed matter-of-factly between two columns: HIM meets Pakistan's army chief, and the US bombs Laos. It promised more details to come.

The thin column announced the death of the two guards inside the palace. It mentioned that one of the Shah's servants and a gardener had sustained injuries. The papers didn't print my name. That's not a surprise. I worked for the Intelligence. I reported on foreign intelligence. I got shot on my way to hand a report to HIM.

That day, the Shah drove from his quarters, something he rarely did. He often walked the three-minute walk hand-in-hand with the five-year-old Crown Prince. On that day, a new boy had joined the school, and the headmistress had asked the Crown

Prince to remain at the Ekhtessassi Palace to put the boy at ease. We like to give lucky misses a supernatural aura. The Shah certainly did.

One of the first bullets ricocheted from the wall to find my tender backside. As I lay down gently on the warm stairs before the Marmar Palace, I witnessed a twenty-two-year-old amateur do his best to kill HIM—amateur because he started his machine gun's flurry of bullets forty meters away. I saw a gardener get up to see what the fuss was about. He received a shot in the arm for his nosiness. The assassin ran past me to get through the door. I couldn't move my legs, an immense frustration.

The Shah had run through the door seconds before. I could hear the assassin breathe heavily from the rush of adrenaline. He hesitated for a moment at the door. Like a cow on a track watches an oncoming train approach, a confused servant stood behind the glass door and watched the assassin. The servant would receive three bullets for his innocent perplexity but lived to tell the story. The killer looked left at me on the stairs. I said something to him like, "Nakon, don't." He repeated two Quranic words and pushed the heavy iron-wrought glass door with his right shoulder.

A guard from behind the Shah's car fired. The assassin entered the building with a limp. I heard bullets inside. The guard from outside rushed past me. He continued to shoot his machine gun. I found out later they fired thirty-four shots; no one-bullet theory here. Two bullets went through HIM's closed office door. They landed in the back of the soft-leathered office chair and his desk. Two more punctured the oil heaters in the corridor.

I saw the bullets' traces on the palace wall for months. I couldn't figure out how one could have gotten to the seat of my pants.

Not for a moment during my prone position on the stairs did I think I could die. I puzzled at my immobility but didn't feel pain. The staff told me I had made humorous comments as they transferred me to the ambulance. I remember none of that. Two guards died—one on the way to the hospital, the other on the operating table. Their families became the wards of the Shah. Each family received $15,000 in compensation, not an inadequate sum. Someone heard HIM murmur, "And this is the Eternal Guards, the Eternal Guards."

Later, we learned it was Ayatollah Kashani who ratified the assassination.

I can see him now: He was from the town of Kashan, whose resident are known for their cowardice. He's pictured with an angelic smile as he caresses the bearded face of Prime Minister Razmara's assassin, the carpenter Khalil Tahmasbi. In the photo, circa December 1952, Tahmasbi, in turn, flashes a kind, subservient, warm smile toward his father figure. Present at the mosque: my uncle, who cradled the bloody head of the Prime Minister in his lap.

Did I mention Ayatollah Kashani was the speaker of the house? Did I mention on his first day, he freed the killer of the nation's prime minister and called the assassin a soldier of Islam? The war of the mullahs had started long before the Shah gathered power, the White Revolution, or the creation of SAVAK. We had a war on our hands. I never doubted it. We built the infrastructure to fight it. While our Ayatollahs used their batons to conduct assassins and kill politicians and intellectuals, we were fighting the communists tooth and nail—the wrong enemy. My anger has no bounds. Imagine if Congress had freed Lee Harvey Oswald and called him a Christian soldier—it sounds absurd. I take it back. These days, we can imagine similar eventualities.

3. 1965: Choose Your King and Lie with Him

HIM visits me in the hospital. He drives himself there from the palace. Simpler times. He wears thick, black-framed glasses with lenses tinted the color of an apricot. He wears a light suit with a dark tie. Not an immaculate dresser. The UK ambassador thought his purveyor of neckties should suffer some ancient Persian torture.

At forty-six, at the height of his manhood, he is handsome with a large, prominent nose and the right balance of peppery hair. He is not tall—he doesn't possess his father's six-foot-four frame—but he's wide-chested and muscled from a lifetime of sports. The eyes behind the orange tint are hooded; rightly mistrustful, but not mean. By the time I arrived, no one in Court or the government dared to refer to him as "the boy." His even younger courtiers call him the Young Shah. He has changed his cabinet. The old, sclerotic aristocracy of the Qajars watch and grumble from their gardens. The forty-something cabinet matches his look. He keeps his private friends private. Nothing wrong with that.

When the Shah enters, the doctors have me on the bed. I lie prone on a heap of pillows. My butt sticks in the air. The bandage offers a modicum of modesty. He approaches me with awkward embarrassment. He can't decide on which side of the bed he should stand. As the Persian proverb goes, I turn my head like a mule who watches his farrier. Awkwardly. I greet him as formally as my position allows. He stands ramrod straight from his army training, his torso back. It affords him a distanced observer position.

"Your Majesty will pardon my *lèse-majesté*." I nod toward my butt. He offers me the practiced benevolent smile.

"You are Alam's nephew, are you not?" he asks.

"I call him Uncle Your Majesty, but he is my mother's cousin. Your Majesty, my uncle favored me with a visit earlier this morning."

"I want you to visit us at Court when you are out. Your uncle says I could better employ you at Court than at your intelligence work. He vouched for your foolishness." He corrects himself, "Your uncle meant it in a good way. We could have more fun at Court. You could divert us."

I answer the call for amusement right there and there. I say, "*Bi kuno o chera sire*," a wordplay on the Persian phrase "*bi chuno chera*." It technically means "with no argument, without dispute," but the best translation to convey wordplay is "with no ifs and without butts." Emphasis on "butts." I could do this style of humor at will.

He laughs uncontrollably for a moment, probably relieved by the lightness my levity brought to the situation. He pulls out a white handkerchief and dabs a tear from his left eye. The tear doesn't originate from my humor; it stems from a different series of bullets from another assassination attempt at Tehran University sixteen years before. One of the bullets entered his cheek. Nasser Fakhrarai, a member of the Fadā'iyān-e Islam and not, as announced at the time, a member of the Russian-backed Tudeh party, fired six bullets point blank. The first three missed. The fourth bullet pierced the Shah's lip and cheek. It knocked out some front teeth. The fifth bullet wounded his shoulder. The sixth was trapped in the gun's barrel. The drive up alone to see me shows his courage.

THE JESTER

In the past ten years, there had been four assassination attempts on his prime ministers, three of which were successful. A series of assassinations spells insecurity for any country. The Fedayeen of Islam committed three out of four at mosques. An Ayatollah sanctioned them all. I stopped going to mosques, even as a tourist. Bad for the health.

"A brave man, your uncle. Don't worry, he will be back soon enough," he assures me.

The previous year, my uncle had resigned as prime minister. He led the government for 597 days. The Khomeini riots started in June 1963, eleven months into his premiership. Thousands rushed into the street. When my uncle saw HIM fret over the promised violence, he joked, "I will weigh Your Majesty's balls. If I find them heavy, I will fuck the mothers and sisters of the protesters. If light, I will resign and leave my post." A good deal, the Shah thought.

My uncle didn't hesitate. His government flashed metal. They borrowed it from his backbone, a backbone nestled in plenty of cotton. The army came out. They used force. His men killed eighty-three people. After the blood and arrests, my uncle drank champagne and slept with a beauty. Finding his position as prime minister untenable, the Shah dismissed him. The *main-de-fer* added thirteen years to the Persian Empire. A pittance. But for me, thirteen blissful, stable years.

"Your uncle tells the truth. You may speak your mind with me. Accidentally or not, you got between me and the assassin." He points at my butt with his glasses, which he has taken off. He smiles now with the benevolence of a royal. The goodwill he shows has a few thousand years of contractual history. The royal nominates the Court's fool. He crowns me with the invisible motley, the three-cornered hat with bells worn by court jesters from immemorial time.

"The doctors tell me the bullet lodged itself in a bundle of nerves. Inoperable, they say. A danger to your sex life if they attempt to extract it." He or I didn't know the half of it. "My bullet exited from here," he says. He points to his cheek. "And out clean here." He scratches on his left upper lip. I detect a slight hiss in his speech. Years later, in a bedroom he used for his romantic interludes, I saw his three-tooth falsie in a glass of water in the bathroom.

4. 1969: Junk Gets Reported

My life as a fool at court started soon after my recovery at the hospital. In my youth, I had learned a great deal about physical endurance. I didn't have much. But I did have extraordinary rarified coordination. I learned how to juggle balls. I could catch a nut thrown by a student on the other side of the long table with my mouth. Later, in court, I perfected the trick with General Khatami, the brother-in-law of the Shah and a born athlete, once the captain of the Iranian soccer team. He'd lob, say, a juicy plum from ten meters away, and I, like a seal, would adjust and catch it mid-air in my mouth to the applause of the Court.

My tennis improved. It angered better players. The Shah and the court watched and found my tennis style hilarious. It fit my jester's persona. It never amused those I played. I had one shot. I lobbed any shot near me high; I mean high, very high. I was ambidextrous, probably from years of piano practice. Or, possibly, I played the piano well because I was born ambidextrous. I would propel the ball toward the baseline, from whichever side it came across, with a quick hand switch of the racquet. I lobbed with an accurate forehand from as far back as I could. I beat any moderate amateur out there; they committed the errors. I looked comical. My long hands, my thin legs, my massive upper body; the crowd completed the picture of what I looked like as I ran left and right, as I switched the racquet from hand to hand.

Sports caused what later became an infamous incident. I even read it in the post-revolution papers. It was presented to represent the immoral ways of the court.

The Royals kept each other company. During summers, most visits happened in the 300-acre Sa'dabad Complex, where the royals lived. The three blood siblings interacted most often. The fourth, younger brother had died in a plane crash. Twice a week, we saw the Queen-mother; her visits were rather staid affairs. HIM and his friends visited Her Highness Asharf, the twin sister, twice a week. Her friends, party types, had the energy to spar. Once a week, the eldest sister, Princess Shams, arranged a cultural event, most often a musical interlude, after dinner. Many of us skipped this event. Once a week, on Fridays, the family and friends visited HIM and HMQ.

On Friday afternoons, we played volleyball. The Queen loved to play. Like her husband, she loved sports. She had captained her high school basketball team to a championship. That Friday, the lunch had more guests than usual. Many of the regular friends, ministers, ambassadors, and members of the family—both of the sisters, their husbands, and the Queen-mother—attended. My uncle, my boss, the Court Minister Nakhai, and curiously, I remember, Seyyid Hassan Emami, the Friday Prayer Imam of Tehran, came as well. An educated man, the Imam slipped out of his mullah garb into a well-tailored suit and back with the ease of the Swiss-educated lawyer he was. To set the record straight, he didn't play volleyball. He was in his sixties. He shared a similar experience with HIM and me; he had faced a knife meant to kill him in 1953.

General Khatami always brought along a couple of officers who played on the Air Force team. They facilitated passes and the flow of balls. One officer played on each side. We played a serious game and then, before lunch, we swam in the freezing swimming pool. The water came from wells dug into the property. We left our swimming trunks to dry on the porch and drank a vermouth or a Campari in relaxed attire: tennis shorts and a sports shirt. Throughout the day, as dice rolled, you heard backgammon pieces thumping with definite energy on the inlaid Khatam board and the accompanying korkori, or trash talk in today's parlance. I remember a tolerant court in those days. We didn't take ourselves too seriously. It was also a young court, but we had serious people by then. We relaxed, but I underscore this, in a Western style. I could count two individuals in the court or cabinet who didn't have diplomas from a US or European university. HIM was one of the two.

We played with the HMQ on one side and HIM on the other. The General played on the Queen's side to balance the teams. I played next to HIM. Several people came in and out as substitutes. Everyone liked to play. I don't recall the individuals who played that day. It was a fluid, fun afternoon. Volleyball, I confess, didn't rank as a strength of mine. I stood short. I scooped up the ball, as usual with comic timing, both hands, palms up, like someone ordering a crowd to stand up. My knees bent as if I sat on a commode. This bordered on earning a carrying-call because the ball bounced up after an uncomfortably extended time in contact with my hand. It exasperated the General on the other side. The two semi-pro officers smiled. Both were indulgent and respectful. The Shah laughed delightedly. "Our *nokhodi* here is exempt," he'd say. "Booby" would not be an inaccurate translation of *nokhodi*— the last kid picked on a team. The game continued.

HIM served. On the other side, HMQ passed the ball neatly to their officer. The man set it up perfectly. The General jumped to spike; our officer jumped for a block. The forceful spike moved horizontally toward me. I stood on the end line, next to HIM. The ball swept towards me in a curve. It wanted to glide out but my head stood in the way. I executed a painful, womanish split like a Romanian gymnast on a bar. The ball sailed over me. I heard a horrendous rip. I fell backward, still in the painful split. My tennis shorts had miraculously transformed into a two-sided miniskirt, completely revealing my hairy genitalia to the crowd. I saw HMQ's face, grided through the volleyball net. Her hand covered her mouth—whether in mirth or embarrassment, I could not tell. My swimming trunks sat unprotesting on the porch, drying off.

I stood up, pushing the cream-colored remains of my shorts together in a womanish, modest gesture—one hand on my backside, the other in the front. It must have looked like I wore a loincloth or some Roman male skirt. I walked off gingerly to the applause of the group, wearing a shit-eating grin. The rip had been complete, and I stood alone as the court fool. In my mind, I still wear that grin, like the lines of a persistent image burned onto a ruined, modern TV screen.

THE JESTER

A headline in *Ettela'at*, under new, unforgiving Islamic management in the early eighties: "It is said courtiers ran naked and drunk during the Shah's Friday lunches and gambled millions." Go figure.

DID YOU READ THIS?

"If you repeat a lie often enough, people will believe it, and you will even come to believe it yourself."

Joseph Goebbels

FIRST THINGS FIRST

1. 1975: Listen! I Hear the Court Jester's Cap and Bells. The King is Coming!

After I returned from G.'s apartment, I knew I had work to do. I took a shower, shaved, and dressed as impeccably as possible. I wanted to communicate with an aura of control. I cried in the shower, away from Annabelle. I explained G.'s death to her; she knew the woman had been HIM's mistress a few years back but little else. I drove to the palace. First, I had to inform my uncle. I wanted to join the audience when my uncle presented the news to HIM. Doubt crept in for the first time.

I walked into my uncle's office, as I did each morning. I knew he would betray nothing once I told him. He didn't. He said, "I will arrange an audience this morning with HIM."

"Uncle, let me accompany you. HIM will ask questions I could answer."

"Unnecessary," said my uncle. "Nassiri's report will have all the details." I replied with a watered-down sketch of the bungled surveyance.

"Also, the report has nothing to say on how we should handle the aftermath with the press, the Queen, and her entourage." He looked at me suspiciously but then assented with a please-yourself shrug. The Shah arrived around 9:00. At 9:30, we entered his office.

He looked tired and irritable. Unbeknownst to all of us, his valet had mixed up his medicines. To keep his chronic lymphocytic leukemia a secret, the prescribed Chlorambucil came in Quinercil containers. When the time came to refill the prescription, the not-in-the-know valet had ordered Quinercil instead. It resulted in an enlargement of the spleen, which made him irritable and, worse, put him in mortal danger. "What's the emergency?" he asked.

"Your Majesty, General A.'s daughter died last night," my uncle said.

"Who?" he asked, puzzled.

"Miss G. A.," I said. I observed him. He got it; it penetrated a layer.

"Unfortunate girl," he said. "How did she die?"

"We await the report. We suspect a drug overdose," my uncle said.

Ayadi, HIM's physician, once recounted to me, over a whiskey and soda, the sudden death of an old servant. "He fell before His Majesty while he served tea; *une crise cardiaque massive*. He died before he hit the ground. A few guests cried out. HIM took it with a *c'est la vie* attitude. Not a word of sorrow for a man who had served tea since his father's reign started. You'd think a bird fell dead off a tree." I recount the incident not to describe a cruel man, which he was not, but rather to illustrate the view he carried, like a curled fetus, of his prerogatives as a king. It was not Europe's, but our nineteenth-century notion of royalty.

"Drugs, drugs," HIM responded. "The bane of the Western world has caught up with our young." He looked at me as if I represented all the young. "My daughter, with that no-good husband of hers, did LSD and has become a religious fanatic. She built a mosque in her house. Don't they call them Jesus freaks?" he asked.

What he meant, and should have said, was "Muhammad freaks." I could never understand the line he drew between his own nonsensical, superstitious beliefs and his daughter's—her being a Muslim earned her the adjective "freak." I didn't answer. Instead, I explained that people could misconstrue it as suicide. It could backfire on us.

"Backfire? Backfire? What do you mean? And why would the girl commit suicide?" HIM looked puzzled. Could I believe he didn't know?

"If Your Majesty recalls, we discussed the rumors a few weeks back. She wanted to write her memoirs?" my uncle said.

"Well, yes, we don't want any reminisces. We thought you said you had taken care of it?" He turned to my uncle. "Didn't you investigate?"

I now had a puzzled look. *What memoirs?* I thought. I improvised. "I found no evidence of any papers, Your Majesty. I searched the premises for any connection. I found none." I showed the retrieved ring as evidence of my thoroughness. They both approved. "Your Majesty, the rumors of her suicide can still harm the Court." I never referred to his person. The "we" of the Court would take all the blame.

He shook his head. He pretended he was listening, but he had moved on. He wanted to get on with the morning's work. There was no other layer to allow the news to penetrate any deeper into the man. I said stupidly would create trouble. Again, he looked at me like I had said something outrageous. "Isn't that why we pay you?" He returned to my uncle. He pleaded, "Can you reschedule the Turkish ambassador this morning?" I tried once more. My uncle gave me his stare with a dismissive head gesture toward the door. My audience had ended. I made my curt bow. I left the room for the two of them to further our position in the world.

My mind focused on how to introduce G.'s death to the Queen. The Queen and her liberal entourage would assume the Shah ordered it. I went straight to her office. No matter G.'s ultimate *lèse-majesté*, the Queen would never have seen her hurt, not two years later. I needn't have bothered. People surrounded the HMQ's office, filled with the helium-like gossip of G.'s death, gliding giddily. They churned the permutations into a plausible scenario—all in whispers like the denizens of some medieval court.

When I arrived at HMQ's office, her cousin, Reza Qotbi, the head of the National Iranian Radio and Television, stood outside her office, having just left. I bent his ear for ten minutes. We had worked together amicably for years. He thought this didn't sit well. I explained that, as long as we limited the damage to the Court, it should pass in a few days. I had worked for years in the rumor mill cloud. I understood the dynamics. The best practice to control harmful news wasn't to promote our narrative silence worked best. Rumors have a short half-life if you leave them alone. Reza Qotbi's priority lay with HMQ, whom he loved devotedly. He looked at me and nodded.

2. 1975: I Exchange My Motley for a Deerstalker Hat

I came out of the palace convinced HIM, oblivious to any plots, had not given any drastic orders. We all played the interpretation game. HIM started it. It traveled through my uncle, Nassiri, and the captains. It passed mouth to ear like a stupid game of Chinese whispers. The starter phrase, distorted with each iteration: "Will no one rid me of this turbulent whore?"

G.'s death awakened in me a resolve to know the truth of what happened. I needed to know. Could Nassiri and his boys have done it? Overlooking the back door to the alley looked like suspiciously sloppy work. Not their MO. The two captains looked far from stupid. I made a note to call Nader, my old colleague, to get some clarity. I wanted to investigate. I had a list of culprits.

At four in the afternoon, I visited G.'s family home. The servant, a curved man shaped like a half-full moon, opened the door. He let me know the General, G.'s father, had left to make the funeral arrangements. A bevy of women cried in the living room. The mother sat in the middle on a sofa at the end of the room. Dressed in black, she wore a black veil. I still remember her suspicious eyes. She watched me come in. Another woman, I guessed her sister, sat next to her. She held her hand. On the other side, a young woman cried into the palms of her hands. Ordinary wooden chairs rested against the three walls. Three older men occupied them randomly. One man used a single hand to shade his face. The rest of the chairs sat empty like a toothless mouth. The men murmured silent greetings to me. They half-rose and sat back again. A military man filled a corner sofa, back straight as if he stood at attention. He ignored my entry. I considered 4:00 early to expect a full house. A baby cried upstairs. I saw the young woman get up and leave to attend to the baby. I got up and went to sit next to the mother.

    I introduced myself and whispered my condolences. She looked at me with a vacant look. She didn't recognize me. I reminded her I had met her four years ago at a dinner at the Imperial Club. It didn't register with her. She asked me to repeat my name. I did. Then she nodded. It dawned on her I belonged to the Court. She had placed me. I expected histrionics.

    "You are the one who accompanied my daughter to Paris," she said. I acknowledged the fact. "G. trusted you," the mother said. "She told me you treated her with respect up there." She nodded in the direction of the palace. Her gaze passed the walls of her house, toward the north of the city. She then brought my attention back to the immediate space in front of us: the half-empty room. "We put in too many chairs. Don't you think? You know my family and friends will not show their faces. My side of the family has applied to change our family's name since her exile."

    Exile? I thought. I wanted to say, "And whose fault is that?" But the grief on her face spoke the truth. All the earlier hankering for power had disappeared, and the years of little plans, schemes, collusions, and maneuvers had melted in some distant past. The death of a child had ironed out all the wrinkles and complexities.

We had here a mother. I repeated a few more formulaic condolences and took my leave.

In the corridor toward the outside door, I saw the young girl who had left the room. She sat on a small bench and hugged and swayed a two-year-old in her lap. A dark twenty-something with blue-black hair and an *air-de-famille* to G. She possessed the same slight droop of the mouth. It had given G. a Bardot pout. On this girl, it came off as a sour smile. The long neck looked inappropriate for this girl's dumpy body, but the head's tilt was elegant. Her eyes sparkled with intelligence.

"I am sorry for the loss of your sister," I said.

"I am her cousin," she said in a familiar voice. I approached her.

"Beautiful child you have," I said. I meant it. Children were not my forte. Children didn't react well when they saw me. Somewhere, I had read that babies recognize symmetry and beauty at an early age. This baby had yet to receive the memo. The two-year-old looked at me with sheer delight, like she had seen the most beautiful apparition. The cousin bounced the baby on her knees. The little one's curly ringlets sprang all over her head. Both tiny fists opened and closed while she cooed and crooned at me.

"I look after her," the cousin said. "I work part-time for my aunt. I study literature at Tehran University." I can't exaggerate the number of wheels spinning in my head. I introduced myself with a voice I didn't recognize. "Azar," she replied when I asked her name. Her clothes looked worn.

"The baby belongs to your cousin?" I asked. She looked at me like someone does when you state the obvious.

I put my hand in my pocket, took some money out, and

placed it on her lap. I murmured something like "to help you with your studies." She looked at me with disgust. "You offer me money for what? I am not my cousin. I don't get bought."

I apologized. I asked if I could sit. The crumpled bills lay on Azar's lap. I sat next to her. The child crawled onto my shoulder. The girl pulled her back. Babies are relentless. "I knew your cousin well," I started. The baby's finger entered my mouth. Again, Azar pulled her back. "Try to understand, at nineteen—around your age, am I right? When the most powerful figure pursues you, "no" is not an option. Your aunt and uncle had little choice. Don't you think?" She looked down. A flush covered her face.

"They had a choice," she said.

"But at what cost?" I answered. I talked to her for a while. I spoke to her in a gentle tone. I did my best to justify her cousin's behavior. The baby was all over my face, her fingers in my nose and eyes, while I talked seriously to the young woman. The back and forth broke the ice. She laughed at the baby and my insistence on my humanitarian mission.

I asked her to call me anytime if she wanted to talk or get any help. I can't explain, but I wanted her on my side. I wrote her number down. General A.'s entry from the street into the hallway interrupted our talk. He wore a civilian suit. He didn't recognize me. He looked at Azar with a venomous stare. "Get this child out of my sight." She went up the stairs. He looked at me suspiciously. I introduced myself. I told him the Court and my uncle sent their condolences—an ugly warning to a man who had lost a daughter twenty-four hours ago. The ugliness, it turned out, was his inability to get ugly. The sudden subservience disgusted me. "Let Mr. Alam know I am his servant at a moment's notice," he said. I left the house. Many variables churned in my mind.

LIFE UNFOLDS

1. 1949: School Bends to a Kid's Will

My father's cruelty didn't spring from cruel acts. He never beat or berated me. Instead, he ignored me. The consistency amounted to cruelty to an only child, an only son. He tiptoed around me. Sometimes, he studied me like an entomologist while I played the piano or read a book. "From where have you come?" the Lord asked Satan. I could feel his ignorant gaze, for he possessed the proud ignorance of country folk who repeatedly declared, "I am a simple man," when what they meant was that no matter how complicated this awry world was, it would never fool them.

Besides my musicality, I can't trace a phenotype linking me to my beautiful mother. I lived with maternity doubt, or the rumor of it, all my childhood. After all, a different man can sneak into a married woman's bed, but what woman fakes a birthing event? Rumors, invisible to any X-ray and far more painful than the pellet lodged in me, always kept me company. I learned their power and how to control their weed-like spread. It made me a ferocious fighter of classmates if they didn't lift their plummeting chins from the floor fast enough when they saw my mother. I responded strategically. When they asked, "How could you have come from her?" I would beat them into a proverbial pulp. I used my already muscular, slanderous tongue over my faking little fists. Before becoming the court jester, I was a mean class clown. Over time, I found I had a better sense of the psychological weakness of other boys. Laughter in classrooms, I found, had little to do with humor. Boys exaggerated laughter to rise against authority.

Classrooms smelled of wet, heavy wool mixed with the odor of thirty unwashed boys, faux leather coats, and orange scent. Teachers often dropped an orange peel on the black, oil-powered heater. The burned peel twisted into a fetus and released a pleasant aroma to fight the pungent smell.

I remember, imperfectly, my first-grade teacher whose kindness left an anthropomorphic image of a broad pair of dentures fixed to a high-rise, beehive hairdo. In it, the dentures smile with the permanence of a single-image memory. Mrs. Dustan, the wispy, large-breasted second-grade teacher, remains an acephalic memory with a lovable, friendly name.

Thanks to the Turkish Mrs. Heidari's slaps, the third-grade image, even though underexposed, is discernable. Her slaps jarred the head like the force of a door slammed by the wind. Her immense ass wrapped in tight, burlap skirts. In retrospect, it resembled a girded computer simulation showing bulged space in the presence of gravity.

Mrs. Heidari believed we all shared the same name. She called all of us, without exception, *ishak*, donkey in Turkish. She'd take two gigantic steps to get to any part of the room. As if to separate him from a pile of sleeping sardines, she would pull a boy to his feet with two fingers grabbing his hair, right above the ear. Once the boy reached his tiptoes, his maximum possible height without floating in the air, she would let go of the hair and land a perfectly placed slap with one sweep of the same hand. The slap, the tiptoe instability, and the pull of gravity would lurch him back into his seat with suitable force to keep the victim quiet for at least a period.

Throughout the process, we all intoned, "*Ma naboudim, ma naboudim*" with the zeal of innocents taken to the stake. "It wasn't us; it wasn't us; it wasn't us," we cried. In my old age, the idiosyncratic grammar used by schoolboys makes me smile. We referred to ourselves as "we" instead of "me." A royal "we" I got accustomed to later in life.

I remember the time before I received my first slap—a rite of passage. Bigger boys scoffed at the pain. These specialists in corporal punishment proclaimed, "It fades away before you are back in your seat." The ruler on the knuckles had a more lasting effect but was less humiliating.

My clowning began when I committed my first heinous offense worthy of carrying her fingerprints on my cheek. It had become a sought-after badge of honor. What I had done and what brought me to the scaffold, I don't remember. I recall, instead, that in a loud, theatrical voice, I shouted, "It was me, it was me, it was me," which confused the poor woman enough that she hesitated for a fraction of a second, allowing me to duck and avoid the usual one-motion slap. The class jeered in unison. I smiled at the class underneath my elbow raised to protect me from the shower of blows that I knew would come. To me, it felt like a standing ovation. A series of random slaps about the face and head followed. It did nothing to dampen my victory.

2. 1949: Tennis Under a Glaring Sun

As a boy grows up, he doesn't remember the first time he saw a distant cousin—say, a first cousin once removed. Children grow up with their world populated. People appear and disappear smoothly. They leave the stage; we forget them seconds later. They come back; we pick up exactly where we left off.

My earliest distinct memory of my uncle, my mother's cousin (almost all elder relations were uncles and aunts) must have occurred when I was seven or eight. My mother, father, and I drove south from Birjand to Zahedan, a five-hour trip. His father-in-law, the prime minister, had appointed my uncle governor of Sistan and Baluchestan a few years before.

I don't remember Zahedan then, but my impression was it was a more modern, or let's say "more newly built" city than Birjand, but much hotter. British interest had caused them to build a railway there that reached Quetta. It felt to me, the kid that I was, like we drove for centuries across a flat, arid country to reach Zahedan,

In the next flash of memory, I rotate a handle on a tennis post to lift the net. I *click*, *click* the mechanism. It gears up a notch at a time. A small steel cap falls on the gear to stop it from rewinding. Two ancient-looking men, who would give Westerners an impression of profound wisdom, water the clay court. They carry heavy tin watering cans with primitive, showerhead-like spouts in each hand. They fill their large cans from a water reservoir behind the tennis courts, which also serve as a green, murky swimming pool. They dip them into the water in a circular motion. Two other men in crumpled, threadbare uniforms made for much heavier men sit on their haunches, wrists hanging off their knees; one lazily slides yellow beads on a tasbih, the equivalent of a rosary wrapped around one hand. Their mustaches compete well with my father's; they look utterly bored.

My strength can't keep pace with the net's weight. The tennis net tightens beyond my power to turn the handle another notch. A boy my size, darker than me, comes and takes over without further ado. He clicks the handle with ease. My uncle measures the center of the net with his racquet and, on the fifth click, shouts, "Hop."

We watch my uncle play tennis with my clumsy father. They both laugh and cut each other's game in good humor. They wear British whites with floppy hats. I sit on the ground. I watch the ball boy, who has miraculously produced a twin. The two distribute balls to my father and uncle while they practice serves. My mother warns me off the ground, "Look what you have done to your shorts, all stained from the red clay?" The boys smile secretly at each other.

They play a set which my uncle wins easily. I cheer inwardly. They switch sides after a set. They take breaks on the veranda with my mother. She laughs with her cousin; laughter from the gut pleases us all. Her laughter is like a bouquet offering; we take it as a compliment. Then I see my uncle look up. His brows knit together like a small wave on his receding hairline. He watches a man approach us. The man wears a suit and tie on a 40-degree day, officious, self-righteous, and confident.

Years later, my uncle told me that the fussy man headed the Financial Office of Zahedan. He marveled at my excellent memory,

"You still remember the day, do you?" he said, still proud of his action then. "Your mother told me you couldn't sleep all night. She said you caught a fever or a heat stroke." I didn't remember that part.

My uncle walks over. He shouts at the man, who stops dead in his tracks. The two guards stand up. They quiver like hunting dogs waiting to hear the mute whistle. I can't understand the back and forth. I have never seen my uncle worked up. I want to go up and chop his knees and make him laugh. My mother pulls me to her side. She tells me to stay by her and not fidget.

I hear the man explain his presence—his arms gesture impossibilities. My uncle walks back to the veranda. He leaves the man in the sun. He crosses our tiny oasis of porch, coffee table, and rattan furniture. He walks over to the two guards and says something to them. One guard goes inside to the office and emerges with a rope. They move toward the bureaucrat. He watches them with uncomprehending dread. His look protests that this is the twentieth century. It all proceeds with civilized brutality. They tie him up to a wooden utility pole—no physical resistance from the man, no physical aggression from the guards—just like they would saddle a horse. My uncle asks my father to resume their game. My mother makes a weak protestation, "*Le pauvre bonhomme va mourir dans cette chaleur.*" My father, pleased with my uncle's toughness, hushes my mother. They play two more sets before I hear the man sob.

My uncle, courteous to his last follicle, invites the man to our table to share a glass of lemonade. He murmurs warm words when we offer hospitality. The man's suit jacket has two boat-like sweat stains under each arm. They reach down to his side pockets. His dark face is shaded to the color of the cooked beetroots sold by hawkers in the streets. His almond-shaped Adam's apple pumps up and down with vigor as he drinks the large glass of lemonade.

The incident scared me. I rooted for my father to win the tennis match. He didn't.

This memory should not mar the reputation of a courteous man whose actions showed delicacy and nuance. At about the same time, my uncle slapped around the English consul in Zahedan. The man had visited a whorehouse during Ashura, a day of mourning and grief for Shia Muslims. The well-deserved beating saved the man's life from the mob. The English government thanked him. I can't imagine a more delicious situation for an Iranian diplomat to mix business with pleasure.

3. 1953: Uncle Fits a Snaffle Bit and Takes Over My Bridle

We moved to Birjand during summer vacations. A few years later, on a warm day in July, twelve-year-old me practiced the piano. The instrument was placed in the room's corner; glass doors to my left opened onto the desert vista. The entrance to the salon, as we called it, was behind me. I played with flair. My mother and my paternal uncles had a relentless admiration for my talent.

Unbeknownst to me, my uncle stood by the door. He listened behind me while I finished the piece in a flourish—just like I imagined a professional pianist did. I threw my head back in a jerk while I slowly removed my hand from the keys. I had just finished Beethoven's *Emperor Concerto*, which was well outside my abilities.

He clapped from the veranda, the clap of sarcasm: three slow, punctuated palm slaps. "Where will all this music get you, boy?"

"Good morning, Uncle. Will you not come and see me at the Royal Albert Hall?" I had a sharp tongue. It pleased him.

"No," he said. "But I want you to come and see me in the morning at the house. Do you have riding boots? No? Can you ride? No? What Alam doesn't ride."

"I am not an Alam," I said.

"If your mother is an Alam, you are an Alam. Come in early. I will figure something out for you."

The following day, the driver picked me up at 8:00 a.m. We followed the pine-lined path to the big Akbarieh mansion, a light, yellow brick Zandieh with Qajar architecture. Two wings emanated from the central core, embracing the garden pincer-like. I clearly remember that garden of Akbarieh. How we took our comings and goings into mansions and gardens for granted. This one was not necessarily beautiful, but it was imposing.

He stood at the door, courteous to any guest, even a boy. What was my uncle like? One could see him as a wunderkind. As a thirty-three-year-old man, he cut a figure. He had served as a governor of Sistan and Baluchestan in his twenties. He had been a minister to two different governments. His face looked like a bent elbow. He looked down with a friendly gaze as I descended from the back of the cavernous Rolls.

"Your mother asked me to take you in hand," my uncle said after we greeted each other. "Show you around the villages. Show you what you will inherit from your father. Come in and have breakfast first. We will ride to a nearby village today. I want you here on Thursdays, the first week of every month." This plan never worked out regularly; he did try, but my uncle was going places.

At breakfast, I rolled feta cheese and jam in lavash bread as he spoke, "Your grandfather and my father and my great uncle, Mohammad Ebrahim Khan, were governors of Qā'enāt and Sistān…" He continued, giving interminable chapters and literate verses on our heritage.

For me, it went into one ear and right out the other. We shared the same ancestors. Identical names, generation after generation, confused me. Amir Alam Khan, Assadolah Khan, Ibrahim Khan, and Ismail Khan appeared regularly, with the numeral one, two, or three at the end of their name. All worked as governors of Qā'enāt. The territory inflated and deflated like a bacterium under a microscope. It depended on who ruled. I had a good memory, but a twelve-year-old boy doesn't care to remember. Not so with him. He had a firm hold of each ancestor's deeds and often reminisced as if he shared their triumphs as he did their name.

I still remember the signed picture of the first English consul, Sir Clarmont Skrine, on the piano in Birjand. It was a glossy, grey-shaded shot of a head and torso in a modern suit and tie. A middle-aged man, he lived forever on the piano among the other four or five silver daguerreotypes of local Khans in their wrapped garments.

I recall my confusion that a large photo in the living room wall was of the Queen. I assumed it was an Iranian queen. Somewhere in my teens, this confusion cleared. The portrait was of the English Queen. My uncle loved the British. The blot follows the Alam family like a rosea rash on all our faces; a few generations of Alams enjoyed British largesse.

After breakfast, we went back into the courtyard, and, to my horror, I saw a silver chestnut horse and a donkey next to it. It didn't take a heartbeat to figure out my role as Sancho Panza. My uncle walked over and checked the fitted snaffle bit. To make matters worse, once he mounted, the stable boy offered him the reins of my donkey. He pulled me as I bounced gently on the ass's back. The donkey, a gelding, had a sturdy saddle made of walnut covered with thick, decorated wool and felt. It let me hang on comfortably enough.

An hour later, when we entered the small village, the guffaws of the dwellers completed the humiliation. Humiliation played a large part in my life. The effect was like a burn victim getting touched by some uncaring person. The humiliated have two choices: hide in shame or double down. I could never let it pass. I quickly swung my legs like a gymnast on a pommel horse and faced the back of my ride. I waved my donkey's tail at the villagers like a fool I was to become. The laughter increased. I took the donkey's tail and waved. To my delight, the donkey, with his tail in my hands, produced a good amount of dung, an excellent fertilizer for the farmers. It angered my uncle greatly as he looked back from atop his horse. Back at the house, he scolded me. "Never forget your station, my boy." I asked him for a horse next time. He obliged.

4. 1975: Spiro Agnew Sings *That's Life*

Today I woke up to Oliver's broad face. He looked at me with interest, so close he blocked the rest of the world. He saw my eyes open and continued to look at me with a dog's curiosity. "What's up, Elijah," I croaked. He straightened like a researcher who realizes he has been looking through his microscope for too long, He used his arms to rub his back and said, "You laughed in your sleep, Mr. Sam." I don't know where Elijah acquired his southern accent, for he has lived all his life in Jamaica Plain, Massachusetts. But he talks like Mammy in *Gone with the Wind*, with the same feminine drawl.

"I do sometimes," I said. I know I laugh in my dreams, an uncomfortable sensation. Laughter takes so much energy, and sleep wants to do the opposite. I couldn't remember why I laughed until around 4:30 in the afternoon. I was watching Nicole Wallace interview John Dean on MSNBC. He gets wheeled in whenever we need a comparison of Trump with Nixon. Poor Nixon. That's when I remembered my dream: Spiro Agnew and Frank Sinatra in Tehran.

The dream was a humorous dramatization of what had happened in real life. HMQ had invited me to attend a Frank Sinatra charity tour for blind people—an unexpected invitation from one circle to another. It was November 1975, one of the coldest winters we ever experienced, a week after G.'s death.

In 1975, the world went sideways. The Palestinians played at terrorism; they hijacked planes and took OPEC ministers as hostages. Lebanon began its metronymic destruction and construction. The Khmer Rouge murdered two million people. Saigon fell. A typhoon destroyed a dam; a quarter of a million people in China perished. The twelve-year reign of Margaret Thatcher as prime minister started. Franco died. And to the delight of our royal, a Spanish royal took the reins to bequeath the disputed Spanish Sahara to Morroco.

Ethiopia abolished its three-thousand-year-old monarchy to the chagrin of our royal. With all the results reported, the Ethiopians beat us as a continuous monarchy by 500 years. At Court, we followed the statistics of monarchies. HIM followed all royal information, facts or gossip, worldwide. Besides Iraq, Egypt, and Syria, I knew European monarchies fell from twenty-two to twelve. You couldn't give much credence to the sorry dozen left; you could hardly claim yourself a monarchy if your royal lived in an apartment.

I sat behind HMQ, her mother, Mrs. Farideh Diba, and a few other hangers-on. Mrs. Diba, who basked in the role of petit bourgeois, had recently asked for the title of Her Highness, to the raucous amusement of both the Shah and my uncle: a bitchy digression. Frank Sinatra walked onto the stage of Talar Rudaki. Built a few years back, our opera house had all the modern stage amenities money could buy. I liked Sinatra—he looked overweight, like an egg on top of a larger egg—but I didn't pay close attention to him. The reasons behind my invitation distracted me. After two encores, HMQ signaled me to walk with her to the customary backstage visit with performers. Her well-rehearsed entourage talked amongst themselves and didn't follow. Her mother left the concert hall right away. Mrs. Lily Amir-Arjomand and Lily Daftari stayed behind. The two Lilys worked hard to look and dress like HMQ. Ridiculous situations arose when people curtsied to one of them, which they didn't find unpleasant. The rest of the crowd made their way toward the exit.

As we crossed the front of the hall, the crowd in the front row curtsied like a drop of dominoes. HMQ bent her head toward me and said, "Sam, my cousin Qotbi reported the unfortunate girl's death to me. Do you suspect foul play?"

"I don't think so, Your Majesty. The evidence suggests she committed suicide. Drugs were involved," I said.

She looked up toward the small stairs, hand on the railings. She stopped like she had second thoughts before going up the stairs. "Sam, are you sure there was no funny business with Nassiri?" She asked exactly the question I had been asking myself. I went to lie to her and assure her, when we both saw a familiar face staring at us with a smile from the stage above. A tall American with grey hair lifted an arm to engulf and invite us to join the group. We could hear Sinatra talking to his group, his American ratata machine gun speech like directed orders. HMQ and I looked at the man; we wondered where we had seen him.

HMQ recognized him a second before I did. "Mr. Vice President," she said with surprise. "What are you doing here?"

She meant, "What's a girl like you doing in a place like this?" She had met Spiro Agnew two years before during a state visit with President Nixon. Agnew had received kickbacks—the paltriness of the amount was a wonder to all of us. Agnew, one of two vice presidents in the history of the US who had to resign.

"Your Majesty, Frank and I go way back," he said without embarrassment. "I manage all of Frank's public relations."

"And how is Mr. Sinatra faring with the public?" HMQ replied.

Agnew took a conspiratorial stance. "Your Majesty, I have put him on a strict diet. The fans want him thin as a rail." We all laughed and joined the crowd.

HMQ and I tittered down the same four steps on our way out like teenage accomplices who had just caught friends in the middle of a sex act. "Poor, poor Spiro Agnew," she said. (My dream had something exaggerated, funnier.) She saw her entourage. They watched us from the empty hall's first row. She remembered our earlier conversation. She had time to say to me, "Sam, about our previous conversation, I don't want it mentioned to your uncle, but if you find out anything, I trust you will let me know." Was she asking me to look into this further? I suspected foul play. Had HMQ joined my choir of one?

Our conspiracy-prone culture had gone into high gear. If someone walked on an ant on Pahlavi Avenue, the whole anthill pointed at the Shah as the culprit. It culminated in the 19th of August 1979 burning of Rex Cinema in Abadan. It killed four hundred people. Later, the Islamists confessed. They had blocked the doors and set the fire, as unembarrassed as Mr. Agnew. Not a soul believed us innocent when the cinema went ablaze.

Fingers pointed at the palace. Our propaganda machine could do nothing to lower them. Our public relations engine died a slow death. G.'s death in 1975, which I kept out of the papers with the help of Reza Qotbi, alerted me that the press couldn't compete with rumors among the ruling class. All this I understood. I needed to control what I found. The last thing I wanted was to feed HMQ's circle with unsubstantiated rumors. I lied to her with conviction, "Your Highness, I have looked at the circumstances thoroughly. Rest assured, the lady had a drug problem. It pushed her to suicide." I hoped she wouldn't ask me to enumerate the psychological pressures that drove her to the act. Too close to the group for further questioning but not reassured, she smiled at me and joined her look-alike Lilys.

I judged Agnew harshly. All these years later, I regret it. Then I asked how a vice president could become the errand boy of a singer. Could Gougoush, our local Madonna, hire my uncle, the court minister, as her office manager? Now I look at it, and he, a humiliated Agnew, could count on a friend even after a disastrous resignation for corruption. I credit Americans for their forbearance. Where can I find an example in our country? HMQ found it in another past American vice president, Nelson Rockefeller, and the Egyptian president, Anwar Sadat, as they looked for refuge. They flew from country to country for 558 days. Not a single Iranian group walked in support of HIM. No one can make a case he was that bad.

5. 1963: Compromised Youth

Despite imagined and real humiliations, I grew into my first forty years with an optimistic, apparently Candide obstinacy about the best of all possible worlds. I was born in Birjand, Khorasan, in 1941, the year the Russians and the English faux-invaded the country and deposed the Shah's father, the older Reza Shah, with an ease nobody likes to talk about; humiliation turned out to be my country's, my king's, and my default emotion. Humiliation requires an outside agency, but its roots reach deep with a nested series of other humiliations. When humiliation blossoms, boy, watch out.

Birjand, a neat yellow-grey city, abuts a rugged, arid country. The most famous site in Birjand comes free: its cobalt blue sky. My family moved to Tehran in my fifth year, but Birjand remained the ancestral home.

By age fifteen, I had grown as tall as my programmed genes permitted. The thickness of my socks wouldn't add to my stature. My mother and I stood back-to-back at 160 centimeters, or five feet, three inches. By the age of seventeen, my hairline had reached its furthest on the beaches of my forehead and receded at an alarming rate. By the time I graduated from university, I considered myself a bald man. Hair sprouted elsewhere to cover me like a blanket. It required the maid to vacuum my bed as if it were an extension of the floor. My lips, a black man's lips, were meaty, shapely. My bulbous nose had mushroomed and resembled the knob of an American closet. It shone at its tip. The circles under my eyes reflected light with a gilded hue contrasting with my darker skin. My large ribcage sat on legs that resembled a cartoon doodle. My arms were longer than a short man deserved; I bent them at the elbow to shorten them, more by instinct than calculation.

I weighed my advantages and skills as I considered my future options. The universe made some feeble attempts to balance the ledger of unfairness: I played the piano like a demon, and I had a salacious tongue a mile long. The fifties society considered me land rich, which was not the same thing as cash rich, as the land reforms of the sixties proved. I didn't tip the scale anywhere near the neutral position.

What nature denied me, I tried to enhance with meticulous clothes. The legs curtained off in worsted wool trousers. I trimmed my chest in well-tailored suits. I wore poplin cotton shirts. Later, I switched to the superior Egyptian and later still to Sea Island cotton. I wore eau de cologne like a Louis XIV courtier. I pared and manicured my nails to womanly perfection and carried a second thick handkerchief to keep my black shoes shined in dusty Tehran.

To my uncle's dismay, my mother switched me from the Iranian elementary school after my fourth-grade teacher lifted my diminutive body in the air with a firm grip on both ears, like he was operating a factory chain hoist. It left a small tear in the back of my left lobe. ("A nothing," my uncle said, convinced my mother mollycoddled me.) I still rub the cicatrix with my left index finger when in deep thought. By the next day, she had transferred me to St. Louis Elementary School, where they didn't exercise corporal punishment. A French Catholic school established by the Lazarists in 1862, St, Louis focused on science over religion. I enjoyed my two years there.

My mother scored one last victory. She picked a French high school for me. My uncle wanted to see me attend Alborz, the best all-boys school in the capital. My mother insisted I attend a French school. She never hesitated to remind my uncle of my French grandmother's heritage. She registered me at Lycée Razi, the high school deep downtown on Farhang Avenue. Long after my graduation, the campus moved to the north of Vanak Square, nearer to the well-off neighborhoods of Shemiran. In those days, it had no policy banning corporal punishment. The French label didn't prevent teachers from justified assault and battery on sixty juvenile delinquents. We had prepubescents to military service-age boys. Boys were held back to repeat the same year multiple times. Most dropped out by ninth grade as mature, illiterate adults.

HMQ attended Jean d'Arc, the girl's section of St. Louis on Lalehzar Street, two years ahead of me. She switched, like me, to Lycée Razi. Neither of us remembered the other from school. We both attended the Persian section, which taught classes in Farsi rather than French—a compromise my uncle wheedled out of my mother. The American schools came a decade later. HMQ favored me for our shared schools. She often told cheerful stories of her time. My stories had an edgier survival element. I sanded them down a bit and offered them as humorous asides.

One such story involved an ink-drinking race, in which two small boys, heads back and open-mouthed (I didn't mention to HMQ that our jaws were held open by the mighty hands of sixteen-year-olds), took drops of ink from a full fountain pen with the filigree lever-filler mechanism pulled down like the handle of a pump until they emptied the barrel. I doubled down. I unnerved my tormentors. I insisted on green ink for aesthetic reasons. It unnerved them. "The first boy to cry loses." I never lost.

Instead, when the teacher, to his horror, witnessed my dark green lips, he sent me home. He didn't want me to die in his classroom. On the way out, I stuck out my green tongue at the last row of boys, three or four years older, whose failure to break me equaled their repeated failure to pass the seventh grade. These "*rofouzehs*," a Farsified cognate of the French word "refuser," had to repeat a year. They sat in the back, measuring their penises with wooden rulers while we, the younger boys, watched their antics in fascination and were awed by the size of these mature penises, another detail not proper for HMQ's ear.

I survived high school. I wanted to study music at the Royal College of Music in London or The Juilliard School in New York. I fantasized that in my late twenties, an orchestra of a European capital—not yet Vienna, that would be in my thirties—would discover me. In my forties, I would write music that would astonish the world. I'd meet world-renowned artists.

Only the last proved true. I met Andy Warhol, Serge Reggiani, Moustaki, Jim Morrison, Roy Lichtenstein, Leonard Bernstein, and Laurence Olivier. I met most of these celebrities at parties in Tehran while I worked at Court. They were on their way to or returning from India or Japan. I could go on name-dropping if my memory cooperated. I remember nothing that struck me as extraordinary; not one anecdote flashed their genius for display or communicated it to me. They were just people standing around at a party in a garden lit by the swimming pool, drunk or high. I slip and slide; let's get back.

In my eighteenth year, my father, that distant figure, now came into greater focus. He stepped into the foreground because my mother now spent months in Paris. He and my uncle had many talks with and about me. The pressure intensified in early 1959, my last year of high school. I resisted their harebrained ideas. My uncle wanted me to study agriculture as he did in Karaj, a town where I could not survive the boredom. Or join the Officer's Military Academy for the Iranian Army like HIM, where I'd be hazed mercilessly. They dismissed any thought of music as a field of study.

A compromise presented itself when I met the future prime minister, Hoveyda—one of the four mentors to direct my life. In 1959, Hoveyda was an official of Iran's National Oil Company. He counted among his friends the most notable writers, musicians, and politicians. I met him in Café Ferdows, where a few of us high school groupies, in love with books, hoped to meet the grandees of literature. In the late fifties, the wealthy bazaaris, the intermarried aristocrats, the ambitious politicians, and the foreign-educated intellectuals were not a cohesive group, but we intermingled. I hazard a few hundred people, ate, drank, and gossiped in cafes, homes, and movie houses. If I hadn't met someone, I certainly knew of them. Relabel and mix each group with the same adjectives of "well-to-do," "foreign-educated," "ambitious," and "intermarried," and the descriptors fit. We lived in a society with two degrees of separation.

I exclude the paradise-lovers. The religious intermarried more amongst themselves and preferred a Qom over a foreign education. The bazaaris acted as the intermediaries. I met and talked to my first mullah, the Imam Jomeh of Tehran, after I started work at the Court. These mullahs revolved around a different sun.

I liked Hoveyda. Like me, he didn't have looks. He came off as a bohemian intellectual without the pedantic, incomprehensible talk of the French intellectuals. He and his ill-fated friend, Hassan-Ali Mansur, created a Progressive Circle Group. They recruited educated youth.

Imagine three high school students in a crowded café, at a small table in the corner, waiters in dirty, white uniforms, a rag on their shoulders, darting from one corner to the other, ignoring us, the non-tippers.

Hoveyda meanders over from a high table, where grandees like Hedayat, Al Ahmad, and Chubak—our local Camus, Sartre, and Kafka—sit. He joins our table and slaps my back like an old buddy I have not seen for a while. He introduces himself and asks us about ourselves. He is patient, with a permanent semi-circle of a smile. He listens to our complaints and hopes. He has the effect of a father, an attentive listener rather than a firebrand: I want to tell him things about myself, so I do. He describes, with a certain nostalgia, his education at the Free University of Brussels in Belgium. A compromise, he says. He wanted to live in Paris, but the war had other ideas.

"By the way," he says, a politician down to his pared nails and careful listening skills, "the Free University also has an excellent music department. I can write a recommendation letter. I know your uncle." Years later, he told me he sat at our table because I had the air of a dandy with a folded silk pocket handkerchief flashing white and poking out of my blazer's breast pocket like two cat ears. He shared the characteristic with his ever-present Carnation-at-the lapel walking stick.

In the fall, I enrolled at the Free University of Brussels. My uncle and father agreed, a reluctant compromise. I suspect my uncle didn't appreciate Hoveyda's interference in family affairs.

I followed Hoveyda's steps. I got my bachelor's in political science and never mentioned my music studies. I graduated with a double major in 1963. I played the piano to the level of a competent professional. Nothing to report: years of bliss. No humiliations.

In 1963, I returned to a dynamic country. I weighed my options for a job. First, I needed to complete two years of compulsory military service. I dreaded uniforms, pointless drills, and dormitories full of testosterone. More than anything, I feared congregating men in a closed environment. They got dumber and more dangerous around me.

On New Year's Eve, my father and mother invited General Pakravan and his wife, my mother's friends, to dinner. She and Tante Fati, as I called her, were more French than Iranian. The General had attended the École d'application de l'artillerie. He followed the path of the intellectual general. I heard during a Hebrew play in Israel, he observed the shirt worn by Queen Mary Stewart didn't match the period by a hundred years.

We spoke French at the table. My father followed with difficulty.

The General wore civilian clothes: a light suit with a dark tie. When I left for Belgium, he managed the external affairs of the Security Intelligence. He ran the intelligence service by the time I returned. In those days, no one except the internal people called it SAVAK. He ran the intelligence agency without a whiff of torture or corruption. He recruited me. "We fight terrorists, not citizens," he explained. He promised me an adventure. He reminded me the CIA and the MI5 recruited the aristocracy of their nations. The privileged responded as a sign of patriotism and the county's health. I don't pretend I had lofty ideals. The clincher for me: My years at the intelligence service counted as time served against the two-year compulsory army service.

A week later, I passed through a low concrete gate by a glass booth where I flashed my ID. I entered the twenty-five-acre brick-walled compound. In those days, fewer than a thousand people worked there. I walked into the SAVAK headquarters east of Tehran in civilian clothes. I worked there for the next two years—a long way from the Royal College of Music or The Julliard School. My father and uncle approved.

DID YOU READ THIS IN A NEWSPAPER?

1. 2023: It Was Like This, Mrs. Lambton of Framingham

I don't isolate myself at the Rising Sun. I play the piano in the activity room, a Sunday multi-faith church. I roll my chair to the piano twice weekly (except on Sunday) when the mood takes me. The upright piano's dynamic range is limited, and the keys are considerably shorter than a grand, but the Rising Sun keeps it tuned.

I made a deal with the manageress, Mrs. Lambton, a woman of considerable stateliness. She agreed to pay for sports cable channels if I played two evenings during the week for an hour after dinner. I play standards to the considerable excitement of the female residents. Mrs. Lambton, a sizeable English woman of a certain age, tells us she will join the Rising Sun as a permanent resident when the time comes. Her peacock of a coiffure could support a circlet of considerable weight. A Julia Child of a woman without the loudness, she laughs a silent movie laugh like she's imitating a laugh.

When I asked, she told me Ann Lambton was indeed a grand aunt of her deceased husband. Well known to us at Court, we ran hot and cold on Ann Lambton. She started as a press attaché of the British Legation to Tehran. She encouraged the move to oust the Shah's father by the British. Cold. Later, she advised the British government to help overthrow Mosaddegh. Hot.

Mrs. Lambton of the Rising Sun and I usually talked after I stopped creating the thick nostalgia flow with my piano. Once the tepid claps ebbed, she sat on the piano bench I had pushed aside to roll in my wheelchair. I remembered her grand aunt. While we worked fifteen-hour days to celebrate the 2500th anniversary of the Persian Empire, she visited a few times to help with volumes of papers we planned to publish on Persian art and history. An older woman with white hair and thick black eyebrows, she didn't look like an English aristocrat but more like a Native American. I detected in her a deep antipathy toward Iranians. She saw us like classicists see Italians: a degenerate, tainted race.

A Londoner born in the sixties, Mrs. Lambton of Framingham and I, aristocrats of nothing, talked of our childhoods and youth. Curious and patient, she listened. It helped me remember how I used to think. Her little prods enabled me, for she remembered her husband's aunt, the professor emeritus of the Diocese of Newcastle. She, our Framingham variety, married into the family. Barclays Bank transferred her husband, an accountant, to Boston. The elder Mrs. Lambton and her nephew died in the same year, 2008.

My beliefs in 1965 had nothing original about them. As an aristocrat, I believed in property. I took the fear of communism seriously. I hated the Tudeh party because I understood the Soviet control of the party. I never changed my mind. Twice, the Soviet Union came close to taking a bite of the Iranian pomegranate. In 1919, they annexed Gilan, a northern province called for a time the Soviet Socialist Republic of Iran. In 1945, the Kremlin kept the province of Azarbaijan in slow motion by not withdrawing to prewar borders. The Tudeh party, not quite in sync, dallied a tad too long after Stalin had backed off. They never survived the shame of the collaboration, a fate not so different from that of so many other national communist parties.

"Please, I don't want to pry, but do you consider yourself a Muslim?" Mrs. Lambton's question in this day and age has as many edges as my crumpled Post-it notes. I played a dah-da-dah on the piano to undermine the gravity of her question with humor. A few hopeful residents picked their heads up. They thirsted for more nostalgia. I shook my head at them in apology.

I grew up as a non-practicing Muslim. I disliked mullahs. We all did. I saw the mullahs as illiterates propagating rubbish. If you visited a mosque and listened to a tirade, you would have heard rhetoric well beyond a Southern Baptist rant. It lifted daily habits like defecation to bizarre instructions that would have surprised a seventh-century ascetic. I didn't grasp the philosophical underpinning. Mullahs never saw Islam as a spiritual religion. They saw it as social order. I should avow my absolute wonder at Cassius Clay. He transitioned to Islam by renaming himself Muhammad Ali. What was he thinking? I only saw a downside. I remember the sentiment, but I was oblivious to the race issue. All this comes off pedantic.

"Mrs. Lambton," I said. "I hope I don't insult you. Frankly, when my time comes, please don't fetch our omnistic pastor at my last hour. His presence might change my mind."

She did one of her imitation silent laughs. "You are a funny man, Sam. We English believe in our religion as we believe in our monarchy. *Noli impedire.* Don't interfere." She translated so as not to embarrass me. I smiled with pleasure. I had an educated woman on my hands. Our religious tolerance was over-hyped in the history books. We didn't bait minorities but ignored them.

HIM never showed his preference; if anything, they accused him as a puppet of the Bahá'ís.

"Can I dare ask you another complex question? Did you suffer any racism in this country?" I looked at her with surprise. I never considered myself a black man. I don't recall a discussion of color or race in my youth. Our skin color showed what province we came from. Our skin color varied from white in the Caspian region to dark, like I am, from Khorasan. People would ask if I was from Khorasan or Sistan and Baluchestan. I shook my head, a definite "no," because I was oblivious to my color.

Mrs. Lambton showed a no-nonsense kindness with the help; when frustrated with Malik and Elijah, like a medieval matron, she'd mumble, "God give me strength." When I told her I called them Laurel and Hardy, she told me Laurel had light blue eyes. Blue photographed white. It made Laurel look like a zombie. He used makeup until the film quality improved.

"How do you know?" I asked.

"Laurel and my family came from Lancashire. I am a Jefferson. Laurel was a Jefferson. Laurel is his stage name. He visited us when I was four or five," she replied.

"Do I have to call Malik 'Jefferson' now?" I used my piano keys to say, "ironic." The residents had left the activity room.

I advance an argument for the US: a woman related to Stan Laurel married into the British Lambtons can have a discussion with a man descended from a thousand years of Iranian tribal lords in a nursing home in the suburbs of Boston with no burden to carry.

"But did you also know the iconic American comedian Bob

Hope was born in England to English parents?" she asked. I didn't know.

I liked Mrs. Lambton. I liked her largeness. She smelled womanly. A trace of perfume didn't hide the woman who ran through kitchens, bent to pick tomatoes from the backyard, and moved furniture when needed. It reminded me of the smell of the women we frequented in high school. See, piano tunes are not required to open the nostalgia faucet.

My sexual experience with legal downtown sex workers started in the tenth grade. I found my erection and lost my virginity in New City, the now-burned-down red-light district of Tehran, not too far from Lycée Razi. My first unpleasant experience shocked me, but not enough. I returned many times.

The woman who transformed me from boy to man lay beneath me. She wanted to do her magic in less than two minutes; not an unreasonable goal for a sixteen-year-old. She had more folds on her stomach than a Spanish flamenco skirt. With the impatience of a soccer fan, she encouraged me to hurry and score. I didn't have the magic bullet in me then. Excited, her earring caught on the metal band of my watch. It ripped the earring from her earlobe. Blood spurted on the already brown mattress, like in the last scene of *Carrie*. Her screams brought the men from downstairs up on the double. I produced, also on the double, all my money from my pocket trousers next to the bed. They spared me a beating. We often returned, not for the quick relief, but the fantasy of choice before and the hilarity among us boys after. We returned to school with erections down, heads held high. Not an ethical thought crossed our minds.

All this from a whiff of Mrs. Lambton? Yes, and more. After the Laurel and Bob Hope comments, I asked her if she had watched movies as she grew up in London.

"Oh yes, indeed," she said. I love how the English can insert the word "indeed" at their most assertive instead of Americans who use "fuck." "Fuck, yes" would have been Jefferson's response.

"Our mother died early from breast cancer," she said. "My father would take us, my sister and I, to the movies on the strip between Trafalgar and Leicester Square. We'd come out of one, he'd look for another film, and we'd go back in. He didn't know what to do with us on the Lord's Day. We loved Sundays. See, no church for us, the damned. We went to pray in the dark of the movie houses of Soho.

"I watched *The Hound That Thought He Was a Raccoon, Pollyanna, The 3 Worlds of Gulliver*, and then," her eyes sparkled as she named her favorite movie of her childhood, "*Swiss Family Robinson*. I thought the Swiss were the cleverest people in the world. Wasn't your wife Swiss, Sam?" she asked, not overly concerned about my emotions. She understood how the old grieve.

"Yes, indeed, she was the cleverest of the Swiss." Fuck, yes. I smiled.

While Mrs. Lambton watched hounds, who considered themselves raccoons, we watched movies in Court. I stood far in the back. A Bell and Howell projector setup in the garden projected on a large screen affixed on a tall wooden pole with a heavy cement base—luxury incarnated. Some movies didn't reach commercial distribution until months later. US, the little fingers of HIM, got to brag. I enjoyed the French films of the suave Eddie Constantine, the Humphrey Bogart of Paris, the Sinatra of the

Seine, who started a mania. We wore his cool chapeaux in Tehran. Just as I didn't know Bob Hope's origins, I never knew Eddie was American, his French accent was so perfect. The ladies swooned at Marlon Brando as Napoleon and Jean Simmons as Désirée. Any Alain Delon movie was an assured hit. I suffered and adored his good looks in equal measure. The portrayal of the Arabs as savages in *Lawrence of Arabia* didn't ring a bell for any of us. The movies focused on action. Ubiquitous sex had not entered the nooks and crannies of our society. It would be coming.

Within eight years, we saw nothing but explicit pictures, movies, and ads in daily papers; not a moment of regret for me. All kinds of liberation washed over the West. It brought down the governments of Britain, France, and the US. Millions marched in the capitals of the West. And yet we wondered at its delayed effect, as though it was something special to us. I remember a censor asking for permission for an ad by Qantas Airlines. It showed a busty woman in a bikini, holding a surfboard under her arm. It went through; not a peep from the religious. It started that innocuously. I thank Mrs. Lambton; not bad for a man with early Alzheimer's.

2. 1965 On-the-Job Training

After I attended university, I worked for two years in the intelligence bureau, which wiped my debt to my country's compulsory military service. My uncle, still fifteen months away from his return as court minister, did light penance. He didn't don a sackcloth and walk barefoot in Qom for the deaths of Khomeini's groupies. He cooled his heels—or convalesced, I should say—as the chancellor of Shiraz University.

Thanks to my uncle's warm relationship with Court Minister Nakhai, I joined the Court's propaganda machine in late May or early June. I became the paperboy for the Shah. No complaints. An apparatchik two doors down from power always beats an apparatchik in the suburbs of power, no matter the hierarchy. We didn't call it public relations, but our job was communicating the Court's position. We played a marketing arm to policy positions.

Crucially, or perhaps fortunately, I didn't serve under the new SAVAK Chief, General Nassiri. Six months earlier, after the assassination of Mansour, the prime minister (it was a pity but no loss), HIM dismissed the most humane Intelligence head anywhere in the world, my beloved General Pakravan.

I worked in a small office next to the small office in which Court Minister Hossein Nakhai sat. A humble man, he took pleasure in humility; it was his *carte de visite*. Few remember his four years as a court minister. Sandwiched between Ala and Alam, two previous prime ministers, he cut a lesser figure.

Hossein Nakhai was an old-school diplomat and a former foreign minister. He had the credentials to become what a court minister ought to be: invisible. Soft-spoken, he tended towards whispering. A poet, he wrote his own Rubayat and translated Khayam's *Rubayat* into English and French. A bald man, he wore glasses whose black frames hugged only the top of the lenses; the smokey tint of the lenses exaggerated the bruised-colored pockets under his eyes. He wore a bemused smile. He could have played the role of the minister who helped Audrey Hepburn, Princess Ann in *Roman Holiday*, to regain her shoe, if it weren't for the atrocious, foul-smelling local Oshnu cigarettes he smoked.

As the story goes, he'd shake his head in agreement with any statement made in a meeting of foreign ministers of CENTO. The Pakistani foreign minister once protested, "Mr. Foreign Minister, you seem to agree with all of us even though our statements contradict each other." He replied that he even agreed with the protest. That is diplomatic professionalism. His kind didn't fit the more aggressive stance HIM envisioned in our future.

He understood the job. He hammered into my head: Thou shall avoid embarrassments to us. "You know who 'us' is? 'Us,' the royal we, is His Majesty. We are part of the 'us,' but it is singular. Think of yourself as a small finger of His Majesty. His brain crooks his little finger, and you come to life and operate." He smiled. "I don't exaggerate." He doubled down on the smile. "It is like jumping in front of a bullet for HIM. I remember you are good at that," he said with a smile. "Any of us in the government should deflect and take the blame when a negative story appears."

In the mornings, a dozen foreign and domestic papers appeared in my little office at the Marmar Palace. I perused them.

I read articles to detect stories that connected or could get connected to the Court and the person of the Shah. I had to relearn how to read for what was essential to the singular "us." I cut and glued the articles.

In my previous job, when the Americans left the Dominican Republic, I would scramble for more information and analyze its effects on the Middle East. The military coup by the Algerian Houari Boumédiène against Ben Bella was all grist for the mill. Let alone Israel's move into Jordan or when the US put boots in Vietnam.

"Someone else now does your old job," he told me during my first week. "You don't have to include foreign news unless you think it might embarrass us," Nakhai instructed with patience. He read excerpts out loud. "What you missed: See this little gem on the last page between the Pakistani plane crash and the ad for the Birdman of Alcatraz? It says because of a worldwide good harvest, wheat imports will be $12/ton cheaper. HIM has a special interest in the weather. He is interested in the weather because of his mania for a good harvest. And did you miss the 2300 hundred people who have waited two years to get their first phone?"

"That's bad news?" I said.

"My job," he said, "is to feed His Majesty the news with a mix of good and bad about the internals of the country. A judgment call, I grant you." As I mentioned, old school.

I learned HIM skimmed over an assassination attempt on the President of Bolivia with a snarky remark. He got more interested when they tried to kill de Gaulle. He loved the man. If the target was any of the royal personages in the world, he took it seriously, no matter where in the world. I had to go through a great deal of nonsense. On his sixty-sixth birthday, the Emperor of Japan published his sixth marine biology book, *The Scorpions of Sagami Bay*. We wrote a small column to remind readers of HIM's autobiography, *Mission for My Country*.

I wrote the Shah's anti-communist speeches during those months. I pushed the point of view with editors. I invited them to lunch. Our war, the wrong war against the communists of all sects, had started long ago. We had the law on our side. It said the Communist Party was an illegal entity. It reduced governmental assassinations but increased the violent toward the stationed Americans.

The Shah appointed my uncle as court minister in the winter of 1966, a private thank you. He had saved the monarchy. My uncle laid down the law: "Never call me uncle at Court, or I'll crack your head. Keep your eye on two groups: the Prime Minister and his friends, and the Queen and her sycophants. Don't underestimate the last lot. Their crackpot ideas will show up later in disguise. Always remember, they watch you because you are related to me." He and the new prime minister, Hoveyda, stayed in power for the next thirteen years, an achieved balance.

Hard to believe, but before him, we burned most of the incoming mail. We didn't have the personnel to answer the correspondence. He redesigned the Court's communication system. I saw and oversaw new people. They joined us by the dozen. We ran a well-oiled machine. He created a government within a government. Two ministries lost their influence and became mere paper pushers. The foreign minister often stood outside HIM's office while crucial decisions occurred inside. The Shah had taken over.

We admired the Israeli lobby. Israelis understood the West. The Israeli representative introduced us to a firm in the US called Yankelovich, Skelly, & White. We got excited. We worked with them until they sent a marketing questionnaire to HIM. The questions seemed hostile to his ear. He closed down the relationship.

We kept the offices in the Marmar Palace. HIM moved his office to the Sahebgharaniyeh Palace in the Niavaran complex. We added larger offices outside the Sa'dabad complex further uptown. I shuttled between the three offices.

My uncle, suspicious of hidden agendas, decided nothing until he exposed an individual's intention. When he did understand, he decided decisively. He had an inscription on his desk. It said, "You told me, and I believed you. You emphasized, and I doubted. You swore, and I knew you lied."

CLUELESS

1. 1975: Amateur Hour with a Breast-Biter

I woke up swearing. I had dreamt of a page heading: Amateur Hour with a Breast-Biter. I don't need to write a Post-it note. How could I have forgotten the worm in the apple—the breast-biter? While she fed him her milk, he bit her breast. I am not a snob, but I don't underestimate the effects of a marked card shuffled in the wrong pack.

HIM's childhood friend was of low origins; the poverty mark was tattooed on the forehead. It was visible to all but the man behind the forehead. A father in the lowly gendarmerie got his son chosen to join the Crown Prince's school of twenty boys. He was not a stupid boy, but he was a dullard. Despite this, his high grades made him a favorite of the old Shah. They chose him to keep the Crown Prince company for fifty years. We Iranians believe the young become the company they keep.

The poor boy accompanied the Crown Prince to Le Rosey, the Swiss high school. The boy wanted to attend medical school; the old Shah insisted that a soldier's calling is the patriot's path. The unneeded friend enrolled with HIM in the officers' college.

I remember that boy as an adult—Fardoust, had a nominal position in the SAVAK organization. No one considered it nominal. His social relationship with the Shah gave him a listening ear you could not take lightly. Later, HIM appointed Fardoust Imperial Inspector General; he was the vegetarian fox in charge of the henhouse, hankering for the eggs. Among HIM's inner circle of friends, he was the one with a portfolio and the person to collaborate with the Islamic Republic.

The execrable book he wrote, or got dictated to under the tutelage of the Islamic Republic, taints my memory. He appeared for them on television. He spewed what he wrote—a series of anti-Bahá', anti-Jewish, and anti-Christian tropes. If you believed his narrative, not one person who served in HIM's thirty-seven-year rule had not been an English spy or placed there by the Americans. He talked on TV as he talked at Court—like a man who didn't want to talk. Long pauses at the wrong parts of his sentences had the regime interviewers on edge. They wished to jump in to help him or drag the word out with their hands. In time, he'd slowly string together four or five words and spew more antisemitic nonsense. I don't believe he praised a single person in his book. He sat at the SAVAK for most of its existence, but then went on to help set up SAVAMA, its Islamic burka-clad sister. With his thick eyebrows and oily skin, he could pass as a member of the Politburo. He sat in his office with the curtains always drawn. He wrote his reports with a pencil to make them erasable.

The social friends of the Shah had specific characteristics: they were charming, humorous, womanizing, from upper-crust families, and uninvolved in the government. HIM kept them separate. General Fardoust, however, possessed none of these characteristics. HIM remained loyal to his friends and his friends to HIM, but for the breast-biter.

Once a week on Thursdays, Nassiri reported to HIM and left a twenty-page report for perusal at the Sahebgharaniyeh Palace in the Niavaran complex. We penciled Fardoust in during the second hour a report similar to that of the second in command at SAVAK. His reports consisted of a tight narrative starting at mid-management level and edited down to the most critical elements. It was a familiar exercise to me. In my earlier years, I fed into my superior's reports—a corporate discipline followed by most multinationals. The Fardoust report could be critical of Nassiri's organization.

A few Thursdays after G.'s death, cigarette in hand, I stand on the balcony of the Shah's office in the Niavaran compound. I see the two men pass each other outside. Nassiri saunters, ferret-like, toward his car and the chauffeur holds the door open. Fardoust walks toward him. The two men are dressed as generals, which both are. Nassiri smiles and makes an awkward mock salute, then bends to get into the back of the car. Fardoust's casual walk and tight smile—which he always wears—say it all.

"General, could I have a word?" says Fardoust.

"Won't you be late for His Majesty's meeting?" says Nassiri.

"It won't take a minute, and I want you to know what I will report to HIM." They move inside the hall. I walk stealthily to the top of the stairs to hear their conversation, eavesdropping on eavesdroppers. I take a few steps down toward the first landing.

Right away, I hear Fardoust question Nassiri. "Who authorized the approach to Tala?" he asks. I prick my ears. "Three secretaries of SAVAK approached her to get information. Can you explain?"

Nassiri, uncomfortable, mumbles, "Routine. You know how it is."

"Three secretaries? Do you call that routine? And you can

spare your personal secretary. This is preposterous. I will let HIM know."

"As always, you are well-informed, General," says Nassiri. "For efficiency, we use any personnel with any spare time. By the way, he knows." Nassiri refers to HIM. Then they both look up as if HIM sits on a cloud watching them. Instead, they see me. I recover. I walk down the last flight. I hurry Fardoust upstairs. "He has called for you," I say.

I am deeply suspicious. The heads of the Intelligence exchanging words over a dead girl? Secretaries had befriended her? It doesn't make sense.

It didn't. Did I forget to mention that Nassiri's secretary was Major General Motazed, deputy chief of SAVAK, who had no spare time? Something Fardoust would know. HMQ asked about Nassiri's involvement. Could it have been Fardoust?

2. 1975: The Bad Guy Makes an Entrance

After the revolution, I watched the Islamic Republic put eleven SAVAK bureaucrats on a platform to be interrogated by the world press. If you listened without bias, they described the running of an intelligence bureau that worked hand-in-hand with the CIA and Mossad. I am sure most of them now worked for the SAVAMA and worked hand-in-hand with the Syrian and Hamas intelligence bureaus. I know this for a fact—I recognized one of the eleven on the panel as Nader Yasin, my old colleague. He sat there calmly. He explained protocol and process without a shadow of fear.

I called Captain Yasin after my detective-like eavesdropping session at the Sahebgharaniyeh Palace. We met in the afternoon at the busy Chattanooga Café on the upper side of Pahlavi Avenue. Willful, fluffy snow covered the small branches of the 18,000 sycamore trees lining the longest street in Tehran. Two trucks on each side drove at a stroller's pace. The street sweepers on top of the trucks used long wooden brooms. They batted the snow from the branches to spare tree damage. It created a horrendous traffic jam. Car horns penetrated, albeit at a lower frequency, into the cafe without effect because tables full of young people laughed and shouted across other tables. The din inside of Chattanooga allowed us to talk without risk. If anything, we couldn't even hear ourselves.

We drank beer. We talked about our families. He congratulated me on my recent marriage. He showed me a picture of his son and daughter. We didn't fake; we liked each other. He understood why I moved to Court. We all did. He sat opposite me with a thin, cream-colored folder under his elbow. It attested to his recognition of the source of power.

"The other night, the General didn't want us to give you all the facts." I stayed placid and nonresponsive. He smiled and tapped his finger twice to his temple. "Our training, right? The pressure of silence will make most people babble. I am not here to babble, Sam. I made a decision. You looked like you cared for the dead girl. Once, you and I worked for an elite institution. I believed in it. Now, people hate us. I can never admit that I work for Intelligence. My family will become instant pariahs. This information I give you, I give to you for my own sake."

"We both can confess to the unsavory side of our work," I said.

"Yours at least gives pleasure to someone," he said. It didn't surprise me he knew what I did. Still, I felt the knuckles of the first two fingers of this bureaucracy reach and tweak my nose. No one likes to know a file living in a cabinet contains other information than his job title as a pimp. I asked what he had for me.

"Earlier in the night," he began, "another man entered the house." Nervous, he looked around. I guess for any sign of 'us.' "The man stayed there for a while. I can't tell you how long because he left from the back door. The thing about it is, Sam, he had been there before with the girl's father."

"What man, what's his name?" I asked. He slipped the folder across the table. I half-opened the file and took a peek. Even today, I could swear the whole cafe stopped all activity. The owners of the cars took their hands off the horns. The street sweepers in the trucks stopped their work. Nader looked at me with pity. "Yes," he said. "Prince Amir Houshang Davallou Qajar. You should also know your uncle knows all the facts. Davallou took a suspicious box in a nylon bag into the house."

I told him I had read my uncle's report and it didn't mention Davallou. Nader said, "Not Nassiri, but Fardoust reported it in person to him early in the morning, right after we left the house." Again, he understood the import of what he said to me. My uncle could also keep a poker face. I didn't detect the slightest waver when I gave him what was second-hand news. My uncle let me in to report to HIM. It suggested he didn't intend to disclose the Davallou's visit to HIM. Or at least not yet.

It didn't make sense to me. My uncle disliked Davallou's undisciplined, corrupt mind. Once, Davallou insisted on an audience for a friend. HIM, suspicious at this persistence, asked him, "What's in it for you?" To the amusement of many but not my uncle, he said, "$5,000." Another time, he dared to offer opium to relieve HIM's tension. My uncle jumped in to remind the Shah of our strict drug laws. HIM refused the offer. My uncle never trusted Davallou.

I got hot under the collar. Davallou wasn't the only person my uncle didn't trust. After all these years, he still didn't trust me. I told Nader I might need his help with the small matter of Davallou. He sat without comment.

I had to ask him about Fardoust and Nassiri's exchange at the palace. I repeated the exact words. He looked at me and joined the rest of the cafe with raucous laughter.

"Don't you know?"

"Don't I know what?"

"Fardoust's wife's name is Tala." He laughed again.

"Why would they approach Fardoust's wife?" I said.

Nader got serious again. "It's what I mean about how the service has changed. No one is above suspicion. I hear rumors, well, more than rumors. Fardoust has left a trail of breadcrumbs that links him to the KGB. The investigations show extensive circumstantial evidence. By the way, his wife sings like a magpie; like the bird, she is bold and intelligent. HIM grants all the requests to investigate Fardoust. He reads them. He never gives credence to any of it. He believes the Russians plant evidence to turn friends against him, which is also not unprecedented. He doesn't doubt Fardoust ever."

Now I started to laugh. "Can you see the traces?" I asked.

"Of what?"

"Egg on my face." My detective work needed improvement. I was no Hercule Poirot.

NLESS, OPIUM, AND GIFTS

1. 1972: Prince Pimp and the Blinking Swiss

I slept poorly last night. A wooly confusion reigned until 10:00 a.m. As I ordered and reordered my notes, I puzzled over three words on one of the headers I had written the week before. I write words because they trigger cause-and-effect remembrances. They act like fast-flowing rapids in the memory river before I arrive at the calm waters of the present. My Post-it note has three cryptic words: Nless, opium, and gifts. I had to concentrate on words I had connected days before.

Opium, its sweet, sinewy smell, masculine hospitality, and ceremonious cooking all come to mind. Our house was known for its *basat* of opium—*basat* refers to the infrastructure necessary to prepare opium. I do not use it as a compliment, but my father treasured those afternoons. I didn't mind them. Today, the dictator in me might require the assisted living community to provide the *basat* for opium use.

With the dispassionate wrist movement of an expert, *woosh*, *woosh*, the servant ever so rapidly spins the heap of coal in an ornamental metal mesh, at the end of a thin chain, to a perfect glow. The host places a punctuation mark of opium on the pipe's pinhole. He offers, with utmost delicacy, a small rock of coal, held with a filigreed silver tong, to fuse and burn the medicine. The red coal resembles something mined from the Earth's center, black veined angry red. The practiced greedy, prolonged breath intake goes on forever. The smoke trapped in the chest stays there for even longer. The desperate exhale shows little evidence of the inhalants. The perfect minuet of sweets, tea, and fruit sent by the lady of the house transforms the afternoon into an artistic performance.

I finally remember the man most connected with opium and how we saved his bacon with generous gifts. The Nless introduces my wife.

It began with an audacious move by HIM—audacious because, under the guise of diplomacy, he broke the law of another country: Switzerland.

The previous Qajar dynasty had fallen in slow motion under the authoritarian Reza Shah in 1921. The rot ran deep. It folded unto itself without a fight. It whimpered into irrelevance. HIM didn't have a mean spirit. He could have frozen the descendants of the previous dynasty, but instead he brought the sons and daughters of the large and well-educated clan inside the tent.

He liked Prince Davallou Qajar, the least impressive of the lot. The Prince loved the Shah. He once cracked his knee when he curtsied with grandiloquent enthusiasm. They took him to a hospital for his dog-like devotion. He had a checkered history and a reputation for buffoonery. He was not a fool like me; he was a clown. A clown amuses. A fool wraps truth in tomfoolery. He dealt in caviar and women. People referred to him as the Sultan of Caviar or called him Prince Pimp. He didn't run exactly the Cali cartel, though some of his operations, run by his wife, had an extortionist's odor. An opium addict, he didn't relish confrontation. A behind-the-back raconteur, he could cut people but without sustained focus. During World War II in Paris, he had charmed half the German General Staff.

In late February 1972, the Shah arrived in St. Moritz. I accompanied the royal family and stayed at the Kulm Hotel, close to the chalet villa Suvretta, where the royal family lodged. The Queen asked her friend Bushehri, another of the band of philanderers, to decorate the house. He represented Jansen. He brought richly detailed carpets and antiques from Iran to give the chalet a warm atmosphere.

And warm it was. The nannies ran around but ran slower than the four kids who chased and screamed through the house. The personal servants offered tea at every chance, holding their silver trays high up to protect the kids. The dogs yapped and rolled around with the two young children. I could see something to be treasured: a happy family.

I want to shout at my brain's director: Freeze, cut, let's call it a day. The tragedy of the family rises to the surface. Besides HIM's death at 61, the two youngest children, who once happily bounced on the couches, died from a drug overdose and a suicide.

On the third day of our stay, at around 3:00, I escorted an officious young Swiss woman from the Bern-Mittelland administrative district. The cobalt blue sky startled me. The Queen and the children had stayed in town to get Grand Marnier crepes. I sat discreetly in the corner as a notetaker. The young woman spoke French well but with a trace of a German accent. The Shah entered. He hadn't taken off his ski Boots. He carried his anorak under his arm, his goggles twisted on his wrist. At fifty-three, HIM looked relaxed and sunburnt. He wore a white turtleneck and black ski pants. I ran forward to help him with his shoes; he shooed me away with his hand without looking at me. All curious, he watched the young woman. He sat on the couch and unbuckled his boots. He kept his gaze on her.

"Mademoiselle…?" he enquired with the pleasant smile he often flashed to women.

She didn't betray any nerves. "Your Majesty, my name is Annabelle Lehmann," she said and nodded in a stiff, head bow.

"Any relation to the American Lehmans?" he asked.

She smiled a warmer smile. "Not even a poor cousin, Your Majesty; I am without a fortune. The extra letter N has proved costly. They are "Nlessly" rich." The question had been asked before. I feared he might ask, "And are you Jewish, Mrs. Lehmann?" I am sure she had an answer to disarm the interlocutor. From a Middle Eastern sovereign, though, the question might have been misinterpreted. The opposite was true; the Shah admired the Jewish people. His father saved hundreds of Jews by granting them Iranian passports before the War. We worked with Israel, albeit without press releases.

The Shah's smile broadened. He chuckled with delight. He never revealed a predatory outward sign toward women. Charm from a powerful man was predatory enough. She was far from his type, a shortish brunette with thick calves, a chipmunk of a face with a hole in her chin deep enough to strike oil. When she smiled, a small gap in the upper middle teeth changed her look from serious to cute, like a traffic light. You had to wait for it. An Alfred E. Neuman kind of face. "How can I help you, Mrs. Lehmann, with two Ns?"

"Miss, without ess," she corrected. She smiled for a fraction of a second. The traffic light changed. She switched back to officiousness. "Your Majesty, I have, here," she pulled out a piece of paper, embossed with a few seals, "an arrest warrant for a Mr. Davallou-Qajar." The Shah could keep a poker face. In the fifties, he played a mean poker game. He stopped playing to kill the rumors he gambled large sums. He didn't.

"And the charge?" the Shah asked.

"Smuggling opium across the border with intent to sell," Miss Lehmann said.

"Ridiculous," he said. He meant it.

I got up right away. I said in Farsi, "Your Majesty, I know Davallou uses the stuff, but he doesn't sell it; he doesn't need the money. Allow us to meet in private. Mr. Davallou has a diplomatic passport." I wanted the Shah not to say another word until we had time to discuss the matter with lawyers.

As I uttered my words, Miss Lehmann took an immediate worried step with her hands up like she wanted to surrender to a gun-pointing Shah. "Your Majesty, I confess to have a smattering of Farsi. I have always been interested in the Iranian culture. I have a double degree in history and Iranian studies from the University of Bern."

"Thank you for the warning." He affected a cold smile and made it disappear like a magician's trick. "As you probably understood from our embarrassed servant, Mr. Davallou has our protection. Is it a coincidence the Swiss government has sent an emissary with your skills?"

"It is not a coincidence, Your Majesty. I volunteered to come. My superiors have probably forgotten what I studied in school. I wanted to let you know right away. With my background, I didn't want any confusion around my mission." She had no idea how suspicious we all were. Coincidences didn't exist for HIM. "Your Majesty, the case against Mr. Davallou is federal. It involves Interpol because the crime crosses multiple borders. The accusation comes from a Mr. Goreishi caught with thirty-five grams of opium, intending to sell it to a Mr. Khosro Qashqai in Germany. When questioned by the prosecutor, he claimed to have gotten the opium from Prince Davallou Qajar." She pronounced the fricative *Kh* and the *Q* of the names with difficulty. Her attempt gave credence to her knowledge of the language.

I saw the Shah's mood shift. The imperious façade always hid the tentative, uncertain man disrespected by foreign leaders. On this occasion, he surprised me with his resolute response. I thought it incautious at the time, but I rooted for him. I shared the humiliation.

"Miss Lehmann, can I ask you to inform the authorities of our continued protection of Mr. Davallou?" The Shah never used the title of Prince. "We know of Mr. Davallou's addiction. We should consider him a victim of the drug. You might not know, but our laws take the distribution of drugs seriously. Anyone caught as a supplier of drugs faces the death penalty. You have evidence of distribution?"

I saw fear creep into Miss Lehmann's presentation. Not fear of HIM; she didn't want to screw up her mission. Miss Lehmann added a few more details: "A Mrs. Vallon, secretary to Mr. Ghoreishi, saw the package on the desk. She got suspicious and opened the package. She found 35 grams of opium wrapped in oil paper. She reported it to the Swiss police." Oh, how Swiss. "Your Majesty, my official role will be as a liaison officer. I will update your office on the progress of the case. I work for the foreign office. His Excellency Judge Weber will keep me up to date. The Swiss government wants to ensure our continued commercial cooperation." There it was. She, or, rightly, the Swiss government, blinked. No one wanted to jeopardize the not-insignificant commercial relations with Iran.

I accompanied Miss Lehmann to the door and handed her half a kilo of caviar in the unmistakable imperial blue round tin box wrapped incongruously with a ribbon. She took it from me without a glance at the package and left. She called me the same night, horrified. "I can't accept such an expensive gift. I thought you gave me a box of chocolate," she said. "I need to return this right away." That is how I got my first coffee date with Miss Lehmann, my future wife, Annabelle.

"Chocolate?" I said. "Chocolate should have been your gift to us." We met in Geneva the next day. HIM encouraged me to go.

Two days later, on the 29th of February 1972, the Shah cut short his holiday. He jetted us out of Switzerland. I glared at the Davallou. He assumed a pitiful pose in his seat and avoided my stare. He looked far older than his sixty-two years. His body pleaded for a few grams of opium. I asked him directly, "Did you do it?"

"He came to my apartment and asked for a favor. I gave him some of my stash to give to Qashqai in Germany."

"Did you ask for money?"

He looked at me with hurt eyes. "I export 50 tons of caviar yearly. I make $150 in profit per kilo. You think I worry about the cost of 35 grams of opium?" *I know you*, I thought. *You asked for money*. But he had given me his first line of defense.

"Anybody see you give him the package?" I asked. He said no.

The Shah sat in the cockpit next to the pilot. He flew the aircraft and landed at the Mehrabad airport at 1:30 a.m. I had some strategies to offer my uncle by the time we landed. I saw the crisis as an excellent opportunity for me.

2. 1972: The Bad Guy with an Opium Outlook

How to characterize the next six months: happy times. My uncle took the lead. I did the work. We flipped a public relations disaster into an image-enhancing opportunity for our boss. The pressure was to make all this poof away before the mid-June International Labor Conference back in Geneva. We had scheduled HIM to give the welcome speech at the conference.

We first had to weather the storm—a dog's breakfast of negative articles. The story broke in the *Bild Zeitung* or *Bild*, the best-known daily tabloid in Germany. The story of Goreishi's arrest at a party had the perfect delicious accident for the tabloid: Soraya, the second wife of the Shah, also attended the party. It was a coincidence, but meant more work for us.

On the 10th of April 1972, *Tribune de Genève* gave more details on the party, and, for the first time, they mentioned Davallou. The paper reported that Judge Weber had been unable to contact Goreishi. Never at his apartment at Grand Sourcier in Geneva, Goreishi escaped to Capri. The judge asked to interview Mr. Davallou.

We worked day and night with our legal team in Geneva, headed by Monsieur Raymond Nicolet with whom I struck up a friendship. I stayed in touch with Miss Lehmann. On all our calls, she advised us to get Davallou to respond to the judge's summons. I assured her of our government's complete cooperation.

As if we didn't have enough headaches, *Le Monde* wrote an inflammatory article unrelated to the Davallou case. It alleged that Princess Ashraf, the Shah's twin sister, was the owner of a suitcase full of heroin found at the Orly airport. The incensed Princess sued *Le Monde*. It exacerbated our public image problems during the late winter. Other papers piled on about the execution of terrorists in our prisons.

The court minister, whose position was comparable to that of the chief of staff at the White House, and his staff at Court, had one *raison d'être*: protect the boss. That first week of spring, we looked inept. If we were to protect the Shah and blunt the press attacks, we had to separate Davallou from HIM.

It wasn't easy to convince the Shah. My uncle and I caught HIM at a weekly Queen-mother's dinner. After dinner, drinks in hand, we retired to an unused large salon full of gaudy, gold-decorated faux-Louis XVI furniture. The room smelled damp. Our voices echoed around the room. We could hear the noise of the dinner party, like a general hum. A large chandelier with hundreds of candle-like bulbs cast a weak light. He sat in the middle of a wide couch, one arm stretched on the back, the other on his crossed legs. I had lived with him long enough to know he practiced postures to communicate his power. Like a male model, he could keep a pose for hours. Seldom at ease in his later years, he would freeze into one of his three or four characteristic permanent poses when the number of attendees at a function rose to over five or six. He had developed a stare. It rested on some point mid-horizon—not quite infinity, but not in the forefront of current life.

My uncle sat in an armchair to the right. He faced HIM obliquely. I stood behind my uncle. We explained the plan. He went imperially impatient in seconds. "The lawyers influence you and you swallow whatever nonsense they sell you."

Except when in the presence of the Shah, my uncle walked confidently and self-assuredly. With the Shah, the posture changed to that of a supplicant; he bent forward, hand crossed at the crotch position. He maneuvered his view in real time to read the Shah's body language. He smiled at all the right times. When HIM laughed, he followed the laughter with his own. He excused HIM's ingratitudes and deflected his petty cruelties. He consoled his minor setbacks. My uncle's jokes belittled himself and aggrandized HIM. It wasn't pure flattery; he believed in the hierarchy of monarchy. I state the rule of power: In the presence of a powerful man, the power of a less powerful man does not diminish; it goes to zero.

I was no different. I bootlicked, groveled, and self-belittled with the best. I uttered exaggerated compliments (remembering them makes my American head sweat with shame), which is why my uncle's reply stunned me.

"Your Majesty is also under the influence of Amir Houshang Davallou. If Davallou doesn't arrive in Geneva in the next two days, we shall lose a major public relations coup." I stood frozen. It is hard to translate the complexity of the relationships into our modern vernacular. There was not precisely fear yet, but I sensed something unhealthy. An Iranian politician, Entezam, once told

HIM, "To your father, no one dared lie; to you, no one dares tell the truth." An early insight, but I quibble with the second use of the word "dare." HIM had a way of not wanting to hear the truth. But a truth-teller didn't face the dire consequences the father had meted out.

To his credit, HIM didn't even notice. "Unperturbed," my uncle wrote in his diary later. HIM changed tack. He said gently, "Davallou won't make it. He will collapse. He has a heart problem. He spent all last week in the hospital."

"Your Majesty, I have spoken to him. He has assured me that, for the sake of Your Majesty, he will make the journey," I said. I felt I could reduce the tension by telling a mild untruth. We had applied severe pressure on the man. We threatened to cancel his beloved distribution franchise of caviar. That's when he agreed to make the trip.

"So, he should. He owes us." The truth uttered by kings can change instantly and still be the truth. He shook his head in agreement with us. "Okay, but," he said as he got up, "he better not get arrested at the airport. That I will not tolerate."

The Shah left to join the party. My uncle and I sat and sipped the Queen-mother's favorite drink: Hennessey Cognac. We didn't say a word to each other.

I called Miss Lehmann. By then, I called her Annabelle. "You got what you asked me to do: the return of Davallou. Our focus now must be to soften the press. Remember, we return to Geneva for the International Labor Conference in June?"

She laughed. In my mind, I could see the small gap in her front teeth. The girl had insinuated herself. "You know, Sam, the judge is happy. But now the foreign office does not want him back. They worry that if Davallou gets convicted, the Shah will be furious."

"That he will be," I assured her. "Let's make sure the judge finds him innocent."

3. 1972: Success with the Swiss and Miss Lehmann with Two Ns

Davallou's return to Geneva meant we had to prove him innocent. Davallou had two charges to answer. No evidence existed to link him delivering the 35 grams to Goreishi.

We pressured Goreishi to recant his confession. He had told an Iranian lawyer, Hassan Matin, that the Swiss coerced him to confess like the Gestapo. The pressure on Goreishi backfired because he kept naming other important people the judge wanted to question. He made wild statements. The Swiss took wrongful accusations seriously. To take back a confession would have landed him in jail. We portrayed him instead as an imbalanced individual. We convinced the third party, Khosro Qashqai, an anti-Shah individual, to repudiate Goreishi's story.

I visited the brother of Khosro Qashqai. He had an office in downtown Tehran, on the third floor of a building on Kakh Avenue. Nothing dramatic. Khosro had debts, and the brother had a shipping business. After much back and forth, we agreed to pay his debts. Khosro paid us back with a convincing don't-make-me-laugh defense. Mr. Keppler from the Swiss authorities interviewed him on the May 8 in Munich. "Don't make me laugh. I wouldn't have needed a middleman like Goreishi; I would have gone to Davallou directly since I know him well. Don't make me laugh.

Why would I need to go to Geneva? I can get all the opium I want cheaper in Munich." And so on.

Judge Weber ruled in favor of Davallou. He accused Goreishi of lying. The judge shook Mr. Davallou's hand on the way out. Monsieur Nicolet released the following statement written by me: "Although Mr. Davallou will not be sad to leave Switzerland, it saddens us not to have his company." The man could charm a snake charmer. The lawyers also obtained a legal permit for Davallou. After some tests, the doctors confirmed Davallou's addiction. They prescribed 15-20 grams of opium with a 10% morphine content. It allowed him to use opium for health reasons in Switzerland.

We had an all-out marketing campaign to combat the press and ensure the narrative favored the Shah. Under the pretext of the New Year, we doubled the presents for reporters. That year, the Minister of Foreign Affairs purchased 900 Vacheron Constantin watches, a line item on the budget called brazenly gifts. We sent special deliveries through Iran Air: caviar, gold and silver cigarette cases, and silk carpets. In our profession, we understood these *douces cadeaux* shaded the reporters' content. Of course, we had reporters who, let's say, could take instructions on what to write. The important ones had to be convinced—the small gifts made for fewer adjectives. Someone said gifts blind the eyes of the wise.

By June, I reported that the Shah's international image had improved. The press treated him with some deference. We operated as any other public relations firm would have, except we lived in our client's compound.

HIM and HMQ returned to Geneva. HIM gave a rousing speech at the 57th International Labor Conference. The press returned the love purchased by caviar, gold cigarette cases, silk carpets, and solid public relations efforts. In our little orbit, we set the standard. Many foreign visitors from the Gulf states desired to learn this all-Court offense. During official visits, the deputy of deputies would seek me out to learn how to do public relations.

On November 27 1972, the judge fined Mr. Goreishi the sum of 30,000 Swiss francs and freed him from jail. So complete was our victory that many members of the Swiss judicial system and police force visited Iran as our guests. The chief of police, Andre Leyvraz, sent a letter of thanks to me on October 17 for the warm welcome. I received a letter from our lawyer, Monsieur Raymond Nicolet. Through a university conduit, we invited Judge Weber to visit. The Shah approved the invitation. The judge flew first class in 1974. I arranged all his accommodations and tourist visits. He never gave a lecture in any institute of higher learning.

The bills, I recall, amounted to 250,000 Swiss francs. This didn't include the promotional materials. I wrote a note to my uncle in December. "We have closed the Davallou file." In 1973, the slick escalator moved me upwards.

Fifty years later, I believe Mr. Weber's decisions would not have differed no matter what we did. I grant the whiff of ethical misconduct. We saw our world as organized by specific rules. I'm not eager to blame a vague mass called the West. Yet, undoubtedly, they wrote the rules. Today's lobbies offer far more rewarding *bakhshish* than we could imagine. Nothing connected Davallou with distribution except hearsay. Gossip is the delicious food Newspapers serve but it doesn't constitute legal evidence. We worked within the system. We bent the rules here or there. We exercised, maybe too rigorously, "the means" to justify our harmless "ends." After the revolution of 1979, Khosro Qashqai returned to

Iran. We paid his brother's debts. The Islamic Republic executed him on vague charges.

Nless, opium, and gifts: I arrive at calmer waters. In January 1974, Miss Lehmann, with an extra N, started work at the Tehran Embassy. I had asked my uncle to encourage the Swiss to promote Annabelle Lehmann to a posting in Tehran's Swiss Embassy. I argued she could be a valuable contact after the Davallou affair. No fool, he thinned his eyes at me. "Let's call it your reward for all your work this year." I will say this for the Swiss: Behind their cold, unfriendly, self-righteous exterior, I know no people so accommodating when they put their minds to it.

IT BEGINS

1. 1973: A Guide to Bedrooms

1973: the acme of the Persian Empire. I exaggerate. Let's call it the first glory year since the invasion of the Arabs. We all felt the momentum. The world's press hailed us. A philosopher friend quipped that Iran lives in its recreation hour. HIM had not yet started his awkward (what my daughter calls cringe-worthy) lectures to the West. We, his younger servants in the background, bought into the Great Civilization trope. We had come to manhood only to witness rapid progress. The work we did felt righteous. The Shah said no foreignisms for us, no ready-to-wear suits for us, a third way for us.

I worked hard. Orders came to me from my uncle, left and right. I scurried to find out the minutiae in ministerial departments. What exactly did I do? I solved etiquette problems in Court. I brushed family indiscretions by siblings, nieces, and nephews under the royal carpet. I moved ambassadors to different rooms to avoid casual contact.

Yes, 1973 was our glamor year. We had the money. The foreign papers had four subjects: the oil crisis, Vietnam, Watergate, and terrorist bombs in Europe. We celebrated the start of the steel mills and oil revenue. The spigot had changed direction. Our newspapers were full of factories, opera houses, and festivals—an embarrassment of riches. No crisis for us.

The Shah had matured. The playboy in love with cars had disappeared. In his place emerged a workaholic in love with detail. No detail was detailed enough. He studied weaponry brochures, commented on reports line by line, and visited factories with unfeigned enthusiasm. He remembered much of what he heard or read in detail. A hard taskmaster, he once, after a military maneuver had gone wrong, told his commander-in-chief that should there be any repeat, he would send him to do less arduous tasks. He didn't threaten members of his government with anything worse than dismissal.

The seventies pared down his lifestyle. He loved exotic jams but ate a light breakfast. He never overate. A shy man, he relaxed among a few friends unconnected to the government apparatus. Contrary to reports, he played cards with friends, never for high stakes, and only consumed a drink or two. I never saw him inebriated. He exercised vigorously, skied on snow and water, and played volleyball.

We operated smoothly. Continuity, without assassinations and coups, had the government, the Court, and the embassies working like constellations spinning around HIM.

Around this time, the Shah ordered the curtailing of the various sources of introduction to women. How do I say it? The job of centralizing his afternoon delights fell to me. The joy of promotion outshone any negative pimping references by Court colleagues. It brought me closer to HIM. He enjoyed me. We bantered.

After one of his afternoons, he joked that he might get barred from entry into heaven. I retorted, "Your Majesty, if you step sideways and let all the air out of your lungs, you can squeeze through the eye of the needle. Nothing to it." He laughed.

Another time, I related an apocryphal anecdote my uncle wrote in his diary as his own. The Russians offered Nasser of Egypt their most up-to-date MIG, a plane of stunning simplicity. They explained it had three buttons: one for take-off, another to guide you to the target, and a third to drop the bomb. The hapless Nasser asked about the landing. "We leave that part of the flight to the discretion of the Israelis," replied the Russian. HIM laughed with the delight of the avenged. He hated the now-dead Nasser.

I don't recall him as abusive. More often than not, he had sex with call girls. No woman walked into his bedroom unwillingly. Power tastes and smells like an aphrodisiac to women. I never heard a complaint of maltreatment, even years after the revolution.

Three weeks after the Persian New Year, I saw G. for the second time. We sneered at each other. She saw the Court's pimp and I took her as whore, which, strictly speaking, she wasn't. It pissed me off because I thought I knew who had arranged it. That clown Davallou continued his shenanigans. He had helped the father, a general, to organize an introduction. She sat next to HIM on a flight from Isfahan. My professionalism smoothed my arched backbone.

As part of the recent reorganization, I had been asked to centralize the activities, a kind of corporate simplification. People sent him photos of women all the time. I bought and brought the women from Madame Claude's stable of courtesans. It reduced security issues. G. was the rare Persian.

The Court bureaucracy had moved the burgeoning Court employees to more convenient offices outside the palace. For this function, we used a house a few minutes' drive away. She walked in, all subtle curves. She had dressed simply but applied too much makeup. I spoke to the mother on the phone to provide the dress instructions and a proper cover story. She was to be a young student, recently back from overseas, invited for afternoon tea. HIM disliked complicated hooks and buttons. That day, my first words to G. were to point out the excessive makeup. "This is not a wedding ceremony. Let's lighten up the powder and rouge." She consented with a nod of the head.

My job on that late April afternoon in 1973 was to inspect her outfit for the rendezvous and impart a series of dos and don'ts for when she approached HIM. She listened intently and stayed silent throughout. She raised one delicate eyebrow when I explained she could not *tou-toyer* his highness. "Always use second person plural."

"Even in bed?" she asked as a practical possibility. I understood the contrariness of bedroom talk and the mode of address. I could not answer. A shy man, HIM never discussed sexual details with a man like me. "You get paid to feel through these problems," I said. I didn't intend to be severe.

She looked at me without malice and said, "You know I have been with him already, and I don't get paid." I didn't ask when and where.

The gentleman preferred blondes; G.'s blonde hair was so thick a swing of her head moved her hair to block her profile, like a waterfall. Impatient with her hair, she looped it back over the ear. G. saw me take notice. She misunderstood. "I have an appointment with the hairdresser at 2:30." I warned her not to be late. You don't keep kings waiting, especially not a punctual one. "My appointment is at the Hilton. I will take fifteen minutes to get back here in midafternoon." She left.

Late in the afternoon, I saw her. She was leaving the bedroom in the house. No walk of shame. Head high, long legs taking high-heel steps on the carpeted floor toward the exit.

I always waited for HIM to finish. Usually, I escorted the ladies downstairs with the agreed sum and a small present: a broach. I would help HIM adjust his shirt and put on his cuff links. I never enquired, but he might comment about the companion like he would about a luxury car parked in his garage. Nothing lewd. "What a carriage, a fine ride," he might say.

That day, however, he had left in a hurry minutes before. I accompanied HIM to the door downstairs and returned to see her off.

I had the side window wall open. I smoked a Winston, one foot forward on the false balcony, dressed to a T. Early in life, I saw the benefits of a well-cut, Savile Row suit on my broad shoulders and short, thin legs. My frame could be mistaken for weight unless naked; I have a large rib cage. The Egyptian cotton, blue shirt (always French cuffs accompanied by silver hex bar links) and a citrus Penhaligon aftershave crisp enough to cut the air. A sober dark tie went against the post-psychedelic wide prints of the time. I understood how the magic of sartorial manipulation complimented the unimprovable as well as any aged beauty. The Court acknowledged my impeccable taste—far more refined than the Shah's, who wore the most atrocious combinations.

G. saw me from the corner of her eye. She stopped in the middle of the corridor and turned toward me with an exaggerated body swivel. She buckled both knees sideways, mimicked exhaustion, straightened, and came over. I offered her a Winston. She took one and laughed with her head back. "An after-cigarette," she said. I saw the joke.

I tried, to my shame, to smell her post-coital odor. My dark color hid a concentric blush that spread outward from inside me like a loud siren. I turned to look toward the small garden. Was it then that she crawled into my large chest? Not yet. She spoke to me in Farsi. "He wants me back," she said.

"It happens," I said. "Don't let it go to your head." I took a small Harry Winston jewelry box from the breast pocket of my dark suit and handed it over to her. I usually played it more discreetly. With her, I wanted a rise. I suppose there was anger in my gesture, a childish power play. She had jumped the line, so to speak, without my consent.

The box hovered between us but stayed in my hand. G. took a long, steady puff, one eye half-closed from the wisps of smoke. She now also looked out into the garden. She took her time, lowered her hand to unclasp her handbag with a rewarding click, and invited me to drop the box inside. I did. With a practiced motion, she twisted the two oval-shaped gold clasps back in their usual embrace.

"And how did you inherit your present duties?" she asked. Humiliate and be humiliated. We deserved one another.

"The way of all inheritances: through blood. My name is my bondage." An inside joke. She looked at me, puzzled. I sighed in surrender. "I do whatever His Majesty asks me to."

"So do I, so do I," she said. She threw her head back and gave a deep chuckle, then flicked her forefinger against her thumb and hurled the cigarette butt out a distance into the garden, like a man would. She walked off, one arm stretched straight above her head. She waved the back of her hand from side to side. "I will see you when he wants me back."

IT BEGINS

I watched her back sway all the way to the stairs and, like in a TV advertisement, saw her body disappear one step at a time. Was it then? Did I fall then, and I don't mean down the stairs? From my addled brain to my writing hand: all details present and ready to report.

2. 1973: Walk in the Palace Gardens with Friends

A nudge of neurons and the next day sat good and proper, ready for me to wallow in. Fourth week of Farvardin, the fourth week of spring: a time of the year in which Northern Tehran had weather pretensions.

She walked in like a shock to nature. She wore a high couture, psychedelic cotton twill dress—two inches above her knees, with two vertical circle cutouts between her breasts and above her navel—and comfortable, white leather loafers. It was her first appearance at the Sahebgharaniyeh Palace, HIM's office in the Niavaran complex. It sat away from the newly built mansion, the family's residence. Five o'clock in the afternoon, light without the stare of the brutal sun. I could draw birds and flowers in this picture. I cannot remember a more perfect balance.

After his second afternoon with her, I returned to his room. While he tied his shoelaces, he whistled. "Invite her to the palace for tea at a convenient time," he said. HMQ being on a two-day trip to Tabriz with her entourage passed as a convenient time. Thinking it was unwise, I talked to my uncle. He also showed concern. "Stay with her at all times. With you there, we always have a fallback." He looked me up and down. "However implausible," he added. By now, small humiliations bounced off me. Sticks and stones would never break my bones.

"You approve?" She did an imitation runway walk in my office. She pouted her lips. She resembled a *Vogue* cover model.

"You have modeled before?"

"It's all there, Sam." She pointed to the papers on my desk, all conspiratorial. She had dropped the Mr. I didn't call her on it. From then on, she called me Sam.

"Not here," I lied. "It all goes through the security office downtown." Did G. arrive one hour early, or was the King delayed? Delays were unusual. The King worked long hours into the night but was punctual. You can't take the hard work away from him.

I could hear HIM talking to someone on the phone. I took her for a walk through the palace gardens. Under the trees, a soft breeze left behind the lightest of shivers on her bare shoulders. I took off my cream-colored suit jacket and placed it on her shoulders.

We walked into the compound toward the northeast. The complex contained six main buildings. She stretched, picked a blade of grass, and held it between her teeth like a man. We walked toward the newly built library in the corner of the 11-acre property.

"Did you grow up with brothers?" I asked.

"Thank God no. Or they might have made a fuss with all this." I ventured closer to understand her better.

"Do you not have friends from school who visit you at home?" She attended the Reza Shah Kabir all-girl school, famous for its tough girls. The file sat on my desk.

"Ah, you are wondering if I am gossiping about HIM? Sam, no one in my school talked to me. A miracle I graduated. I know people think that because of this," she used her hand to signal her whole self, "girls flock to know me. But no one likes the comparison, don't you see? Besides, my father has become a tyrant in the last month. He won't let my mother even invite family to dinner. He asks for details. If I let him, he will want to know what happens in the bedroom. Sam, one minute he gets excited, another minute he looks scared like a kid. He wants me to ask HIM to move some of the purchasing responsibilities from General Toufanian to him." I thought the father had lost it. Toufanian had headed the purchasing department of the Iranian Armed Forces ever since the General escorted HIM back from Rome in '53.

I tried gently to warn her. "Tell your father to handle this with care. If he pushes, your father will become the loser," I said. A nineteen-year-old's ear heard wave compressions from an older man and nothing else.

I saw HIM walk toward us. "Well," he said, "*la belle et la bête.*" He went up to G. and kissed her on the cheek like an uncle would. She kissed him back, a slow kiss near his ear and jaw. He laughed. "If you kiss him this way," he pointed to me, "you might change him into Beau Brummell." She smiled awkwardly. HIM thought me vain for how I dressed. "You can leave us," he said. I didn't. I hung ten steps back. HIM didn't insist. He understood my function.

An awkward moment passed in which I didn't know if I should take the coat off her shoulders. I didn't. HIM took her hand and placed it on his arm. His other hand covered hers, all avuncular and proper. HIM asked after her mother. They walked toward the library. I walked ten steps back. Not yet complete, the library planned to add philosophy books and modern art. They had just hung the famed 300 cylinders of light. HIM took her inside to show her the future plans. I had the sense not to follow.

I wondered at her confidence, thinking about that kiss near his jaw and ear. I can attest that reality wobbled when you were in HIM's presence. I suspect the phenomenon happens with all recognizable figures. They turn into icons. I saw it repeatedly when we introduced new ministers and ambassadors. I wondered if Iranian women who first kissed him as the prelude to sex weren't repeating in their heads, again and again, the mantra, "What am I doing here? Am I in bed with HIM?" Did they miss the act? On the other hand, there is nothing like nakedness to bring home our mere humanness.

I stood outside. They emerged ten minutes later. They both smiled like teenagers. I saw the streak of a small boy running on a pathway toward us. The boy came out of the primary residence. A comic guard and a woman from a Buster Keaton movie chased him. I approached the couple, swiped my pocket handkerchief, and offered it to HIM. I gestured toward the right of my mouth and, with my eyes, directed his glance toward the oncoming child. He wiped off the lipstick before Alireza, his six-year-old son, jumped into his arms, squirming around to look at us. G. and I stood next to each other, apart. The governess arrived out of breath, all panicked and apologetic, and behind her, the guard beamed. HIM, all love and affection, introduced his son. "I saw you from the windows," said Alireza. He again wiggled and pointed to G. "You look like my sister's Barbie. Can I kiss you?" We all laughed. The Shah handed him over. He let go of his father's neck, grabbed G.'s neck and swung like a small monkey into her arms. Alireza landed a kiss on her cheek before the governess took control. They moved back to the residence.

IT BEGINS

As they walked away, the governess held tightly to the recalcitrant boy. We praised the small boy, to his father's delight. I saw the circle of the Shah's friends come out one at a time. Bored by the indoors, they walked with drinks in hand. Most of them were unimportant governmentally, but let's not mistake their importance.

First out came the lanky, bold, horsey-toothed Professor Adl, a surgeon full of wisdom and integrity. All those years ago, he refused to operate on me to remove my metallic companion: good call. A humorous man, but not a clown and far from a fool, he parlayed for mercy for condemned men and had a high success rate. Behind him emerged Ayadi, HIM's physician, a shadowy Bahá'í with a finger in every jam jar. He had an isosceles face and a symmetrical, curly smile, with no teeth visible; he always looked like someone who knows something no one else does. The courtiers accused him of graduating from a veterinarian school.

Short, squat, and almost hidden from view by the other two, the Armenian lawyer Felix Aghayan emerged. He smiled the genuine smile of an experienced hedonist. Like the pit bull he uncannily resembled, he defended his piece of the pie, the sugar industry, and headed the Ski Federation of Iran. The last two men appeared outside as the sky used its dimmer: the mild Mehdi Bushehri, car-salesman-handsome, brother-in-law to HIM, husband to the fiery Ashraf, and General Fardoust. Bushehri's sister married HIM's brother. Fardoust had one hand on Bushehri's shoulder, pushing him onto the lawn in a kidding gesture. The General was not a kidding-man.

As if to underscore his separateness, Majid Alaam, not one of our relations, came out a few minutes later. He was a civil engineer. He had met the Shah as a kid before HIM became Crown Prince. A while later, doing a faux jog as if late for an event, the most harmless of HIM's friends, Hadjebi, came toward us. He drank a gin and tonic. I can still smell his gorgeous cologne mixed with the smell of gin. He dressed better than me. He looked like a retired colonial gentleman, with a roseate face and unkempt eyebrows. He played bridge from the cradle to the grave.

My memory takes a bird's eye view because it can. They all gathered in a spontaneous garden party; the tight group that kept HIM company throughout the reign. I watch them spread on a perfectly manicured lawn. I knew them all well. In the refrigerated retrospective of the Rising Sun, I can see that none of them, except for Fardoust, took exaggerated advantage of their thirty-odd years as courtiers. They could have. I never credited critics who accused HIM of encircling himself with craven fraudsters. A harmless, charmed group, they were loyal to HIM, and he was loyal to them. He didn't involve them in politics and government. That's how he protected them. Yes, they, in various ways, drank from the royal tit, but in moderation. Except for Fardoust, they shared family, humor, and bonhomie.

They held scotch and sodas, smoked through cigarette holders, and cracked indecent jokes as they petalled around this beautiful nineteen-year-old who basked in their attention on a beautiful spring day. None of us thought this picture odd when we next curtsied in front of HMQ in her home behind us.

I heard HIM repeat the Beau Brummell aside. They laughed and patted me on the back. She joined in. I walked back to the office and left them to enjoy the dusk. I don't know what happened to my coat.

IN JUNE, ICE MELTS IN PARIS

1. 1973: The Lambton Affair

Mrs. Lambton visited my room on Friday, the day after one of Marie's visits. She walked in and inspected the ceiling. The rain had drawn a yellow map of an ancient fantasy world on the gypsum ceiling panels, the seven continents separated by the aluminum grid. She muttered, "God give me strength. I told Jeff to fix these weeks ago; my apologies, Sam. By the way, you have a *ravissant fille*." The English could not do the uvular trill if their life depended on it. We Iranians speak French with better accents than we speak English. My daughter mocks my English pronunciation all the time. Still, I appreciate Mrs. Lambton's effort to keep up a cultural banter.

"We talked for hours." She made a conspiratorial hand-to-mouth gesture. "All about you." I laughed with pleasure and made my standard retort. "A fortunate girl," I said. No Laurel or Hardy, she saw a joke creep up a mile away and fed me the line. "How so, Sam?"

"She is my spitting image," I said. Without access to the piano, I used my hand and the table like a drummer to deliver a Johnny Carson band close. "I meant to ask you a question, and I forgot. Was Lord Lambton also a relation to your husband?"

She flushed. "Yes, Ann Lambton's younger brother. He named his daughter Ann also. She flushed, remembering the sordid business in the seventies. "Did you know my paternal grandmother moved in after my mother's death? She lived with us. She died the same year as the scandal." She mentioned death like someone who has seen hundreds of deaths, which she had. "Our grandmother wouldn't let my sister and I watch TV for weeks. Imagine what my mother and grandmother would have said if they knew I married into the family."

"All families have a black Lamb," I said.

"Did you know Lord Lambton?" she laughed.

"I didn't. Knew of him," I said. Unbeknownst to Lord Lambton, he started a chain of dominoes. They slid and fell against one another to Framingham.

Toward the end of May 1973, my uncle called me to his office. "Have you read the papers?"

"Yes, Uncle," I said. The have-you-read-the-paper question hounded me through the years I worked for him. He required that I read both foreign and internal papers. The increased workload didn't leave enough time. I read the first page of most papers. In those days, I had an excellent memory. It served me well. "Did you read the *New York Times*?" he asked.

"It looks like Mr. Nixon's goose will be served *à point*. Mr. Magruder admitted guilt and will be a witness for the prosecution," I answered.

"No, not that," he said.

I went on a fishing expedition. "Kissinger and Tho's peace talks?" He looked at me with the exasperated look reserved for family members. I felt the pressure of the high school classroom.

"Second page," he said. "Lord Lambton resigned." I looked at him, baffled. Who was this Lord Lambton? I waited him out. "A prostitute's husband took pictures of him in *flagrante delicto*. I want you to increase the house's security from any photographers." I understood.

The next day, I paid particular attention, and, sure enough, the *Times of London* reported a second member of the Heath government, Earl Jellicoe, caught pantsless. This time, I reported it to him. I assured him we kept a lookout on a wide perimeter of the house for anyone nosing around.

Then, the daily papers in Tehran covered the story with verve and vicious interest. The last week of May, page 2 of *Ettelaat* brought out a new angle on the pleasures of Lord Lambton and Earl Jellicoe. S&M descriptions. One article claimed the lords lashed the girls. The next day, the articles described the girls in charge of the whip. Lord Lambton, in a typical English aristocrat's nonchalant manner, dressed in a double-breasted suit, showing a mountain peak of a white handkerchief, gave BBC an interview. He normalized sex, opium, and hash, something the entire world had digested already in the sixties.

My uncle continued to rant each morning. No one in 1973 who followed the Court was unaware of the dalliances. The rumors hung over like the pollution covering the city. The newspapers, powerless to criticize the boss, used parallel stories to present a mirror. Sometimes, an overzealous editor might cross the line. We knew they had crossed it with Lord Lambton. By the end of the week, my uncle had me talk to the editors. "You have had your fun. Let's move on." Nothing dramatic. We all played by the rules.

A week later, I read a small column in a small Farsi language magazine that I couldn't ignore. Jean Huron, a purported prostitute, had told an interviewer that some of her clients from Iran and other Khaleeg states had contacted her to keep their names out of the papers. My uncle and I wondered about the identities of these clients.

The next day, my uncle had a name. In a good mood, he laughed aloud—on a day the Mojahedin assassinated an American military aid in Tehran, no less. "I give you ten thousand guesses. And you won't succeed." He named an old industrialist known for his religious piety. "Never would I have thought the old goat had it in him." We laughed.

"The West in the Grip of Call Girls," a headline shrieked. We shouted in the quiet woods of Islam. The Islamic population had consumed the sordid, bowdlerized stories. You couldn't find a movie advertisement without a half-naked actress at the center. We devoured the news with tolerance. We, the courtiers, saw it as forces of civilization winning over the reactionary and the ignorant. I agreed with the censors not to show *The Last Tango in Paris* in Tehran. We had limits.

A month later, toward the end of June, I walked into my uncle's office. He had a copy of the *Khandaniha* magazine; he flopped it back and forth at me. "I will put Amirani in prison for this." He referred to the editor of the popular bi-weekly magazine.

"But he is our guy," I said. "I saved him from the wrath of Tehran's Imam." His conservative magazine, published colored pictures of famous beautiful women on its cover twice weekly. The Shah competed with Jacqueline Bisset, a favorite. The week before, he had run a photograph of some actress, I don't remember who. It showed a nipple where the red cover ended. I called him to ask what on Earth had made him do it. He spluttered. He thought the photo shown to him had a tighter crop. I told him I had spoken to the Imam Jomeh of Tehran. "Send him an apology."

My uncle bade me sit. Then, he asked me to read a two-page article a university professor wrote. While I read, my uncle raged. The professor pointed to Lord Lambton and Earl Jellicoe with a wink. He used the metaphor that men might want to try green cheese when they tire of chicken. Then, in an attempt at humor, he pointed to a rooster's behavior in the coop. He overworked his analogy. He even attempted to explain the English penchant for sadomasochistic acts like choking.

As I read, I planned arguments to advise my uncle to forgive and forget. Then, the author ended with a bomb. He quoted a translation of a foreign article. He reported the collaboration between the European governments and the centers of prostitution to gather information about their clients. The paper printed the phone numbers used by MI5 and the French intelligence agency, DST. France, England, and Germany had footed the bills for prostitutes. Ulrich Althof, the head of a prostitute ring, confirmed the cooperation with the intelligence services.

I read the last few lines and understood the enormity of the problem. The author mentioned Madame Claude, who ran the high-end call girls. We were her most prominent client.

I raised my head from the article. "I don't think this jackass Amirani knows about our involvement, or he wouldn't have dared reprint this article," I said. "If we make a fuss, rat that he is, he will smell his kind." The Court Minister agreed. My uncle lowered his head to think. I stayed quiet. I knew him. Minutes could go by while he searched for a solution. I had learned to remain silent. He straightened and instructed, "You need to go to Paris to understand the damage. You know the Madame; find out our exposure. Then we will decide how to deal with the French government."

"When do you want me to go?" I asked.

"Go when His Majesty takes his trip to the US. That will be on the 24th of July. In a couple of weeks," he said. I got up to leave the room when, as if a thought had occurred to him, he stopped me at the door. "Close the door for a moment longer," he said. Awkwardly, he explained his request. "His Majesty, in his munificence, wants to reward G. with a parting gift." I looked puzzled. "He has agreed to pay for some surgery, some small enhancements. He wanted me to accompany her," he said with a sense of outrage. "As a favor, can you take the whore to Paris with you? Buy her some clothes. Then, take her to Germany for the surgery. When you are back, we must find her a husband posthaste. She has spread nonsense about becoming the Shah's second wife."

I explained the seventies to Mrs. Lambton. "You see, Mrs. Lambton," I said, "those were the final years of the male species. They had their cake and ate it with impudent appetite." She smiled.

"I promise to have your ceiling repaired by the end of the day. However, I doubt the solemn finale of male impudence. Look at our ex-president."

We Americans try not to talk about politics, religion, and sex. Mrs. Lambton and I had bonded in our relationship. After all, we have discussed all three taboo subjects.

2. 1973: A Thawing Doesn't Melt the Steel Edge

When I bring up our aristocracy in the twenty-first century, we should not confuse them with the dukes of Norfolk, Somerset, or Richmond nor with houses of Orleans, Dampierre, or Bourbon. The old Shah took away our titles. The last Shah took our lands. We retired into our city gardens. The town planners crisscrossed our gardens with highways. Contractors stole our privacy and built high-rises around us. The Islamic Republic hounded us for the last scraps. This aristocracy lost without a fight. No one recognizes the families' names, not even our American, French, and Swedish children. You can hear the squeak of the historical squeegee as it cleans the decay of the well-mannered, old-fashioned, educated. Not a whimper. No regrets. I am a thoroughly American man.

Our diaspora is an independent lot. We are more independent than redneck Texans—none of the by-the-bootstrap struggle for us. We believe in the family but don't care about the community. We have the highest self-employment of any ethnic race. Which ethnic race in its first generation has one of the highest numbers of Republicans? We do. The US doesn't recognize us as an ethnic race. If push comes to shove, we admit we are Aryans…you know, Iranians. Shucks. I don't know of any ex-pat community that helps each other less. We distrust each other for good reason. We cheat and lie to each other. When we recognize a compatriot in an airport, we warn our companions to be careful, for "the fellow is Iranian."

Our diaspora of 1.5 million has bled into the American population without backlash, even from the city of Oroville. They win the race for the reddest necks in California. Undoubtedly, we are the most flexible group of immigrants to dapple the shores. We have mixed like milk in hot chocolate. Our elite didn't serve like a grand duke as a doorman or the Vietnamese general in a carwash. I might have driven a cab or played the piano in a lobby for a while. Americans cannot distinguish us from their own. Where did you go to college? Texas A&M. Go Aggies! Who did you work for? Bell Helicopter. Where do you live? Mendocino, California.

We have elected no one to Congress. The best we could do was to select the mayor of Beverly Hills. It tells you something. We dream of Tehrangeles life, the life imagined by the Shah in Tehran. Our kids are now indistinguishable from natives. Accents are gone. Language gone. We can barbecue, drink beer, and show our bloated bellies with the best of them. Good. I hate all of them. No, I hate those above fifty-eight years old—the self-selected irreligious population that went out into the streets of Tehran and destroyed pure promise.

I accompanied G. to Paris during the last week of July. Security had ratcheted up even then. The day we left, or the day before, the Palestinians blew up a Japan Air 747 airplane in Benghazi— without the passengers on board. It was a more civilized time. We stayed at the Hotel Plaza Athénée on 25 Avenue Montaigne: two rooms for three days. The hotel's façade was a collection of balconies with squares of red geraniums shaded by little, rectangular red canvas awnings for each room. The concierge never performed a false note. He welcomed us with delight. G. walked next to me with the assurance of a much older woman. We traveled first class; no such thing as Business Class in those days. Neither of us gave way or showed our unhappiness at each other's company. In those days, the Air France champagne flutes could break, the food was fresh, and they picked the hostesses for their beauty—all taller than me and none prettier than my companion.

I recall my primary school days when my mother convinced my father to move to Tehran. I suspect the motivation included factors other than my education. Each day, the driver fetched me from school. My blonde French governess, a young woman of loose morals, accompanied the Armenian driver. To my horror, schoolmates often pointed her out as my mother. The two never talked in the front seat. The silence lasted for two years. Each saw their role in a household full of servants as more elevated than the other's. All the household referred to our driver as Musio, a bastardization of Monsieur. They called the governess Mut-muzzle, the corruption of Mademoiselle. When the silence broke, it broke like a damn.

To my shame, G. and I resembled them. Petty servants might even have behaved better than the pimp and whore of the Shah. High summer in Paris, with luxury all around us, we looked for an opening to make a Parisian pax. It occurred in the elevator ride to our rooms. The elevator arrived from the floor below. To our surprise, we came face to face, in the small French elevator, with the corpulent body of Orson Welles. Good-humoredly, one eyebrow raised at G., he invited us in. A tight squeeze but more comic when you considered my height compared to Mr. Welles's. G., taller than me and in high heels, fitted herself sideways. I turned to face the door. I felt Orson Welles's stomach pushing my back toward the elevator door as we ascended to the third floor. The hilarity showed in our faces, mine hidden, hers a rictus of a smile. She resisted the funeral giggle. She hadn't recognized the Hollywood mogul, but she saw the comedy of the situation. When the elevator doors opened, we spilled out into the corridor and walked fast in the wrong direction to our rooms. We ran and kept tight control. Far from the elevator, which had stopped one floor above us, we giggled. And then we heard Orson Welles shout down the winding stairs that hugged the elevator, "I can hear you." And then the *fou-rire* overtook us.

I knew Paris. After a friendly divorce, my mother moved to the 16th arrondissement in the early sixties. I studied at the Free University of Brussels in Belgium. I often went to Paris to stay with my mother during that time.

That night, I took G. to dinner at Brasserie Lipp. For the first time, we talked unencumbered.

I talked to her, no lectures, more like a family member. I warned her of the dangers of the slippery slope with an inconstant man like HIM. I erred when I raised her father's role in the introduction to HIM. She took me to the shed for hypocrisy. She understood the power of her beauty. She argued if a kid were a math prodigy, you wouldn't criticize his father for placing him in an élite school. Her beauty had disfigured her life, she told me. She gave me a bitter smile. "Look around you," she said. "There are five tables within a few steps. The table on the periphery of your right eye has a husband and wife. The man has his back to us. Watch him use little, discreet gestures. He drops his napkin while he steals a glance at me." She waited patiently. The man leaned back to ask for the check and, at the same time, stole a glance at G. "Now look at the table of four behind me to my left," she said.

"You have a perfect view. Four businessmen, Lebanese, if I am not mistaken. They are shameless. They talked about me from the minute we sat down. Look at them." I had noticed the table. I had also shamelessly enjoyed their envy. "Now look to my right." We both looked at the table for two. A French elderly couple, clearly wealthy, enjoyed their meal as the French do. They saw us turn toward them. The woman and man lifted their wine glasses toward us. Had I sat there alone, no one would have drunk to my health. "Against the wall behind you is a table for eight." I could see them in the mirror on the opposite wall. It had four couples of different ages. They talked and laughed loudly, oblivious to any other table. I protested. She smiled with her lips, but the eyes were joyless. "Pick one of the couples and observe them. The men know their wives know of my presence. It isn't an ego thing. The men will not glance over unless their wives get involved in a serious conversation." Sure enough, she nailed it. "The fifth table behind you, I consider safe territory. A mother with her children, a boy and a girl. My," she observed, "the French allow their kids out late at night.

"You must understand, I have lived this way since I turned thirteen. I knew…" She twirled her slim index finger 360 to include all the tables. "After the first minute we sat down, I knew all you observed. I am the math prodigy, you see." She made a wry smile. She pressed her lips tight like that was the end of the story. She understood the torch of her beauty. She carried it erect into any room she entered. The monotony of her beauty imposed a dictatorial hold in the company of others. Furious at her beauty, she used it to get ahead. "And nothing wrong with that," she said.

I took her to my business meeting the next day. I also had something to teach her.

3. 1973: The Paris of Madame Claude

I woke in my hotel room in Plaza Athénée as coffee arrived with a copy of the *Herald Tribune*. Out of habit, I went through it to check HIM's reception by Nixon—nothing but Watergate and the White House tapes. I found an article on page six. The paper misspelled the Shah's first name—a friendly report. It called "Riza," a friend of the US.

When HIM returned from the US trip a few days later, more than a million people lined the streets, and the capital's primary papers' ledes gushed like the oil whose price had been rocketing all year. His return coincided with the end of the oil consortium. The oil companies would not share in our revenues anymore. The signing of the Sale and Purchase Agreement came down from the oil refineries on a day with the Air Force jets, 21-gun salutes, and half-day national holiday. A hundred thousand people gathered at the Olympic stadium to celebrate. He stood in his black Rolls-Royce and a general sat hunched in the front seat. I saw the pictures when I returned: his torso straight, wearing a blue suit, he waved to the crowd with a kind smile. He was at the height of power, but sadly missing the slave in the back to whisper in his ear, "All glory is fleeting. All glory is fleeting." In six years, he would see similar-sized crowds: this time, no waves, only fists. I threw the *Tribune* to the side of the bed. I deserved a break.

Paris in the 60s and 70s: the world of Castel, Régine, Maxim's, and La Tour d'Argent. I had met Madame Claude some years before—a no-nonsense woman who ran a strict call girl business. By 1973, she had learned to switch her focus from the European male to the more lucrative Arabs. She had to find girls who spoke English and pleased the new clients—larger women, less linear, less aesthetic. She didn't like the change.

The Shah, more comfortable with French, could be called a dependable traditional customer. She considered HIM a sophisticated European. She understood the Shah's preferences for blondes. We had much to discuss. I wanted to persuade her to send my office a facsimile of the girls who flew to Tehran. She resisted because the black-and-white facsimiles didn't do justice to her girls. I wanted to ensure that the "larger girls" preferred by the new clientele didn't arrive at Court. His Majesty desired.... well, not worth more detail. My job was to infer from jokes and asides by the Shah if the latest had pleased him. I couldn't ask for more information.

G. and I sat at Fouquet's around 11:00, sipping coffee and enjoying the sun-filled summer day. I explained Madame Claude's role to her. Fernande Grudet, Madame's proper name, came toward us. She smiled with a slight swing of the hips and slalomed through the tight-set tables. Dressed like a Parisian woman, she must have been fifty—a tiny woman with a sculpted face and blonde hair sprayed into a sculpture. She reminded one of a bureaucrat in a ministry. She wore a conservative Chanel dress, heavy for a summer day. I could smell her perfume, also Chanel. I had met her a few times. Not a problematic woman, if you avoided a few minefields: Never refer to her girls as prostitutes, never ask about her clientele, never haggle, and never, never call her a *mère maquerelle*, a brothel keeper.

She sat and stared at G. with an expert's eye while she greeted me and settled her handbag on the fourth empty rattan chair. "Who is this swan?" she inquired. She called all her girls swans. G. spoke French well enough. I introduced her as a friend of HIM. I didn't expand.

"A Madame Pompadour?" Fernande said. "How unlike His Majesty. I thought he didn't want *des soucis*." I had brought G. to the table to hear the sexual philosophy we espoused—to witness the transactional quality of the enterprise we operated. If you understood it, you knew no one would sacrifice a queen to gain a pawn. Nothing wrong with serving as a pawn. She wouldn't have anything to do with any of it.

"I am not one of your girls, Madame. I will be the Shah's future second wife." It was an outrageous statement. My uncle had warned me but it still shocked me. Did she think HIM would consider such a move at the height of his power when he sought the approval of the West? Then, I took it as a taunt. I had exposed her to the pleasure infrastructure we had set up for a man she slept with for weeks.

Fernande laughed raucously. "I like her. My girls all have high aspirations. Suppose I tell you where some of my girls have ended up. By the way, wouldn't you be his fourth wife?"

"In the Muslim world, a man can have multiple wives," G. said. "His Majesty's father had four wives. The Queen-mother didn't like it but accepted the younger wives at the palace." I wondered where she had gotten the notion. Had she thought about the mechanics of the arrangement? I suspected the parents had filled her head with nonsense. We lived in the seventies; HIM was an international star, Iran was a strategic partner to the US in the Gulf. The backwater Iran of the thirties didn't exist. Did she seriously think she would get a house at the Sa'dabad complex, where the other royals lived?

Fernande now looked at G. with cold eyes. She considered herself a women's libber. Notwithstanding the money she made from her girls, she believed her girls, like hedge fund managers, were mistresses of the universe. To be called a Claude girl was an honor, not an insult. Her women embraced their pasts. She saw men as sniveling little beings on the other side of the telephone. They begged for special favors—polygamy, to her, was an uncivilized practice that stank of surrender.

"Be the fourth sole wife," she counseled. "Take no prisoners, but if you don't get married, come and see me. I like your spirit. You can always be one of my *jeunes filles*." G. smiled, pleased with the retort. Peace restored.

"And nothing wrong with that." I forked-tongued my words to four ears—a sarcastic warning that echoed G.'s words the night before and accepted Frenande's business as another valid human activity.

Fernande saw through me. "It's a difficult job that I offer," she said. "Pleasure is not a harmless thing. I believe it is more dangerous to discover it than ignore it." She looked at me pointedly.

I have often wondered, why we should make a fuss about the sexual adventures of a monarch? We understood the requirement for discretion, but more deeply, I understood its unimportance—the so-whatism of it. A man paid a woman once or twice weekly for an hour of physical intimacy. A bureaucrat or a garbage collector uses the red-light district of Amsterdam or Rue St. Denis in Paris on the way home on a Friday afternoon. I understood my work as a waste of life in a world that considered the sex act similar to a lunch with a friend. We didn't live in that world.

I explained to Fernande that, as a *cadeau*, HIM had agreed to pay for some minor plastic surgery with the famous Doctor Pitanguy. Fernande smoked with one eye shut, took G.'s chin gently in hand, and examined her profile back and forth. "*Oui alors...*you can tuck the small droop of the nose, but be careful. The chin... well, a tiny fraction less square. Touch nothing else. Don't touch the breasts," she warned.

"Why not?" G. asked, even though she didn't intend to alter her breasts.

"Men come to regret that change because it never looks natural. Only God creates *une belle poitrine.*"

We talked and gossiped while G. listened with interest. Like us, Fernande was at the apogee of her female empire. We all suffered similar fates. Our fall began over financial issues in 1975. The taxman, Capone-like, came after her. They charged her with *proxénétisme*, pimping. Napoleon had legalized the sale of the sexual act. The law forbade earning a commission on a prostitute's earnings. I read of her death in 2005 in the *Times*. She died a pauper at ninety-four.

Over the next few days, we shopped for dresses. HIM had asked my uncle to spare no expense. Guilt makes us generous. Later, rumors spread that G. had bought copies of HMQ's clothes. Not true. She was not a Lily. She had her style and my guidance, and HMQ had hers.

SIGHT, SEEING,
THE QUEEN OF SENSES

1. 1973: Plastic Germany

The famous Brazilian plastic surgeon Ivo Pitanguy worked in Europe for a few weeks a year. In Brazil, he reconstructed burn victims and people with severe physical disfigurements. He established pro bono clinics in Brazil. He saw no difference between reconstruction and remedial surgery. Either nature had been unkind at birth or unkind later by accident.

In Europe, he charged top dollar. Familiar with more than a few royals, he kept a daguerreotype of our royal family in his house. I know this because I sent it to him after a minor procedure for the Queen. His office informed me that the doctor would be in Wiesbaden in August and gave me an appointment for the first week. I had a photographer take pictures of G.'s profile as specified by Pitanguy's office. They wanted them sent to St. Josef's Hospital in Wiesbaden.

We flew directly from Orly to Frankfurt. From there, we took a taxi to Wiesbaden, known for its thermal baths and spa treatments. We drove to the Schwarzer Bock Hotel, a fifteenth-century building. A large crew worked on the facade. The hotel straddled the old and new like many European hotels struggled to do. The effects of two wars had created an ornate hotel with its share of Art Nouveau. Thin, rectangular pillars of red-hewn marble gave the mostly round reception a tasteless appeal. The corridors to our rooms had pilasters of brown marble. They stood floor-to-ceiling on each side of the bedroom doors. The Art Nouveau touch gave a militaristic impression of guards at attention. The rooms were German unimaginative; the workers outside had yet to reach the bathrooms.

We dined on a small sunken terrace at the back of the hotel. We sat at a table under a large yellow umbrella. The sun did its best on a summer night at 7:30. I continued in the Higgins role to my Pygmalion. I ordered a sizeable Choucroute—sauerkraut with assorted sausages and salted meats—and an Alsatian Riesling to help the dish's sourness.

G. and I had become chatty. She recounted her isolation. I amused her with Court stories. A pleasant evening. I walked her toward a loud concert. She comfortably put her arm through mine. I took her through the Bowling Green Wiesbaden, and a weak yellow light came off the Kurpark building. It perfectly matched her dress—a light yellow one falling two inches above her knees. She wore flat white sandals. Still a head taller than me, yet I felt taller than everyone else as we walked in the park. Did I see her then as more than a Van Cleef & Arpels watch?

On the loci of Oval Park, two beautiful fountains poured water down the three-level stone basins. We walked to the end and found the concert attended by a filthy, in the hygienic sense, crowd. I saw a small sign with an arrow pointing to a casino. We gave up on the concert. Instead, we made our way to the casino.

The doorman looked at me apologetically. He barred me from entry. I had on a double-breasted blazer buttoned with silver lion heads. I wore no tie but a gentleman's square tucked in a crisp blue shirt. The doorman, in the ridiculous costume of a Russian grand duke with gigantic epaulets, offered me a variety of ugly ties. I argued and brought out some bills to pay my way in. G. jumped in with hilarity and chose the most hideous tie on offer. She then worked the tie for me. She moved to my back and draped her long arms from behind, her cheek next to mine. She looked down with pure concentration as she crossed the wide end over the narrow. The silk rasped with each crisp movement. "I always tied my father's ties. He didn't know how," she said in my ear.

"I know how," I said. And I gently removed her from me. She looked at me sideways with a voice full of fun. "When there is no choice, make the worst choice possible."

I tugged the knot toward my Adam's apple and said, "Let's go in and win you some money." Casinos had a trick. If you paid the table manager, he would let your partner win. Give them $5000, and they let the lady win $4000. In those days, they understood noblesse oblige, a win-lose-win scenario.

The casino was small but right out of central casting. Wall-to-wall red carpets with printed black tiled lozenges decorated the floor. Brown wooden panels with a tinge of red covered the walls. A narrow gallery extended around the room, a faux second floor for non-existent spectators. Like the fountains outside, two enormous chandeliers dominated the modern, individual fixtures above each green baize baccarat, poker, and roulette table. The only cheap effect was the noise of the few slot machines outside. No casino could resist the profits.

That night, I had G. win at the roulette table and drink enough champagne to make her dizzy. We came out well past midnight. We left the roulette table's hilarity and people's cheers behind us. The streets had emptied from the earlier concert. I heard the clatter of our footsteps and the klaxon of odd cars. She leaned on me for support, one hand through my right arm, the other across her twisted body resting on my right shoulder. She walked with a sideways gait, her face severe and uncommunicative.

In the elevator, she whispered, "Sam, I am scared." Disingenuously, I told her not to worry. The surgery tomorrow will take an hour. We would then go to Baden-Baden for the recovery. She looked at me, disappointed. "Sam, what will become of me?"

I lied to her again. "I don't know." Her vulnerability still tugs at my heart. Why could I not see the little girl? I insisted on seeing the woman she wasn't.

She said, "Please stay with me at the hospital tomorrow." I said I would.

2. 1973: Hospitals at the Beck and Call of the Rich

The next morning, she followed the hospital's orders. She didn't break her fast. In support, I only had a cup of coffee. The hotel's Mercedes drove us to St. Josef's Hospital. In her whites, a pert, piggy-nosed blonde nurse awaited us at a side door. She took us to a conglomeration of rooms at the back. I filled out a few forms. She escorted us to a bare office.

There we sat in front of the famous Pitanguy. A Brazilian, he could be pompous one moment and charming the next. He had a balding, round head with a rich man's—or a supporting actor's—face, and his entire face broke upward when he smiled. He looked at G. with interest. "Mademoiselle," he said while a Brazilian nurse, also a beauty, translated into English for him, "nature didn't quarrel with you. But I can do her one better. That is the job of all artists." Charming and pompous. In an interview with *Paris Match*, he said his life had changed after a 1961 fire tore through a circus tent in the nearby city of Niteroí. He used private money to fund his clinics but didn't spare himself a good life. He lived a life of luxury and died in 2016.

The photo I had sent of G. lay on the table. His magic marker had drawn squiggly lines over it. The nurse translated. He would shave the chin into a thinner representation of itself. "Your nose is delicate, but I will lift it at the tip. You might get the prettiest nose wrinkle if you smile. Will it please you?" Charming or pompous. He then asked how she was related to the Shah. "I will soon be," she replied.

"How so?" he said.

She repeated what she had said to Madame Claude. "He asked me to marry him." The doctor frowned with concern. He changed into a business-like demeanor. "Mademoiselle, we will see you in surgery in fifteen minutes. Monsieur, you will wait outside if you please."

I could now answer her question of the night before with confidence. I counted on Madame Claude's discretion not to repeat what she heard. Doctor Pitanguy knew the Queen skin deep, but well enough; he, however, had none of Madame Claude's obligations not to chatter with the next royal who waited for perfection. Sooner or later, the Court would hear of her foolish boast. "Be scared," I wanted to say. "I can count your days at Court."

The nurse rolled her to me three hours later. The Brazilian translator walked behind them. She sat slumped, her head bouncing off her chest. I got up in a panic. "Is she all right?" I reached out. She straightened like a jack-in-the-box puppet and gave me her manly laugh. "Me? Am I all right? I am more than all right." G.'s face was a patchwork of rotten banana yellows, Roquefort greens, and bruised violets. Some cotton was visible in her nostrils. A surgical net covered her hair. She smiled, took off the net, and vigorously massaged her golden hair onto her shoulders with both hands. "You are next, monkey face," she said.

I told her no amount of surgery would put things right with my face. "Too true," she said. "You may be a monkey face, but you are my monkey face. What are we waiting for? Let's get out of here." The deed was done. I had fallen for her.

3. 1973: Performance by the Narrator with a Recuperating Dulcinea

At my age, the brain prioritizes the flow of blood rather than the loins. All is relative. When Oliver Wendell Holmes was about my age, he spotted a beautiful woman and said, "What I wouldn't give to be seventy again!" Girls be damned; what wouldn't I give to be seventy and prance to the toilet and piss my heart out.

My early condition hardly ever betrays me anymore. The hardness no longer produces pain. In my youth, I carried a pin in my wallet. Like all excellent tailors, my tailor understood a client's *petit* embarrassments. He tailored my trousers with skill to hide my long hours of discomfiture. When desperate, I used the pin, like an anti-grenade, to deflate and relieve myself of the pain.

Our driver drove the two-hour trip to Baden-Baden at 200 km/hour. She slept first on my shoulder and then on my lap in the back of the Merc. I had never seen Baden-Baden. The travel itineraries of the royal family after surgery had the stay as a prerequisite before they showed up in public again. Nobody wanted a battered face in a crowd, or wanted to admit to the vanity workup. We live in different times now; girls wear their Band-Aid on the bridge of their noses as a badge of honor. And why not?

The car dropped us off in the afternoon at Brenners Park Hotel, one of the Vielles Dames hotels of Europe. The magnificent baroque building, without the style confusion of our Wiesbaden hotel, stood in a park. They wanted to build a grand hotel, and they built one. They employed the architect of the Karlsruhe Palace and Speyer Cathedral. Columns and arches give it grandeur. The canthus leaves and laurels on the building showed restraint. The mint-striped awnings gave it its wings. It fell shy of ornate.

We had a suite with two rooms in the new wing furnished with Art Deco pieces. Patients walked the corridors *sans-gêne* with black and blue faces. The staff expressed no sign of surprise at the horrors of surgery. G. went straight to her bed and slept till the next day. The young can sleep.

I sat at the empty bar and sipped Black Label from a seriously heavy crystal tumbler. I wondered how a cravenly ambitious man changes. One day you don't give a shit if someone lives or dies. The next day, you are prepared to commit treason for her? She had not given me the green light, but I knew, no wooly confusion, about my intentions. My confusion lay in how to justify it. I imagined my uncle's harsh questions.

"What were you thinking, you ass?"

"But uncle," I would say, "His Majesty was done with her."

"And you think you can have the sloppy leftovers?"

Then I thought about her. Not yet twenty. Didn't she need my protection? What would this protection even look like? Would I marry her? Let's not get carried away—a shallow girl without an education. Her ambition dwarfed mine. She dreamed of replacing the Queen, for God's sake. I had not asked her what exactly HIM had promised her. Did it even matter? In no scenario was it possible. The Queen was the mother of the heir to the throne.

Should I tell her about HIM's intentions of retiring her? I scurried through those thoughts to find uglier, more ruthless thoughts. Would it be easier to bed her or more difficult if I told her of HIM's intentions? After a plate of *saumon fumé*, dainty toast squares, and a glass of Blanc de Blancs champagne, I gathered these thoughts and took them to bed with me. I spent a sleepless night imagining she might walk into my bedroom. Then I dreamt of my uncle. He caught us in bed. He laughed like he laughed at the religious man after the Lambton case. More complex scenarios ensued. The liberties of the last few days expanded in my mind to unfettered touches. With each advance, I saw crowds in Court whispering behind us. I denied it under one set of conditions. I stood proud in different circumstances. Why do we get so unhinged at night? One fact never varied in my hallucinatory night: If she asked me, I would not hesitate.

The morning came. She woke me with a military shout, "*Khabardar*, at attention." She jumped and stood on my bed in jeans, a white T-shirt, and bare feet like the teenager she was.

"We need to go."

"Where?" I said.

"Explore."

"Come here," I said. I took her chin gently and inspected her face. Like an expert needleworker, the good doctor had sewn a small cicatrix underneath her chin. He had earned his keep. The bruises had all taken on a soft yellow color. They disappeared in the background of her thick blonde hair. She had removed the cotton from her nose. All changes so subtle. Her excitement had her green eyes sparkling like emeralds. "You okay?" I said. See, tiny liberties.

"I can hardly breathe," she said. "Can you see the wrinkle on my nose?" She mimicked Pitanguy. She had the mimic talent.

She got the perfect caricature of the doctor. "I had some blood ooze out in the middle of the night. It made a mess of the pillow. I washed it."

"What? The pillowcase?" I said. "But they clean up soiled beddings."

"Come on, let's go. I am famished."

The day began. We walked in the park; it was a birds and bees day. Warm, the sounds of summer all around. We bought swim suits and visited the pool in the afternoon. Outside, next to the pool, we lunched on scrambled eggs and strong coffee. I wouldn't get her a Campari and orange juice because of her antibiotics, nor did I allow her to sit in the sun. "Okay, Papa," she said. Her confident look belied the diminutive. We walked around the few shops in the hotel.

In the mezzanine, she discovered the ballroom. I saw a grand piano in the corner. She didn't know I played the piano. I had never shown her much of my shenanigans, humor, or any other talent I possessed. With a loud screech, I dragged the leatherette-padded piano bench in the corner of the room over to the piano. She covered her ears exaggeratedly. The bench had a small knob on the side. I adjusted the seat up the telescopic inner mechanism to fit my stature. I knew the effect a musician could have on audiences. Most of my pickup successes came from my skill at playing the piano. Years later, I played in hotel lobbies and bars to put food on the table. I knew how to throw a wide net out there to fish.

At first, I banged some of the most untuned notes I could muster. G. walked on the shiny parquet floor in the far corner. She held her palms to her ears. Her two sandals were hanging from her fingers like a Spaniel's ears. I played an atrocious version of *Happy Birthday*.

"It's not my birthday," she shouted. Her voice echoed in the high-ceilinged room. She moved to the center. I played a smooth version of *Jingle Bells*.

"Not Christmas," she said. Her voice had doubts at the skill in view. I played a complicated version of *Twinkle Twinkle Little Star*. She had never heard of it. "You know how to play?" I smiled.

I dove into Scott Joplin's *Maple Leaf Rag*. This was before *The Sting*. The movie relaunched its popularity. She mimicked a version of the Charleston she might have seen in a film. Bare feet didn't allow for smooth dancing. Nobody who grew up in the sixties knew how to dance. I slowed her down. I played her *Put the Blame on Mame*. She came over. She undulated and leaned on the piano. "What's this?"

"It is from your namesake movie," I said. "It's story of a young man who discovers his old flame married to an older man."

"Does he win her back?" she asked. I didn't answer. "Play something different," she said. I launched into *As Time Goes By* as a private joke. "What's this tune?" she said.

"A piano player's view of the world," I said. Nineteen years old, and she hadn't seen *Casablanca*. She removed my right hand. I continued to play with the left hand. She threw her leg over my lap and straddled, facing me. She replaced my right hand behind her on the keyboard. I didn't flinch. I allowed my right hand to rejoin the left one. *Old enough*, I thought. I played as I looked up at her face. I never lost a note. A wrong note would have blown it. *I learned the piano for this moment*, I thought. She looked at me with an I-didn't-know-you-could-do-that look.

She bunched the fingers of one hand in a mock telescope, put it against one eye, and watched me as I played. "What are we going to do, monkey face?" she said. She then kissed my thick lips with the tenderest touch of hers. We starred in *Beauty and the Beast*, the story told by Gabrielle-Suzanne Barbot de Villeneuve. I read it after the comment by HIM in the palace gardens.

A benefit of adulthood: The home run is implicit when you get to first base. You don't need to spell it out. Being an adult also meant I would not turn into a prince at the touch of a beloved lip. I stopped playing the piano.

Can I compare our few hours to when I first held my daughter? The question itself reveals the answer. The moment you first hold your daughter stretches the present to an eternity. You reflect on a few moments for the rest of your life; consciousness does not allow you to stay in the present for long. Moments in the present flicker.

The first kiss. She shook her head up and down for more, like an infant getting fed. I search my memory to remember what magical transport took us to our suite. I don't recall it. I remember I ordered caviar and champagne; both rested on ice. It arrived on an amputated rectangle of a table to fit through the hotel door. We didn't complete the table's round existence. The leaves rested downward while we wrangled.

Among senses, sight reigns. During sex, eyes best reserved for pornography lose sovereignty. In bed, the eye takes on microscopic responsibilities the brain rejects on aesthetic grounds. It prefers to lower the lids and defer to touch, taste, and smell. The ears prick up, but primarily for signage. I don't claim eidetic powers. But that day and night, I can roll forward and backward like a microfilm reader.

In our nakedness, we all surprise our lovers. My thin legs surprised her with a guffaw. The heat of her body shocked me. I can't describe it as pleasant or unpleasant. The skin was hot to the touch but had no sheen of sweat. Close, real close, her skin smelled of an orange grove a mile away. The olfactory memory rushed to lock down the datum forever. Her breath smelled of fresh air. Not warm. Fresh. That's how young she was. A tad vulgar at first, she was no delicate flower. Between the sculpted collarbones, like an ancient gold necklace, and fragile ankles, you wondered how her bones supported her. She had shapely flesh and toned substantial muscles—arousing, not girlish, but womanly. The light in the living room suite cast a distant glow on her limbs.

I kissed her clavicle first. I traced my fingers around her clavicle, the slender curvature of a bridge of grace, a crescent, a sculpture of fragility, a hollow spoon between her collarbone and throat. Her throat, soft, white, and pliable, changed shape under the touch of my lips. Can surface beauty have this profound effect? It does. It tattoos itself on the brain like leatherwork on a saddle.

I kissed her lightly spittled lips that tasted of salt. I stroked and kissed the crescent of her Achilles tendon, as thin as a wishbone. She made a clever, tittering remark. I didn't hear it. I traced the narrow paths of hieroglyphics: her bra straps and shoe straps stamped on her perfect skin. I knew by morning, the youthful skin would bounce back, and the prints would disappear like footprints on sand smoothed by waves. As I caressed the last few vertebrae of her back, I felt, against the tips of my fingers, the soft blonde hair down like the tip of a feather.

I saw her want to take control. She asserted the polished ceramic of her character. To get it over with, as she had learned. I saw her earlier amusement evaporate as she got down to business, beginning with moans, their falsity divulged by their unimaginative repetition. She wanted me happy and showed me how a queen gives favors, expecting nothing back. The straddle had her head tossed backward with each stroke. I had other plans. I had many years over her. My insomniac bullet had other plans.

She dreaded the idea of a man bringing her off. She dreaded the loss of control, even for a short time. My tenaciousness surprised her. I played with a stacked deck. She was in her upright straddle, eyes closed, the spread of her shoulders with two delicate, smooth blades that sharpened and curved in rhythm. Her S-shaped, serpent-like sinuous movement, learned in dance clubs, I detected it as fake. I traced the chain of tender bumps on her vertebrae and steadied her.

We had brief intervals of loss of control—her anguished face showed not a trace of the pleasure to come. She acted the not-acting with difficulty. I even detected anger during the intervals. Those intervals had the quality of enthusiasm that caused shame at the unashamedness. I remember the flat of our tongues touching. I remember her orange scent grew more humid, no longer a mile away, overpowering me. I felt the keys of her teeth biting. It dawned on me she was a novice as we worked our way into each other. I'd say she was an innocent with a will to dominate. I felt the soft scratch of her hair down there against my cheeks, the skin taut, pliable, wet, dry, resistant, smooth, and clingy. I wished my hirsute body away; I wanted to take it off to have better contact. The awkwardness of bones, shins hurting shins. Elbows desperate for freedom under the other's shoulder.

Yet these were the moments I later confused with her love for me. How could we have had such a physical commitment without an actual commitment? We would go through a cooling time, a wrong expression, a grind I could pull off all night if necessary. I recall intervals of possible pain for her. The vibration of her body. The lightest shudder in her shoulders, like a car's engine not starting. You wait and begin again. Like a marine signal coming from the depth of an ocean, she signaled. She was proud. I imagined a motto floating in her mind: "No complaints, ugly man. I will satisfy you yet."

The cycle of her emotions would start again but at a more surprised level, like the piano face she showed me an hour before. I saw in her eyes an agreement to explore with her ugly satyr. Then, a change of mind and an attempt to pull away. I wanted to make her quit acting sexual and *feel* sexual. I pulled back. No quitting. I experienced the slides and the frictionless frictions, and I might have even come. I did. I carried on. I didn't require any further sexual satisfaction, a role reversal. I floated like a hard cork in a sea. I uselessly bobbed up and down on the sea. My male ego told me I raised the sea level by immersing myself in it. The lushness of it all overpowered me: a humid, warm tropical continent.

When it all made sense, sensation was made. At most, it lasted thirty seconds. I saw G. bloom not like one flower but a bed of flowers, all of her, in slow motion, in total acceptance of me as her lover. Her pleasure deepened and sank into her. Not a moaner when all act melted. Her mouth opened, mute. She opened with all her body—no possibility of an act. My brain experienced the cliché flash of a fifties camera, which takes time and works like a unicolor firework, an even worse cliché. In the light, I saw her gaze. She accepted me. Her green pupils speckled in all directions. I imagined I saw my reflection in them.

Her face flushed down to her chest; the chest goose-pimpled. She watched me with wonder. She called my name twice: first from deep inside, a "Sam" that sounded far away, then a "Sam" with a growl full of pebbles. For thirty seconds, she transformed me from a beast to a prince. I recognized the miracle. The possibility was the gift she gave me to last a lifetime. A light flickered in me. It repaired my confidence like a blowtorch. You can't put out the light. The reversal of the humiliations of a lifetime, unconnected to the sexual act.

She broke down and cried as she climaxed. The end of the flash had darkened everything to a deeper black, like flashes do. She continued to weep on the side of the bed, a low animal whimper. It communicated defeat—no smart-aleck talk from either of us.

I, in turn, experienced physical pain. I moved to the bathroom. I quietly used the ice in the champagne bucket to detumescence. Why was I insistent with her to prove myself to her or HIM? Why the sexual boastfulness? Perhaps to prove I could attract her because of *me* and not by sitting on a throne. Or to communicate, "Can you see me now, O King, not a fool." Or, indeed, I was a fool. I had done something dangerous and without purpose for once—no hidden agendas, Uncle.

4. 1973: Cigarettes, Regrets, and Deafness to Reality

The frail line thickened over the years between what I performed as love and what I judged as intrusion, exploitation, and stupid boastfulness. But the light flickered. And I lost my humor. In my bed, forty-five years later, I saw myself in the mirror. Her youth didn't tickle my conscience. The combination of her and me insulted my aesthetic affectations. Surviving a few more years, I now see myself uglier than ever; I see her as an Egyptian mummy, preserved in all her beauty, a refrigerated memory. I thaw her at will as a memory of a memory. Distant but clear. I see me from the mirrored high ceiling of the hotel room, which wasn't mirrored, like an ugly virgule next to her, head and limbs wrapped in a mess of expensive sheets. And I say no, this isn't right. I don't belong in aesthetic considerations.

Later, we talked. More relaxed. We drank the champagne and ate the caviar. She used her pinky to scoop it out while sipping from the bottle. She left an indelible sturgeon roe trail across the snow-white, starched table spread that would take a few washes to restore. We talked about our childhoods. More me, for she still lived in the neighborhood of her childhood, sitting cross-legged, elbows on knees, crouched like a kid eating and listening to me as if at a camping trip around the fire.

We talked about the future. I didn't have the heart to tell her what awaited upon her return. I tried to explain to her our relationship with the King. "We serve him," I told her. I explained how dire life was a few years before her birth. We had come far, thanks to HIM. "We owe him our service," I said. "We don't question the trivia. What I do is trivial. What you do is trivial. The trivial matters up to a point. He works all day, you know. Disciplined."

"I know. You think I don't know?" G. said. "When he comes to bed, I can hear the clank of armor being removed. He always folds his clothes before coming into bed. He changes. He turns into a boy. Right after, he smiles like a boy. By the time he finishes the cigarette, the armor is back on. He becomes super polite. Immaculate, not messy like you." She pointed to me and the sheets.

"I am proud of giving him the respite," she said. I nodded my head in agreement. *She gets it*, I thought. Then she jumped up, sheets around her, walking around the hotel room like a Roman senator, one arm bare. "But you see," she bunched her fingers in the Iranian way, like a pine cone, to explain something, "I can give him so much more. He relaxes with me. He tells me things I cannot repeat."

I asked myself about her sexual ignorance. The bluff when in bed. How else could it be for a nineteen-year-old? Yet she had conquered an experienced monarch. I further asked myself if that was the attraction for him—an innocent after so many professionals. I remembered her comment about how he turned into a boy. Was it intimacy he needed? A girlfriend, a girl who was a friend to a boy who had experienced so much trauma. No demands. And now so demanding.

Her speech brought me back to Earth. I didn't want to hear details. Not then, even though my ego wanted to listen to it. It shocked me how we both talked about serving a man who transcended our lovemaking. He sat between us, joining in a *partouse*.

We made love one more time the next day, around 10:00 a.m. before checking out. I allowed her control, a quick affair. It gave her some satisfaction, as it did me. I still needed time in the bathroom. I used a needle from a flat sewing kit in the sliding drawer. A swelling of blood balanced at the tip of the needle; it dropped into the basin with a lush raindrop splash—relief for me.

We checked out. We took the flight to Tehran. We arrived past midnight. Her father picked her up. I heard him say, "His Majesty wants you at Court tomorrow afternoon." I looked conveniently for my delayed suitcase. I didn't talk to them. He assumed our relationship had harked back to our departure a few weeks before, a lifetime ago. I drove to my apartment near the Court.

5. 1973: The Nose Gets Tweaked

The next day, I stayed home. In the afternoon, my uncle sent me a sarcastic message: "We missed your presence today. Tomorrow 8:30. Tennis at the club."

I knew the routine. I drove and entered by the upper gate of the club; I knew the guards. They waved me in. I had the Hilton Hotel in the rearview mirror. The clubhouse roof was visible down the large, dirt-packed avenue as you drove toward it; halfway between the gate and the clubhouse cars parked on the right. Further to the right, the grassless golf course, dirt-packed, filled the horizon.

Twosomes and foursomes already sprinkled the golf course; many Japanese took advantage of the low fees. I could hear the sharp, metallic ping of golf balls in the distance. I parked and went down two sets of stairs. The club had built five courts in a tree-lined ravine between the golf course and the road. I could hear the tennis balls' clean, crisp, percussive pops. The center court had a small platform. I saw Asghar, fifteen years old, the loopy ball boy, walking in circles. He waited for my uncle. He laughed uncontrollably behind his hand, elbow held high from congenital shyness. "Your uncle wants us to play double—you and me as a team." Aside from the head pro, Asghar could beat anybody. "Who's my uncle's partner?" I asked.

"Mr. Bozorgmehr," he said. He reddened, hid behind his elbow, and laughed nervously. Bozorgmehr was the general manager of the club. An irascible, moody man who could slap the help in a moment, but, at the drop of a coin, turn on the charm. A few years later, he threw one tantrum too many at the aristocratic wife of a famous architect. By the close of the day, the board fired him.

I advised Asghar to play soft shots at my uncle. I would take care of Bozorgmehr. He looked at me and laughed, more at ease. He knew my clownish game. He also knew I was a player and could beat most people.

Bozorgmehr and my uncle walked down together. The clay courts were moist. I smelled freshly opened tennis cans. The weather was still cool from the evening desert wind. It wouldn't last past 10:00 on an August day. By 11:00, no one played in the 40-degree heat. We all wore white. Tennis hadn't invented color yet.

The game went as I had hoped. My uncle handled Asghar's shots just so. I had to lob to our red-necked general manager (actual rings of red around the neck). It looked like the three of us conspired to get him angry. He directed his vituperation at me. Nothing new. "You call it tennis?" he'd shout. Redder in the face, he directed vitriolic tropes at me. He'd turn to my uncle and say, "I play with a monkey." We won two sets. We gave them a few games out of respect. Bozorgmehr left in a huff. Asghar had his elbow up for most of the match. The raised elbow showed how hard it was to hide his disturbed, uncontrolled mirth. Years later, he joined the Revolutionary Guards. He saved my life. He sat in my apartment lobby for ten hours to warn me of an impending arrest. He died in the Iran-Iraq war, probably elbow raised at the hilarity of it all.

My uncle and I retired to a table on the platform while a mixed couple took over the court. We ordered two Sekanjebin sherbets made of cool mint and vinegar syrup. We sat down. "Tell me how it all went," he instructed. I gave him a quick precis. I told him we indeed needed to worry about Madame Claude. After our meeting in Paris, I called a few of my contacts in the Sûreté from my time in Intelligence. She helped them. But we got the horse and the cart backward. She didn't divulge the names of her customers. The French Sûreté brought their targeted customers to her, a classic honey trap. My contacts told me Madame Claude had developed a too-visible profile. The government showed excessive interest in her taxes, which meant they could get hold of her records.

"The hypocrite, Giscard," my uncle said, referring to the French Minister of Economy and Finance who would become president the following year. "He sleeps with a twenty-two-year-old actress who played Emmanuelle. What's her name?" We knew Giscard slept with Sylvia Kristel. I advised my uncle to switch to establishments run by Catherine Virgitti and Susi Wyss; Wyss was a socialite but also a former call girl. Her first client was the notorious Lord Lambton. Susi claimed to have done a threesome with Lambton and Christine Keeler—Keeler of the Profumo scandal. I note these details not to spin conspiracy theories but to underscore our tiny world.

In 1975, Frenande's memoir *Allô Oui* gave me a few sleepless nights. Jaques Quoirez, a friend of mine, the brother of Françoise Sagan, author of *Bonjour Tristesse*, wrote the introduction. I called him in a panic. He assured me of Frenande's total discretion. "The book doesn't reveal any of her clients' identities," he said.

"And the whore?" my uncle asked. I winced. I told him it all went well. "Too well," he said. "His Majesty has taken up with her again. I haven't seen her yet, but the Queen-mother said she looks more beautiful, more captivating than ever. Did you explain to her the sun will set soon?"

"I did, Uncle, but she was not receptive."

"As I told you before, you must find her a husband." My uncle watched the couple play and sipped from a beautiful, long-stemmed silver spoon shaped like a grape leaf. The metallic stem also served as a straw.

"If you want, Uncle, and if it makes it easier for His Majesty, I will marry her on a one-year contract. A suitable solution, don't you think?"

He turned abruptly from the game, the spoon tip still in his mouth. He watched me with sudden suspicion over his moist glasses, his forehead wet with sweat from the game. "You haven't done anything stupid, have you?"

"Of course not, Uncle," I said. I hid my misprision. No hesitation. I no longer stumbled easily. If you lie, lie briefly. "I offer a solution. It would allow her to be around without too much gossip."

"She has to go," he said. "The other day, her father asked me if he could replace General Toufanian. Can you imagine the nerve? Also, have you forgotten your family name? You can't marry a whore. What would your mother say?"

"My mother," I said, "would die from wonder. How her ugly duckling did the second best and married a swan." He laughed. I didn't.

THE RECKONING

1. 1975: An Islamist Marxist Has My Daughter

I got a call from Azar, G.'s cousin, three weeks after G.'s death. She wanted to see me in Café Naderī in downtown Tehran on Hafez Avenue. At 10:00 a.m., I walked in. She sat in the middle of the room. Her table abutted a thin, white, smooth pillar—the floor had a geometry of narrow red marble accents on the perimeter of the large square white marble tiles. The servers wore red uniforms. They matched the marble accents. Lengthwise floor-to-ceiling windows allowed light into the room.

I joined her. We both ordered tea. The waiters all looked like remnants of the old King's era. Our waiter, youngish compared to his colleagues, arrived lickety-split, with a tray balanced on the palm of his hand above his head. He rested it on his shoulder. He grabbed two saucers from the tray, which he slid with a flourish in front of us. He added two medium-sized water glasses with a clatter. Iranians don't like cups. The glasses dangerously wobbled on the verge of overturning, but no chance. Each glass did a short dance and settled back on the saucer. Part of the show. He poured two fingers of concentrated tea from the shiny metal teapot. He made an arching stream like in a young men's pissing contest. He placed the teapot in the middle of the small round table. He talked with one of his colleagues, not looking as he topped the glasses with boiling water, and left without a second look.

Unlike most women of the seventies who wore a Hermes scarf like a shawl, I noticed she wore a head scarf. She wore it tight, cream-colored, and with a goal: to cover her hair. The scarf emphasized her mouth and the tight smile she bestowed on me as I arrived. It disconcerted me. She acknowledged the confusion. "I know," she said. "My family says I look like my cousin. The ugly cousin, right?" Her smile was mirthless. It didn't help. "I know you are busy, but you asked me to let you know if anything unexpected occurred." I returned the tight smile.

"Since G.'s death, the General has become a tyrant. I mean, he always was a tyrant, but this is worse. He hurls insults at us, the women, every day. We keep the baby out of his way. He calls the baby a whore's child. He shouts, 'Keep the whore's baby out of sight.' If the baby cries, I take her into the streets until she calms so he can't hear us."

I encouraged Azar to play it safe. "Take the little girl to your mother's house for a while."

She shook her head. "You don't understand. We are changing our name. My father hates the General." I conceded the problem. "But that isn't why I called you." She took a conspiratorial pose. She leaned over the table and cupped her hand around her mouth to explain.

I smiled. I told Azar to sit back and talk like she would talk to her father. "Are you an Islamist Marxist?" I asked. She looked at me in horror. "Don't fret," I said. "You aren't in any danger from me. If you want to keep your secret, don't wear your head scarf like an Islamist Marxist. I should warn you. Don't go down that road. It will catch up with you. They know most of your names. Now tell me what you saw or heard."

She looked at me, worried and hesitant. "Mr. Sam, please don't report me. I am a listener in the cell. I am not active. My boyfriend introduced me. I have not committed any crime. All this," she circled her hand around her head, indicating she meant the whole world we lived in, "my cousin, the people at Court, it all feels rotten."

"I promise you, Azar, I will not report you. Your secret is safe with me. Tell me what you have to tell me."

"I heard the General make a call to someone at Court. They had a heated exchange. The General shook from anger. I heard him say the baby belonged to the Shah. Someone must have contradicted him because he said, 'The dates don't match the marriage dates.' Then he couldn't talk for a good while. I could hear the squeak of the caller like a rush of noise, like lots of tiny gibberings. I heard the General say, 'You want me to give the child up for adoption?' It calmed him down. I couldn't hear the caller's voice. The General now talked as if the solution should have come from him in a moment of sudden insight. He asked if 'His Majesty, in his infinite wisdom, would once again refocus his affection on his humble servant.' I am appalled," Azar said.

I sat with her for ten minutes. I assured her I would work out something. "Does G.'s mother know about her husband's intentions?" "No," Azar said. She heard the conversation only yesterday. I asked if she knew who the caller on the other end of the line was. Again, she didn't. I had a good idea. I questioned if she knew the exact date of the baby's birth. No, she answered. For the last trimester, or thereabouts, the General had sent her to a small village-cum-town called Amlash in the Province of Gilan, where the family came from.

I left with a complicated situation. We had a baby with four potential fathers, not two: The husband, General Khatami, HIM, and I were possible candidates. Knowing the child's birthday could eliminate either the General and the husband as a pair, or me and HIM. We had our turns at least thirty days apart. HIM had to either dilute with me or with the other two. I couldn't eliminate HIM. No one knew about G. and me. The time had come for a talk with Annabelle. Like always, I had a plan.

2. 1975: Sam & Belle Reach an Agreement

In early 1974, Annabelle arrived in Tehran full of dreams of the Oriental life she'd read about in her books. Instead, she found an energetic, ugly city filled with lunches and dinners. At times, she was a guest at Court, at others among my family, and at other times among her consulate colleagues, who all talked a Persified Franglais. She loved it all. She plunged in. She went native. She learned this third language, the Persified Franglais—hers a dash more Francais, but a little German.

We dated from the first week of her arrival. We hardly slept. We lunched and dined outside. I had a cook, Ousta Taghi, who mostly cleaned as he had so little to do. She, the adventurer, tried Chelo Kebab in the Bazaar one day, a steak in midtown on another day, and another time Jujeh Kabab over red, fiery coals while hiking in the mountains above Shemiran. She never suffered a day's illness, not even the Tehran Tummy. I changed my flat but stayed close to the Niavaran Palace. From our balcony, you could glimpse Mount Damavand, if you craned your neck. We treated Damavand like Parisians treat the Eiffel Tower. We boasted about the tiniest view and paid for it in higher rent.

We visited tourist spots in Isfahan and Shiraz that no native had ever visited. She loved our home in Birjand. My mother's biannual visits from Paris, with her interminable complaints, were no longer a bore or a duty to bear. She loved Annabelle. They happily shopped in the Bazaar, in the newly opened boutiques and were taken as Farangis. But if an unfortunate shop owner dared to overcharge them for their foreign look, then hell had no fury like a woman cheated. Annabelle brought men to tears. It confirmed for her the existence of a genetic marker to cheat in all of us.

We danced at the discos to the Bee Gees, Donna Summer, Gloria Gaynor, and ABBA, and accompanied it with shots of vodka at the bar, lines of coke in the bathroom, weed outside with friends, and the single rose stem sold to us at 3:00 a.m. before we went home to make love. When couples get called by the moniker of a mono-name, you either reject it or it fits like an honest compliment. They called us Sam & Belle, which works better in English. The odd practice continued even when we immigrated west, first to Europe and then to the US, with different friends. It was like a conclusion: We, the shortest of all couples, never talked about ourselves as individuals; we were like a Snakes and Ladders toy set. We married in 1975.

In my happiness, I missed so many telltale signs of our economy. Lines: People waited in endless bus lines and railway waiting rooms while ships on the Gulf lined up for months to unload goods. Traffic, inflation, and even water shortages. Nothing to cause revolutions. Enough other countries fought the same battles in those years and worse. The US experienced the most prolonged economic downturn since the Great Depression. I missed the general malaise, irritation, and disappointed expectations. Our economy had grown during most of my adult life. We saw ourselves outside the economy. We followed a third way even if oil revenues dropped 15%. When, in a forum, the economists warned HIM of too many projects, he asked, "Have you not read my book?" No irony intended.

I don't remember many factual statistics. But I remember a mid-year report. Whiskey consumption had increased. In six months, our country had consumed 80 million bottles of alcoholic beverages. Someone had added an unsigned note: "And on the day we buried Ayatollah Behbahani. How does this conform with Islamic precepts?" *It doesn't conform*, I thought. It didn't shake me.

That evening in 1975, I poured a couple of whiskey sodas from one of the 80 million bottles—a weak one for Annabelle and a stiff one for myself. Did she know what I did during the day at Court? Yes, to a point. I had risen in the bureaucracy of the palace. I still organized the inflow of women, but I had become a troubleshooter, a Swiss knife, if I might borrow her country's expertise. Annabelle had witnessed the year of bribes, the year we changed witnesses' minds, and our reach with editors of newspapers. The Davallou case had distressed her at times. She accepted it like a good pragmatic Calvinist. She didn't have jejune ideas. She regarded voluntary prostitution as a woman's choice; involuntary prostitution she likened to human slavery. She ticked all the boxes.

G.'s narrative had too many warning signs. Nineteen years old. Three out of the four men were more than twice her age. Indefensible. And there was always the question: Why did I take this long to tell her? Did I still love the girl?

It all came out differently. I told her everything, including the humiliations I had suffered back in childhood, in school, at Court. I sketched my night in Baden-Baden. I closed with the possibility of my paternity.

The question of love came up much later. "Do you remember, Sam, what I told you when we met the second time in Geneva's Mövenpick?" I could not recall. "I told you I don't want children. I told you I would not bring a child of mine into this world. We weren't yet dating. I have always said it to potential suitors. I haven't changed my mind." I didn't contradict her. She then asked the hypothetical. "Sam, if she came back to life and asked you to marry her as you asked her the last time, would you?"

I had one shot: I explained to her that G.'s gift to me wasn't imaginary. It righted a life-long breakage. It sealed a fracture in my psyche. "Without it," I told her, "there would be no Sam & Belle. You have to understand; she acted like a bridge. I don't love her. I am grateful to her."

Annabelle observed me as I talked. Like a good European, she didn't interrupt anybody midsentence, an Iranian's regular habit.

"The child," I said, "she exists, Annabelle. I have seen her. You will not burden the world with an extra child. I will respect your wishes and never ask you to give me a boy or a girl. We, I mean, the men who put her through this, we owe her," I said. "I cannot bear the idea of the child in an orphanage." She sat on the sofa. She thought for a long time. I went to bed.

First thing in the morning, she said, "I want to see the baby."

3. 1975: It's Her

I asked Azar to meet us at the same cafe. We arrived earlier. Predictably, Annabelle delighted in her surroundings. "I have read about this café, built by Reza Shah, which resembles the Dôme Café in Montparnasse, a center for intellectuals. Do you see any writers or artists you know?" I looked at her with awe. I didn't know anyone more curious, even faced with a tense meeting. It's not every day you go to get a daughter.

Azar arrived with the baby in her arms. The baby turned back and forth like she couldn't get a good look at the big picture of life. Her black locks bounced as wildly as the last time I saw her. Her coal-black eyes glistened. She stretched her arm toward me. With a gleeful little scream, she made out as if she recognized me from our previous encounter. We all laughed. Azar sat, bewildered. I had not discussed the reason for the meeting and didn't intend to do so. I introduced Annabelle as a colleague.

The waiter came over, and I swear he looked a hundred years old. He performed the show to Annabelle's delight. Azar started right away. She told me the grandmother now knows the General's intentions. It took a few fights, but he convinced her to give the baby up for adoption.

Azar bounced a finger off the side of her head, a gesture of I-have-had-an-idea. "I want to adopt her," she said. "I have talked it over with my family. They don't like it because I would have to stop my studies. I can get my old job back. I can type and take shorthand with the best of them." I tried to dissuade her. Annabelle understood the gist, but it was hard for her to follow. Azar talked a fast and unadulterated Farsi. Annabelle took the baby from Azar. She cooed to her. I tried to convince Azar of the folly of her plan. I painted a problematic future for her. I reminded her the grandparents could change their minds at any time. Or not even accept the child to live in the extended family.

All this she swatted away. "We will have the adoption agreements signed. Mr. Sam, adoption laws are strict in Iran. I have read them. My law student friend couldn't find one example where the original parents got the child back. Our families, my mother and father, never liked the General. If not for me, my father would have moved us from the neighborhood by now. Can you help me?" she said. I said yes.

We left discouraged; Annabelle thoughtful. In the car, she looked at me and said, "The baby is yours. The bone structure of her head is identical to your uncle and you. I have no doubt. You are the father. She belongs to you and not her cousin. She belongs in our home."

4. 2023: Questions of Choice

I cannot pretend I wasn't puzzled when I left Marie and Marianna in the Nordstrom coffee shop after their announcement—not of their marriage, but of their decision to adopt. I feared I might have blurted out the circumstances of her adoption. Her questions would have created other questions. I needed to think about the order of the presentation. I did my best not to wreck a day she wanted my support. I thought about how to explain the complications of her birth. How much to reveal? Would I tell her about her genetic mother's life at Court? The paternity explanation scared me to death. How would I explain the doubt about my paternity? If not me, who? Could I tell her she could be the daughter of a deposed monarch?

After a few innocent attempts to pull me out of my funk in Nordstrom, I noticed Marie and Marianna glancing at each other as if diagnosing a rapid advance in the progression of my dementia.

The following day, a Sunday morning, back in my room, while most of the "guests" (employees were trained to refer to us as guests) attended a nondenominational service, I wrote my daughter a short letter.

I explained the barebone facts: I had a brief affair with a woman, your genetic mother. Maman and I had just been married when your mother died in a tragic accident. She died at the age of 22. Maman, at once, agreed to adopt you. Then, with great difficulty,

I worded the last sentence about the doubts about my paternity. I dissimulated: "At the time of my affair with your genetic mother, she had other men in her life."

On Tuesday, my daughter walked in with a large bag of goodies from the supermarket on her shoulder. She ordered Laurel, with a wink that transported him to Elfland, "Malik, please take the groceries and put them in the shared refrigerator." She placed some cans in my tiny refrigerator in the room. "Mind, you don't forget to put my father's name on the package." Did I see another wink?

She sat beside me on the chair beside my wheelchair, where I looked at her. She held my hand. "I read your sweet letter, but know about the adoption. Mum told me before she died." I thought I had lived a life of secrecy; the whole world knew without me knowing the entire world knew. "Baba," she said, "I need to tell you more. It could make you happy and mad at the same time."

I looked at her face, all eagerness. "Has the stork dropped a baby girl down your chimney?" I asked. Her smile vanished. "No, not yet. Even in Massachusetts, gay couples must jump through a few extra hoops."

I tried to apologize to her. I was over the moon for them even though I had not shown suitable enthusiasm for their decision to adopt. "I wanted to tell you about your adoption, but I had promised your mother. Sorry I interrupted you. What were you going to tell me?"

"Mum and I agreed to send away your and my genetic samples. Mum never had doubts. I didn't care. But Mum said you tortured yourself over it. I am yours, Baba—all yours. The DNA test showed a 99.99% match." She beamed, like when she received a *grand cadeau*. I got angry, I laughed, then I got angry, then I let go and enjoyed her happiness. The source of my anger didn't come from their complete invasion of my privacy. But what if the test had proved negative? My wife and daughter didn't understand. Only HIM or I could have been the father. From Marie's birth certificate, I knew neither the husband nor General Khatami could have been. The possibility had always frightened me. "You will always be my princess," I smiled.

The door of my suite opened. The source of the wink revealed itself; Laurel and Hardy walked in with a cake and a candle. Behind them, Mrs. Lambton, her hands in prayer fashion on one side of her face, walked behind.

"We will celebrate this day as my birthday. I will have two birthdays," Marie said. Laurel and Hardy wagged their tails with unencumbered enthusiasm without a clue how someone could have two birthdays.

As I anticipated, I couldn't quench the curiosity of an English professor with a simple letter. During the following weeks, Marie's questions followed one after another. I could see how entangled my explanations were. I lifted my hands in surrender and begged her to stop. "I will write it all down for you," I said.

"And I will edit it," she said.

"No," I said. "I have written a lifetime; I can perfectly well edit what I write."

"From the little you have told me, Marianna and I want to publish your memoirs with the help of the Boston University Press, if we give it a literary polish. Don't you see, Baba? My biological mother's death fits our model world. *Zan. Zendegi. Azadi.* Baba, do you see?" She quoted one of the recent chants by Iranian woman against the Islamic Republic: Woman. Life. Freedom. "It will also give you something to do. Keep your mind sharp."

"My story will distort how it was," I said.

"Then make it clear. Personal weaknesses don't hold a candle to what happened to women in the first three-quarters of the twentieth century."

She goaded me like she always did. At ten years old, she could walk in from school and take all the oxygen out of the room with her plans, birthdays, societies, and United Nations projects. Not a moment of peace; she pushed us about like a Russian Gulag guard. We conformed, heads down, on the double. We loved her drive. If not for her, we'd sit and watch TV after a day's exhausting work. Here's what's worse: I look back and wish I had granted her even more. Why not paint her room all pink? Why not hire in a zoo for her birthday? Why not agree to camp in New Hampshire?

The Post-it notes started because she asked me to write. I have to gather a few loose ends before I hand over my notes for the "literary polish" they promised.

THE SHORT GOODBYE

1. 1973: The Lèse-Majesté of a Mistress

I saw her walk out of the bedroom of the same house behind the Niavaran Palace. This time, HIM left in a hurry. I watched her before she saw me down the corridor—a moment of true déjà vu. I remembered the same exit a few months back. Had it only been a few months? She looked less confident, more thoughtful, head down. She raised her head and saw me. Zapped me a hundred-watt smile, then saw me in a better focus. Her smile vanished. "Why the face?"

"We need to talk," I said. "You couldn't leave it alone, could you?" We walked downstairs. I took her by the elbow and pushed her into the pantry next to the kitchenette. I saw a white-uniformed servant with tea paraphernalia. I told him to make himself scarce. He said His Majesty had ordered tea. "His Majesty had to leave on urgent business," I answered. He scurried out.

The night before, HMQ had thrown a party. Rumors said G. appeared dressed in a similar dress to HMQ. Stories about the exactness of the dress were highly exaggerated. A female friend told me she wore the same Courrèges dress as Her Majesty. Of course, it was nonsense. I bought G. the dress in Paris. Her Majesty never wore Courrèges. Court-speak was, by definition, an exaggeration. "Tell me what happened."

"You know I am friends with Khatam's sister? I asked her to take me to the party." She referred to General Kahatami, the

Chief of staff of the Imperial Air Force, who was called Khatam by most. He had piloted the Shah to Italy during the days before the Mosaddegh coup in '53. He later married the Shah's half-sister, Fatemeh Pahlavi. Rumor had it the Americans had picked him to help the Queen and the Crown Prince if the Shah died. Even after Khatam's death, HIM never liked to compete with any popular figure.

"And she took you to the party?" I couldn't speak. To gate crash HMQ's party took an impulsive disrespect I could not digest.

"The General likes me a lot. He asked his sister if he could see me last night. I figured no one would notice me with all the people milling about."

"But G., HMQ invites individuals. Did you see me there? She makes up her guest list."

"I know now," she said. "All the ladies had lined up to receive her. When she got to me, Farah asked my name. When I said it, she turned and went directly to your uncle."

"You don't call her Farah. You call her Her Majesty the Queen. And then?"

"Right away, your uncle called the General over. Oh, Sam, if looks could kill. He ordered Khatam's brother-in-law to take me to Chattanooga, the place on Pahlavi Avenue, for dinner. Toward the end of dinner, the General arrived. We laughed a lot about nothing. He," she pointed to the ceiling, "said the same thing a few minutes ago." She didn't wait for me to ask. "Much about nothing, he told me."

I looked at her, gobsmacked. "Well, he," I mimicked and pointed to the ceiling, "wants you married inside the week."

"I know," she said calmly. She mocked my mimic. "He told

me." She pulled her tongue out, accompanied by a kid-like body bend. "So, find me a husband quick."

"What if I told you they want me to marry you?" I lied.

She looked at me with genuine pity. "You? No one would believe it. It would look like a put-up job. Me and you, the thought of it." She laughed and twisted the knife; words haunt a man years after. "It must be someone believable. Whoever you pick needs to know he can't touch me. When there is no choice, make the worst choice possible," she said.

She took the sting out of my back. I had to admire G.'s flexibility. She rolled with punches. She looked for a quick win, no more talk of marriage to HIM. The vision had shifted to the role of Madame Pompadour.

I already had picked the ideal husband. I had been searching ever since my uncle ordered it. I found a university student ready to graduate with a diploma in philosophy and ethics, not a bad-looking fellow. I enjoyed the cheap irony. His father had lost his pharmacy after the town planners had seen fit to build a road through his shop. They paid for the worthless real estate but not for the business. I promised his father a new pharmacy in a better location. I told the young man a higher-up had forced the girl. I explained the Court always made amends for the oppressed. He saw his role as a martyr to help a poor, innocent girl.

We wanted to convince the Queen that the girl had nothing to do with His Majesty. My uncle asked me if we could publish the wedding ceremony photos. Most editors rejected the request because they didn't see a story. Amirani, the editor of *Khandaniha*, explained it to me. "Two no-name couples get married. What's the fuss?" I couldn't tell them the biggest story of the year sat under their ink-stained nose.

We arranged a full dinner with many guests. Friends of G. and some actors and actresses of the Iranian cinema attended. The clever editor of the magazine *Sepid-o-Siyah* saw the photos and recognized the famous actress Jaleh Sam, another beauty at the table. It gave him the excuse to publish Jaleh Sam's picture as the lead. The headline said: "Jaleh Sam, the famously beautiful actress, attends a friend's wedding." The two beauties sat next to each other. You could mistake one for the other in the blurry black-and-white photo. In the caption for the picture, I insisted G.'s name accompany Jaleh's name. The magazine appeared discreetly in Niavaran Palace. It also showed up in the Queen-mother's palace. She took much interest.

In Court, we circulated that General Khatami kept G.; it turned out to be a prophecy. We knew Princess Fatemeh, the Shah's sister, wouldn't care. The two-pincer move didn't convince the Queen; it merely soothed the hurt. It did stop the talk of divorce and bigamy. I took the win.

The self-righteous Italian reporter, Oriana Fallaci, dared to ask HIM in an interview about the rumors that he planned to take a second wife. He answered coolly. One only takes a second wife if the first wife has health issues and certainly with the first wife's consent.

2. 1973: The Smooth Transition

I saw G. once more at the house a few weeks after the marriage and the disastrous party. We sat downstairs in the living room after her last visit with His Majesty. I am being funny now. Iranians seldom use their living rooms; in this house, never. It smelled musty—old, large furniture with antimacassar, silver daguerreotypes mostly of the Shah and the Queen. Little ironies abound. I drew the curtains beforehand. A draft waved them about. It let in a thin, shaky vertical light that halved the room. A small but overly intricate chandelier hung from the ceiling with a dozen faux electric candles. It shed less light than a 100-watt bulb. She showed me a ring the Shah gave her; a farewell present worthy of the Iranian Crown Jewels. He wasn't generous with money except with his women. Several of the Claude girls still show off their jewelry.

Later, the Islamic Republic accused him of giving away the Iranian Crown Jewels. Lies. We bought (I bought) jewelry from Van Cleef & Arpels in Paris, Harry Winston in New York, or Mozaffarian Jewelers in downtown Tehran. The ring she shined at me I bought for her during our trip to Paris because…well, it was my job.

We sat side-by-side. We waited on the uncomfortable couch. A heavy coffee table oddly close to the sofa had us sitting primly. I knew the next act. I heard the small klaxon horn of a car. A second short double scream of the impatient klaxon followed. "On my way," the doorman shouted. He hurried and opened the green metal gate of the small garden with a loud creak of the rusted hinges. I heard the gravel crunch as a slow car approached. The brakes made a lower register rusty sound at the front door.

I heard General Khatami's authoritative shout of "G.," like he applied the horn of the same car. I called out to the General. He stood at the door in civilian clothes. He was in his early fifties, athletic, not handsome but good-looking, spare, clean cut, with the skin of a well-tanned South American soccer player. He pursed his lips; his smile mocked.

The light shimmied through two perfectly matching oval tears in G.'s eyes. On command, she drained them guilefully dry. I almost heard the gurgle of the last swill down a drain. She stared back at me through the jeweled beauty of her crazed green pupils. She looked up at the General. He stood behind me. "Where are you taking me to dinner, General?" She was all in. She preferred preferment to all else, a brutal habit of careless craving, or so I thought. A smooth transfer occurred. This was the Berlin Checkpoint Charlie and there was no going back. What was I thinking? Silk wide-colored shirts, Anderson & Sheppard suits, Dunhill lighters; we passed the nineteen-year-old girl I loved from man to man.

I didn't see G. again until I saw her dead. I heard she stopped her affair with Khatam. The General had bought her a two-storied villa in Dezashib, in Shemiran. I received a report that the shotgun husband died in a car accident a year later. When did she give birth to a child? I mean, on what month on what day? I didn't know then.

BAD DEEDS GO UNPUNISHED

1. 1975: The Ripe Empire Requires an Amateur Detective

My neck twists like Rodney Dangerfield's. I am uncomfortable in my wool dressing gown made for winter. It reminds me of my childhood. It scratches my neck like eighty-grit sandpaper. I once wrote a manual for a corded Bosch sander. Even with my circulation, the heat in the nursing home is unbearable. I asked for an air conditioning unit. They tell me it will cost me $15 a week. The thoughts march on. I look at the dates on my Post-it notes; I know what is missing. My thoughts twist as my neck does with deeper scratchings. I don't want to think or write more about 1975. I prefer to visit the older memories.

My work gave me less pleasure by then. I must not give the impression that my lack of keenness at Court had brought down an awning on the proceedings of the empire. It still felt like high noon to most of us: no shadows of Islamic dusk discernible. They should have been. It is easy to mix and confuse retrospection from 1975 on. Minor signs now loom large.

The tenth anniversary of my move to the Court had changed us all. When I started, the Shah drove around the city. He went to dinner at friends' houses. The circle of friends ribbed each other. My tomfoolery made them laugh.

By 1975, I was another Court bureaucrat. HIM only visited the Sa'dabad complex of palaces, where the rest of the family resided. He traveled by helicopter. Pictures show a man who walked alone when he went to Noshahr at the Caspian or the Island of Kish in the Gulf. When in company, he sat aloof, focused on the horizon. He had the vision thing down. Few people engaged him in conversation. His humanity showed only when he was among his kids. You could live in his delight.

HIM and my uncle worked fifteen-hour days regularly. HIM read reports from the Foreign Ministry daily for an hour and a half. On Tuesdays and Thursdays, we shepherded the army, gendarmerie, police, and SAVAK heads. We handled the confidential foreign policy decisions (not the Foreign Office). Ministers saw him fortnightly. He attended the weekly Economic Council. Dinners with Arab ambassadors, meetings with US members of Congress, tea with French businessmen, negotiations with oil executives, site visits with state governors, ribbon cuttings of spanking new factories, and personal and family matters boggled a sane mind. We kept the not-for-profit Court corporation in a regular orbit for $20 million annually.

HIM became taciturn, more exaggerated by the day, as my uncle became morose and fawningly obsequious. All, of course, explainable years later, as both fell sick with cancer. It killed my uncle in 1978. It spared him the empire's fall. The Shah died in 1981 from Waldenström macroglobulinemia, a type of non-Hodgkin lymphoma.

Each man knew the long history of the other's disease but not the extent of their illness, due to a farce played by the doctors. Not to disclose to a patient the consequences of a terminal illness is unthinkable today. It happened to these two men. I hear it repeatedly when a new doctor visits me in this benighted Home for the

Dying. Have I taken care of my wishes with my loved ones? The emphasis borders on perversion.

HIM conducted preposterous interviews with foreign correspondents, lecturing the West. To an innocent audience, my uncle reported that General Azhari had made a gaff by telling someone any good work in the country happened because we feared the Shah. From the back of the room, I started my best buttering-up smile at the General's stupidity. "Why gaff?" HIM asked sharply. My smile froze in midair, then retreated from my cheeks. I sensed danger. "Because we want people to do their jobs on their merit and love of country," my uncle responded with a slight question mark in his intonation. He also sensed the danger. HIM looked at both of us, "No," he said. "No gaff. Learn your lesson and keep your noses clean." Fear had crept up on the emotional priority list.

Another time, I submitted the *Daily Telegraph's* review. The exchange underscored HIM's complete change. The interviewer asked, "What do you suppose this word 'megalomania' means?" My uncle defined it as greatness. "Greatness be damned, greatness to the point of madness," the Shah replied. I noticed he didn't drop "greatness" from the definition. Of course, the word means the delusional belief in one's importance.

The Court had become a suspicious place rife with nasty whisperings. We suspected each other. The country blamed the brothers and sisters of the Shah for unimaginably corrupt acts. They were not innocents by any stretch, but the accusations were exaggerated to ridiculous lengths. Rumors accused the Queen-mother of nightly orgies. Imagine: She had just celebrated her seventy-ninth birthday. Any new company requiring a license to operate had to pay 10% to SAIPA, Son Altesse Imperiale Princesse

Ashraf, Shah's twin sister. No one did the math. Still, they accused. On and on, unsubstantiated stories with kernels of truth weaved in and out of the Court. By then, we had lost the narrative. We only fire-fought the rumors about HIM.

I don't remember the Queen smeared, but it was open season on her entourage. They suffered. The HIM crowd hated the HMQ retinue. The HMQ people pointed to the SAIPA entourage as centers of corruption, but many joined their parties willingly. On the periphery, the Prime Minister's lot, mostly technocrats, whirled like lone constellations. They also overlapped with the other groups. I, with a foot in different camps, heard it all. All I could do was laugh it off with Annabelle. We lived happily enough in our circle of friends, mostly embassy people.

After the meeting with Nader at Café Chattanooga, like an alcoholic, I went on a bender of investigative minutiae. No piece of paper going through my uncle's office went unread. I read his correspondence with care. Desperate, I called Nader Yasin once more. "I need a favor," I explained the favor. He thought me mad. I told him if I could do it, I would. But Davallou would recognize me. "You are asking me to kidnap a favorite of HIM?"

"Not a favorite these days," I argued. "I need to know what Davallou said and did when he visited her at her place. Two days with a couple of your men should put the fear of God into him." He refused. I dropped it.

I saw all official documents addressed to my uncle. I suspected he kept a journal. You can't work with a man for thirteen years and not have a good idea he keeps one. He mainly wrote late at night at home. Sometimes, I saw him write on loose-leaf paper at the office, again late at night. He always gathered the documents from his desk and moved them to his house. When I visited his home, I saw the same quality paper on his desk, different from the office paper. I wanted to read them.

Let me set the record straight. Alikhani, the late editor of my uncle's papers, correctly stated, "Mr. Alam dispatched regular installments to Switzerland for safekeeping." Alikhani didn't know I had delivered three of the six volumes: one hard-back notebook and two stacks of papers. Old-fashioned melted wax sealed the wrappers. At the time, I didn't know the contents. I delivered them to a woman I chose to call Madame Vincent, a banker. I tip my figurative hat to the Vincent family (Papa, Maman, Jean, et Marie).

I didn't know the makeup of the notebooks when I delivered the package to Madame Vincent. For the last couple of years, I visited Switzerland around May 1973, 1974, and 1975 to accompany Annabelle to visit her family. The spring deliveries, I deduced and later confirmed according to our calendar. It started on the first spring day. I set my appointments with Madame Vincent in mid-morning to catch up with my uncle in Tehran in mid-afternoon. With me present, Madame Vincent would call the Minister. She would let him know his nephew had arrived.

I knew the 1975 and 1976 installments had to be in his house. He had switched from notebooks to loose-leaf sheets. I sneaked into his office a few times but aborted the idea.

He certainly wouldn't have minded me in his office; I had leeway to go in and out. People came in and out of my uncle's home, from morning to night, like the house of a Turkish Sultan. The well-dressed executives wanted his enormous thumb on the scales of a contract. Fruit sellers offered him sweet pomegranates from Yazd on their scales. They hoped to reverse water rights taken by a landlord.

He screamed at me once, "My house looks like a stable of asses! These donkeys trot in and out. They ask for reasonable, little favors. They figure the house is open. What is to lose? Ask away, they think. Five minutes with each them; that's two hours of my day not in the country's service. Two hours in which I cannot unburden HIM from his heavy load." Yes, a whiff of self-righteousness, but not without a misty scent of love for HIM.

I had scruples. Yet, the notes sat somewhere in his office, with possible crucial information about G.'s death. I finally dared to go through his office in January 1976, a week after he returned from Morocco and the US. He had started the usual Thursday lunch routine after a long trip. A house filled with guests was ready to welcome him back. After lunch, the house calmed to smaller groups. They talked, drank tea, and played Belote.

He asked me to attend to some of the mail stacked on his desk. He had invited a thief to walk into a bank safe. I rummaged through his office. He had locked the bottom drawer on the right side. I found the keys in the top middle drawer, left carelessly among the rubber bands, paper clips, loose change, and tiny rosette honors from unimportant countries. I envied those who wore their rosette on the lapel of their suite. My uncle threw them into his drawer or the garbage, probably after a tough day with a Gulf princeling. There sat the 1975-1976 diaries unlocked in the bottom drawer.

As I thrash around to pick up the strewn pearls of memory, I must explain this upcoming eidetic, total recall from a man with early dementia: I had help. I reread all this—not in Tehran, but in my bed in Framingham, Massachusetts. A six-volume set, bound in imperial blue, of all his journals came from Marie. My grandmother would have said, it was a *grand cadeau*.

Today I read five pages at a time during the two hours after lunch. My interest was to read what he knew around the time of G.'s death. I found the pages written late at night a challenge to decipher. As the page fills right to left, older Iranians economize paper. They write pell-mell on borders, at angles. Aesthetic, but hard to read. The people from Kohrasan speak more ornately. His writing was always flowery. I helped him with reports. In the diaries, the flattery of the Shah bordered on the worship of a deity. I detected a whiff of fear. A worried courtier feared the discovery of the papers. What he wrote reflected my life as if I had written it. Through uninteresting minutiae, that time was made interesting. I read the period of interest; the rest bored me.

He wrote about the first Cuban ambassador, about the Juan Carlos coronation after Franco's death. We bought a house for Prince Davood, the crown prince of Afghanistan, and another home in Paris for HIM's ex-wife, Princess Soraya. It boggles the mind. I wrote a commencement speech at the University of Pennsylvania for him. He wrote: "HIM read and approved." It shows HIM at his most detailed.

I found this note from the day after G.'s death about our meeting with HIM. "I arrived at the palace in a sour mood. Mrs. Alam is responsible. The Shah had a toothache but was in a good mood [probably the administration of the wrong medicine]. I informed HIM about the young lady. HIM commented that Qotbi, the Queen's cousin, should notify HMQ, not me. HIM showed no particular emotion. God has given us the wisest ruler who ever walked the Earth." My uncle writes with relief. The relief came from not having to break the news to HMQ. I, of course, contacted Qotbi.

On Saturday, 25 October 1975, he mentions, "For an hour or two, I saw an Iranian young lady." He comments, "It was terrific," which suggests it refers to his afternoon pleasures. The next day, he writes a similar line. It doesn't say if it was with the same young lady. The time he mentions tells me a different young lady was at play. "For half an hour after lunch, then I came home," he writes.

A thread? It's unlike him. The half an hour makes it too transactional for his taste. No comment on the good times. That is also atypical. I quote these two passages from memory. I could not reread them in my bed in Framingham because I had stolen the pages forty-seven years ago. I reread and studied the five pages many times at home. I am confident about the two entries, even if I missed an "and" or a "but."

He writes, "In the morning, we visited a factory. The factory produces tractors in Tabriz. I enjoyed it more than if I had the most beautiful young lady next to me; I couldn't have enjoyed her as much as this visit. All of it is because of this great man. He is Iran. I will do anything to keep this man safe, even for an extra hour. We flew back late afternoon. Dr. Ayadi, Davallou, the Shah, and I sat alone tonight. We played backgammon. Out of HIM's earshot, for I don't want to pile on his worries, I bent Davallou's ear about a young lady he had introduced to HIM a few years ago. We can't have young ladies reminisce."

Unclear how he had heard about G.'s plan to write a memoir. I conjecture she called him. I suspect she made monetary demands.

My uncle entered his office while I had these five pages on the desk. In an excellent mood, he smiled at me benevolently. I calmly placed the correspondence on top of the pages and got up from his seat to offer it back to him. I shut the top drawer with my gut as I stood up. Thank God I had placed the key back. Once on my feet, I used my right foot in a Chaplinesque move to close the bottom drawer as smoothly as I could muster while I smiled back like a prodigal son. The bottom drawer remained unlocked. I prayed the next time he tried the drawer, he'd blame jetlag for leaving it unlocked. I didn't sweat the five pages. More recent memoirs sat on top; I doubted he'd check into the pile. I promised him action on the correspondence by Monday morning and left the house.

I sit in my nook, which our pretentious management calls "en suite," in Framingham. To my absolute pleasure and hilarity, I read the editor's note in the fifth book in the period mentioned. Verify at leisure as God is my witness; I translate the editor, Mr. Alikhani's, comments verbatim: "From November to December, we don't find any commentary in Mr. Alam's journal. During this time, he traveled to the US and Morocco. After a foreign trip, he typically remarked on his trip before he resumed his daily diary. Probably a few days of his journal are lost in history. The sub-editor, Mr. Sadegh Azimi, double-checked the file in Geneva without results."

It's hilarious. He never mentioned me in six volumes, and there are few mentions of my subordinates; my invisible handiwork, commented on by Mr. Alikhani, is there for all to see. Annabelle would have enjoyed the irony. Much of our best work at Court left no fingerprints for posterity to enjoy.

2. 1975: An Opium Addict Needs No Torture

The diaries had no more new facts to add to what I already knew. With all my uncle's reticence when he wrote, he confirmed that my uncle and Davallou had collaborated with a plan in mind.

G.'s daughter—I should say our daughter—came into play about this time. Annabelle's consent to adopt her spun my planning head into gear. Annabelle remains blameless. I told her all of my life's misdemeanors, felonies, and offenses. But not this. I can hardly examine it today. No doubt I took her consent and her certainty of my paternity as carte blanche. With the criminal mind, like water looking for a crack or a fissure, we let thoughts rush and swamp our scruples. The word scruples originates from rough pebbles: exactly. Water over rough pebbles; the pebbles remain. I never told her. Even when I held her hand for weeks in Mass General, until she succumbed to her cancer, I couldn't tell her about my deal. The deal is what allows Marie to visit me on Tuesdays or Thursdays.

I called Nader again two days after the visit with Azar and the baby at Café Naderī. Here, I record the words I said to him. They have permanently lodged in my criminal conscience forever: "If you get me Davallou and get out of him what he did in G.'s house, I will reveal to you a Marxist Islamist cell at the University of Tehran." He remained silent, skeptical.

"How would you know?" he asked. He sounded intrigued. The Islamic Marxist activity had increased. Since 1971, thirty attempts and bombings against American personnel had taken American lives. We understood that American lives cost more than ours. In 1975 alone, they assassinated US Air Force Colonels Paul Shaffer and Jack Turner while they drove to work in a US military staff car. Later, they killed three American civilians. They worked on a sophisticated electronic surveillance system (IBEX). HIM, the United States Embassy, and even Gerald Ford wanted answers. The intelligence services were under intense pressure. SAVAK needed some wins.

"I know one of the cell's members," I said. "But I want you to promise you will treat her gently." I know. Despicable.

"I cannot make a promise I can't keep. The treatment depends on the extent of the girl's resistance. Women can endure more than men. You understand." I did. The neatness of Azar as a sacrificial lamb at the time had a certain ruthless elegance: I got to the bottom of G.'s death and gained a daughter. Once implicated as a communist, no one could take Azar's adoption request seriously. Another power rule: Neat solutions always trump moral scruples. I had to confront my uncle as a last move. He could make the adoption happen.

Davallou, now a sixty-five-year-old man with a severe opium addiction, lived in a house in Shemiran. He visited the palace, but less often. He attended mostly lunches with the Queen-mother or the Shah's twin sister. He stayed home to smoke his pipe till late evening. His wife, an energetic woman famous for corruption, jetted between Switzerland, France, and Tehran. Nader rejected the abduction idea. "An hour with a man with addictive weaknesses will be enough to get the information. We have to pick a time when he is alone. We will make it an official visit from the Intelligence office." I questioned the official visit idea. "Not to worry, my man will use counterfeit IDs, so make sure he remembers the fake names. Any complaints will backfire. I studied the man's history. Nobody takes anything he says seriously. He makes it all into a joke. A Friday before dinner looks like a good time to visit him." On Fridays, the West's Sundays, the staff always left for the day. Only the cook stayed behind. He cooked behind the main building in a kitchen detached from the house. Nader sent me the visit report on Saturday, the first day of our work week. Nothing dramatic emerged, but it clarified:

We rang the bell on Friday at 6:30 in the afternoon. We rang three times. We heard the shuffle of feet. The subject opened the door. He wore a pair of mules, a white shirt, and grey slacks. We introduced ourselves as instructed by name. We also showed official IDs. He showed no surprise or fear. He turned, and we followed. We strongly suspected the subject was under the influence of opium. The pungent, sweet smell emanated from the upstairs quarters. It confirmed our suspicions. As agreed at our general meeting last week, we disregarded the subject's illegal drug use. The subject guided us to the living room. He offered us drinks. He recommended a label of expensive whiskey, which we refused. We questioned him. The subject, a frail older man, at no time resisted or lied. The last comment is a subjective observation by both agents. The subject cooperated without the use of physical force. My colleague agent Behrouz Javadpour (real name) asked the prepared questions. I (agent Hossein Rezvani) took notes in accordance with the service's interview process.

"Mr. Davallou, my colleague and I have been investigating the death of Mrs. G. A. (the victim's married name). Can I ask you if you know the victim?"

"Yes."

"Can you tell us how you know her?"

"I have known Mrs. Alavi since her teenage years. I knew the General [name blacked out] from my visits to HIM's Court."

"What year would you say you first met her?"

"I'd guess in 1971. She couldn't have been more than fifteen or sixteen years old."

"How would you describe your relationship with her?"

"Like a father, more of an uncle. You might say I played the role of a guide. I helped the poor girl through the intricacies of the Court."

"Did you have an intimate relationship with Mrs. A.?"

"No. I am not stupid?" The subject showed emotional disgust at the thought.

"Why is it?"

"Mrs. A. was spoken for."

"Spoken for?"

At this point, the subject explained Mrs. Alavi's relationships at Court. One of the men mentioned was the late General Khatami; God rest his soul. The report has expunged six lines of conversation. As discussed in the general meeting, we moved on swiftly to the night of Mrs. A.'s death.

"Mr. Davallou, you were seen twice, once with the victim's father on October 28, 1975, and a second time on November 3, 1975. You entered the victim's house alone. The November date falls on the night of her death. Can you explain your presence on both occasions?"

"I am unsure of the dates because I never remember exact dates. I take your word for the accuracy of these dates." The subject paused for about ten seconds. He tried to recall details. "The first visit came about when His Excellency Mr. Alam called me to his office a day before I visited Mrs. A."

"Mr. Alam, the minister of Court?"

"Yes. Before I entered His Excellency Mr. Alam's office at the palace, contrary to all my meetings with him, I could hear his raised voice through the door. He is always courteous. I knocked, and he bid me to enter. His voice returned to his regular register. But he looked agitated. A man sat with his back to me and wore a military uniform. I can never tell about the military rank. All the rows of medals look alike to me. The man turned his head. I recognized a much paler version of the General, the lady's father, who I also know."

"Can you tell us the source of Mr. Alam's anger at the General?"

"I couldn't tell at first. I knew Mr. Alam had called me because he wanted me to do something for him. A bit strange."

"Why strange?"

"Well, he never liked me much. Let's say we had a history. I will skip the details." The subject pointed at me, writing the answers in shorthand. My colleague made the only aggressive comment of the whole interview.

"Let us be the judge," agent Javadpour said. The subject sighed and recounted his 1971 head-butting with Swiss law. We agree with the subject. We left the ten-minute conversation out of the report. We checked. All the details are available in our archives.

"Please tell us what you discussed in Mr. Alam's office."

"Mr. Alam had heard Mrs. G. A. wanted to write a tell-all memoir. For reasons I have recounted that would embarrass several people. Mr. Alam knew I had affection for G. from her teenage years. He wanted me to accompany the General to dissuade our budding writer."

"And was your visit at the end of October successful?"

"Yes, and no. We arrived at the house to find her with her cousin Azar Enferadi and an infant child in her arms. The General asked Miss Enferadi to leave. Mrs. A. transferred the baby to Miss Enferadi's arms. 'Take her to my mother's for the night,' she said. Miss Enferadi looked scared. The General, a martinet, acted harshly with his daughter. She reacted with composure and nonchalance, which surprised me. My apologies, gentlemen, if I sometimes use a French word: nonchalance means casual or calm. Daughter to a general, she was the general."

"What do you consider harsh?"

"He called her a whore in my presence. She ignored him. She talked with me like he didn't exist. I explained to her writing a memoir would be a terrible idea. She agreed."

"Did she agree not to write it?"

"Not quite. But I could see our way to an agreement. It looked like she wanted financial independence, if you see what I mean. With a father like the General, who could blame her? I had to get back to Court to get approval."

"You mean she blackmailed you, or let's say the Court?"

"Too harsh a statement. She played the hand dealt to her. She overplayed it."

"What do you mean?"

"When her father left the house, she let her father get out of earshot, then she said, 'Guess, the father's child.' She smiled all innocent. As I said, she overplayed her hand."

"Is it why you returned the night of her death? Did you kill her because she overplayed her hand?" The subject didn't react to my colleague's accusation. He sat there, his head on his chest. He picked up his head with a sad smile. He looked terrible and tired.

"Gentleman, look at me. Could I throw a woman of her size off a balcony? She would flip me over before I could stretch my arm." The subject showed typical signs of an opium addict. He slurred words with an over-emphasis on the shhh sound.

"You carried a box with you. What was in it?"

"Your men had the home stalked well. I looked for you but didn't detect a soul in the neighborhood. The box contained her favorite dry pastry—elephant ears—made by a Zoroastrian couple. They have a pastry shop on the corner of Shahreza and Lalehzar Avenue. It is fried dough but so delicate it breaks at the touch of a hand. Powdered sugar covers the top of the large clover-shaped pastry. She loved the pastry. My driver can confirm. He picked it up earlier in the day." Our finding of powdered sugar on the victim's lips confirms the subject's veracity.

"What was the deal?"

"There was no deal, you see. Once Mrs. A. had made the accusation, the Minister offered a different solution. To stop her from writing her memoir, it took money, money the Minister would have paid. He had a generous heart. But the paternity thing was something altogether different.

"The message I conveyed while we munched on the pastry had a promise of money." The subject's head dropped to his chest like he had fallen asleep. I want to say he had dropped asleep. My colleague nudged his feet with his own. He picked up his head and continued.

"My second message was to prepare the child for a pickup at 10:00 a.m. the next day. The child would move to an orphanage, or a family would adopt her. Her name would change on her birth certificate. She cried and begged me to reconsider. She kept saying *Qalat kardam. Qalat kardam.* I screwed up. I screwed up. I explained to her that some statements, once made cannot take back. 'My dear,' I said, 'you raised the guillotine blade. It hovers over HIM. What if you change your mind when she is sixteen and she asks for her father's identity? Can you refuse her? I don't think so. In an orphanage, the question won't have an answer. It's better this way. You can have other children. You are young.'

"'I won't change my mind, I won't,' she cried and begged. After I replayed the same arguments and she begged with the same cries, I left. Of course, with her death, we left the child in the care of her grandmother. The problem solved itself satisfactorily."

"What time did you leave the apartment?"

"You know what time I left. You know what time she jumped."

At this point, we took our leave. The subject blurted a few humorous asides, but he wanted to shuffle along to his upstairs den as soon as he could get rid of us.

Of course, we don't know when the subject left. He left from the back door, which was not under surveyance by our crew. Our professional opinion has not changed. We determined Mrs. A. committed suicide. The interview clarified the cause. The trauma of a lost child, combined with drugs, addled her brain enough that she threw herself from the second-floor balcony onto the flagstones in the garden below. The report attached shows death occurred from head trauma and not poison, as one theory maintained.

The report gave me an advantage because I learned of my uncle's recent telephone conversation with the General. My uncle, like me, couldn't resist neat solutions. He detected an ultimatum nestled in the General's flattery. He regretted the delay in the adoption after G.'s death.

I provided him with a neat solution. Cleverness gets a bad rap: It convinces when disguised as truth. I had to act fast. For two days, I walked around with a long face. At first, with all the work, he didn't notice. I performed efficiently but stopped the jokes. I placed papers in front of him, and he'd sign. I'd whisk the paper away and leave the room. He'd crack a joke. I would acknowledge the joke and say "Hilarious," but not crack a smile. We would play a game of tennis; I'd let him win. When I lost, I didn't warn him how badly I'd beat him the next time.

During our Thursday lunch, we sat at the table with two Camparis, a rare moment for us without people about. Annabelle and Malektaj, my uncle's wife, the daughter of Qavam Al-Molk, a former prime minister, walked in the wintery garden.

"What's the matter, my boy?"

"Nothing." I faked a smile to convince him otherwise. He and I had played together for over thirty years since I was ten. I won some, and he won some. It was hard to win against this complicated man. I had to play this without arabesque curlicues.

"I have known you all your life. You have your faults, but being morose isn't one of them. What's the matter?" he asked.

I again feigned a look at the women as if I didn't want them to hear. "We had some terrible news, Annabelle and I. I don't want to upset her more. The Swiss like their privacy."

"I am not other people. I am family. What terrible news?" he asked.

"She can't bear children. She has, the doctors say, a primary ovarian insufficiency. Whatever it is, we cannot have children," I said. I achieved the perfect sob but still held it together manly.

He looked at me. His eyes could achieve perfect pity. "I am sorry to hear it, lad. We have enjoyed our two daughters. You will, I am sure, find happiness in other pursuits."

I perked up. "Oh no, Uncle, we want children. We could not live without children. Annabelle has made it clear. She and I have looked to adopt a girl. She wants a girl badly." For the briefest moment, I thought I had pushed too soon, too far. He looked like he wanted to say something, then thought better. I kept my head. "We have applied for adoption. Uncle, the paperwork is horrendous." Then, like an idea occurred to me, "Uncle, do you think you can help with the bureaucracy without Annabelle's knowledge? She doesn't want anyone to know until all the T's are crossed."

He grinned. I could see the hook marks on his gums. "Let me see what I can do for you, my boy." Like I said, neat solutions always trump moral scruples.

EARNING AN ENDING

1. 1987: The Beginning of the End

Historians have scrutinized my uncle's diaries. In 1987, his wife and two daughters turned to a family friend, Alinaghi Alikhani, to gather and publish the notes. No one consulted me; I didn't even receive a phone call. Not to disparage Alikhani, whom I knew well. He served as a respectable minister of economy until 1969 and was chancellor of Tehran University. We met at SAVAK as young recruits. When I joined, he had recently resigned. I admit that Alikhani's choice stung. My uncle knew my facility with writing. I wrote so many of his letters. I could easily mimic his style with Hafez quotes, his favorite poet. After thirteen years of service, I smarted from this exclusion.

The diaries begin in 1969 and end in 1977, a year before his death. The family gave Alikhani complete freedom to include or delete material. He excluded our names and many others still alive to protect us from the Islamic Republic. In all fairness, my most significant contributions to my uncle came during the crazy year that marked 2500 years of monarchy in Iran—from March 21, 1971 to March 21, 1972. He didn't keep a diary that year because no one had time to keep a journal. Others speculate he kept diaries before 1969. If so, no sign of them exists.

My uncle took an unnecessary risk. He put many of us in danger. I could never breach the subject with him until 1978, on his deathbed. The diary's value, I think, has been overblown. The history buffs (and a history buff, by definition, is an amateur) point to these documents as products of the one witness without 20-20 hindsight, unlike so many memoirs written after the revolution by people who claimed to have warned and told the truth to power. My uncle wrote to publish these dairies. Let's not underestimate his manipulation to self-aggrandize; he wasn't an egomaniac but possessed a healthy ego.

When he referred to HIM, he fawned with highfalutin, pompous verbiage. The later diaries make the head prickle with shame. I attribute many motives for this extravagant flattery in documents meant to remain out of the public's eye for at least ten years after his death. The change in language alone explains the evolution of the Shah's reign. My uncle didn't see, though many attribute this to him, the fatidic end of the dynasty. His worries, sprinkled throughout his journal, resemble the concerns of any astute politician. We predict the sky falling all the time. The last flight with a dove in its engine proves us correct. We don't credit the boy who cried wolf as a prophet because he got it right before his demise. I am confident of one conclusion: He envisaged a continuation of the dynasty or hedged with a Pascal-like wager.

In his last few years, my uncle suffered much from acute lymphoma—mostly due to his exhaustion and the brutal chemo he underwent during his interminable hospital visits in Paris. Chemo in those early years affected the patient with even more complications than it does today. It took a long time before he had an accurate diagnosis. They allowed him to think he had a virus. He understood back in 1975 that the lumps under his armpits and chest resembled his sister's, who had died years before from the same disease. Not until late July 1975, during a visit to his doctors in Paris, did they warn him about the gravity of his cancer.

HIM encouraged him to take it seriously and go to the US. Both men straddled a similar line where, at times, they understood the deadly effects of lymphoma. They shared empathy for one another. Neither could imagine his demise in the cold light of day. Abdol Karim Ayadi, the ignorant personal physician to the Shah, never broached the subject with either man. He also died from lymphoma. It spawned more conspiracy theories.

2. 1978: Lost a Mother, Gained a Daughter

I visited my uncle in New York days before his death in early April 1978. He had not yet entered the New York University Hospital, where he'd die. We met in the lobby of the Pierre Hotel. He looked diminished, with a face pinched by the physical stress of pain. He couldn't stand up from the armchair. He tried. No Iranian worth his salt would willingly stay seated. My uncle had gotten up when I entered his house as a boy of ten. I ran forward and bid him to stay seated. He looked relieved. I asked him if the therapies had helped him. He answered they had not. "I should have come to America years ago. They understand the disease better than the French. Now, I am kept comfortable." A wan smile crossed his face like the shadow of a bird flying off. "How is your daughter, Marie?" he asked.

My smile broadened and was genuine. "Marie is four and talks like a teenager," I said.

"And your wife?"

"The Swiss Embassy has promoted her as the second consul. She commutes to Shiraz once a week. Your recommendation helped her a great deal."

"Nonsense," he said. Annabelle deserves her position. She's a clever girl. Don't lose her." He then went into a gloomy rant about Iran and its economy. He had resigned the summer before. I attributed his overly pessimistic view to his isolation from daily affairs and his visceral dislike of Hoveyda, his replacement at Court. My uncle never studied abroad. I never gave him enough credit for his knowledge of ordinary people. He couldn't guess the total collapse but worried for the right reasons.

"Uncle," I said. "Can I ask you a question? I have been curious about it for a few years." He lowered his skeletal face to assent. "You remember the girl G.? Three years ago, you visited her a few weeks before her death. Did you go to her house to warn her about her memoirs?" He lifted his head sharply. I composed my face to depict the innocence of a husband clueless about a wife's infidelities. He watched me for more seconds than I cared to count. He then relaxed. He took on the affability he used to show me when he confessed with pride to one of his "young lady" adventures. In those days, men talked openly with one another about their adulterous affairs, sometimes including detailed blow-by-blow descriptions.

"You always had a special interest in the girl," he said. "I didn't go there to prevent her from anything. While I was there, giving it a go," he made a small back-and-forth Italianesque hand gesture, a semaphore for sex, "she told me of her intention to write her memoirs." He smiled, not a dirty old man smile, but triumphantly. His admission caught me off guard. G. could not resist powerful men. The needle of her moral north spun out of control like a compass placed near a power line. I didn't expect my uncle's "giving it a go," as he called it, with HIM's past mistress. I burned with anger and not jealousy. His behavior made shame gush out of my pores. You can't consciously achieve genuine vulgarity. Vulgarity rents space inside us all. The attaining act is invisible to the person who commits it but visible to everyone else.

"Did you know then she had a child?"

"After I asked Davallou to pay her..." My uncle rubbed together his fingers, thumb across his index and forefinger, to denote the substantiality of his munificence. "He told me about her child. Then she solved all our problems to your benefit." I feigned surprise.

"My benefit?" I said.

"Your adopted daughter, Marie, was her child. Someday, she should know about her mother," he said. I didn't ask him about his threat to take away the child, which was clear enough to me from the Intelligence report by my friend Nader.

"Speaking of memoirs." He pulled what looked like a wrapped book from the side of the armchair. "I know we have had our differences in the last few years. I trust you, nephew. I wrote these papers in the last few months when I lived in Birjand trying to recuperate. I can tell you the packages you delivered in the last few years contained my daily notes. You will do me a great favor to deliver these on your way back to Tehran to 'Madame Vincent.'" He enjoyed my nickname for his banker.

"I know about your diaries, Uncle. I'd have to be blind not to know you wrote these diaries. How could you risk it?" I said.

"Of course you do. Of course, you do." He didn't answer the question. He fell silent while he passed the package wrapped in a violet silk cloth with gold embroidery of the type we kept Korans in for protection. He had wrapped a red ribbon around the package; it replaced the usual red wax seal. Where would you get sealing wax in New York?

We sat silently. We looked at the package now in my lap. My uncle said, "My boy, you can open the package and read what I have written, but for your protection and that of others, I urge you to deliver it and forget about it. I will tell you what pertains to you." Then, like a teenager delivering a retort, he said, "I want to let you know your mother adopted you."

"Adopted?" A bitter sequence of logic, feelings, and childhood scenes flashed across my mind. Then I smiled. "What do you mean? I have seen her pictures. She carried me. Did she use pillows to fool us all?"

"She lost the child. Your mother nearly died," he said. He shook his head in the Iranian way, a long pendulum swing communicating disasters or tragedies.

"Yes," he confirmed. "Your mother adopted you a day after her tragedy. The doctors warned her she could not bear children." He watched me and a look of concern came over him. "She loved you, you know," he said.

"It explains my father's dislike for me," I said.

"Not at all." He shook his head vigorously. His loose jowls followed with difficulty. "He never knew. Do you think he would have contained himself if he knew?"

In all these remembrances of people living and dying, I forgot to mention my father's death, an uncelebrated affair, during the celebrated affair of Davallou. He suffered what the Shah's doctor, Ayadi, called *une crise cardiaque massive*. Born in the early twentieth century, he died in the nineteenth-century life of the landed gentry.

I remember one memory of him above all.

We received a tablet of chocolate from the American consul in 1946. We sat at the dining table. He smoked one of his noxious Oshno cigarettes and relentlessly ate one bar after another. I had never tasted chocolate. His obvious pleasure intrigued my six-year-old imagination. He left a solitary bar on the table to answer a phone call. I, ready to make a meal of it, had the readiness of a hundred-meter sprinter before the crack of the gun. Two steps out of the room, he remembered. He returned and picked up the last bar. He chewed as he hurried down the hall. Unforgivable.

"Your French grandmother also knew of your adoption." Each time my uncle used the word adoption, a lifetime of scenes rearranged in my head. *Le grand cadeau* and *pauvre garcon, pauvre Sam* fell into a rearrangement. "I never thought your mother should have married him. Your grandfather insisted on the match. Few of us had the luxury of choice in those days. He thought, I mean, your grandfather thought that his wife, your grandmother, had far too much influence on your mother. She wanted her to live in Paris."

"And your hard behavior toward me, Uncle?" I asked.

"My boy," he said, confused. "I hope you know my professional demands never crossed my view of you as family. I mean, look at your daughter. You adopted her. You love her like she's your own."

With a particular evil pleasure, a vengeful me said, "Uncle, you are mistaken. I didn't adopt. She is my own. She is my genetic daughter," I said with a fifty-fifty confidence. I sat back and watched him puzzle over the import of my statement. Gears worked furiously. He remembered when we sat at the table, and I asked for help with adoption. The gears didn't mesh at first. How had I tricked him? "You and G.?" he said. Yes, me.

"Looks are not everything, uncle," I said.

He had lost flesh but none of his sharpness. The vast, planetary structure of his suspicious mind in full gear, like a clairvoyant, he said, "Ahan," a linguistic cousin of the English "ah," more movement of the chemical gears. "Ahan. You read my diaries. That's how you knew about my visit." He paused for a moment, remembering. "The unlocked drawer, but I wrote no names." I silently watched. The face questioned. Understanding dawned. It changed to display a clever man. Unpleasant as the conclusion was, he congratulated himself. He had grasped the complete picture at a suitable speed. "Of course, you didn't know until seconds ago. How can you be sure you are the father? If I am not mistaken, you competed with three other men," he said. He thinned his eyes with a remarkable similarity to my sly look.

"Uncle, you forget that I saw the birth certificate. Unless she arrived a month early, she is mine or has a claim to the title of Princess. I claim her as mine if you get my drift."

"Be careful, my boy." He said it kindly like he had lost patience with the subject and had grander worries, like attending an end-of-life ceremony.

From the end of the corridor, I recognized one of his daughters. She walked toward us. I got up. "I will do as you wish. I will deliver your manuscript to Madame Vincent." I didn't call him Uncle. I bid him goodbye and walked in the opposite direction toward the Fifth Avenue exit. He died two days later, on the 14th of April, 1978. I went from a fool to a pimp and back to a fool. The last fool is a different fool. Of course, I didn't obey his last wish. I threw away the package in a Fifth Avenue trash can. My secret remained safe for another forty years. I didn't discuss it with anyone.

3. 1980 The End is Near

"Did Maman know it all?" Marie asked. We sat in my terminus of a room. My little girl has lived almost thirty years more than her genetic mother. Hard to put that in perspective.

These days, politicians of all colors quote Justice Brandeis: "Sunlight is said to be the best of disinfectants." I have come this far. I have used *eau de javel* with the most potent concentration in my stack of Post-it notes. I answered, "Mum knew it all. I never told her about Azar, your biological mother's cousin, which you know now. I wanted to tell your mother. I couldn't. The year after the revolution, we lived in our Parisian purgatory. You remember, don't you?"

"Vaguely," she said.

In Paris in 1980, we read of the Shah's daily humiliations. He traveled from place to place as he wasted away. His was a harrowed face, emaciated to a permanent question mark. Annabelle and I talked through a harrowing night in the waiting room of the Pitié-Salpêtrière Hospital while my mother suffered and worked hard to die. Doctors walked in and out of the waiting room. They commanded us to come in or go out. My mother was also in and out, coherent and incoherent. She never spoke of my adoption. I never let her know that I knew. I had passed my fortieth year; my childhood phobias lay behind me. Our marriage, like all marriages, had its varied heartbeats. Fast and turbulent, like a good game of tennis. Slow and methodical, like a rope-pulling contest. Never in doubt except for the night at the hospital.

I lived a life of guilt. A revolution acts like Control-Alt-Delete; the reboot simplifies life. I destroyed a life. Azar's end didn't come because of me. Freed after a traumatic few months, she never contacted me again. In August 1981, the People's Mujahedin of Iran (MEK) bombed the Prime Minister's office, killing some of the highest-ranking members of the Islamic Republic. We celebrated their end with champagne. The Islamic Republic never lets a good crisis go to waste. They fell on the MEK more zealously than they believed in Islam. They executed an untold number of the MEK. Azar was among the dead. They returned the body to the family and ordered them not to mourn. I shudder at my twenty-four-hours-in-the-ground message to G.'s family the day after her death. It was different, right? The family changed their name and emigrated.

I dig deep to relive the night at the hospital while my mother sank deeper and deeper into a coma. I shed a few tears beside Annabelle as I hug my head over my bent, parted knees like someone ready to throw up. Annabelle, a most discerning human and a rational Swiss to the last cell of her body, asked, puzzled, "Why cry? She lived a long life. She lived it selfishly. Your mother never suffered a day. She did what she liked."

"Do you know, last month we went to the butcher with her dachshund Leontine? The butcher told her, 'Madame, don't you know you can't bring dogs inside,' and she said 'No, I've never been in a butcher shop.'" I smile. Our savings had dwindled fast. She had to fire—or I did—her maid Marte and her servant Mamadou a few months before the hospitalization. She kept a small jingling bell at the dining table to summon Mamadou. She lived like a Proust character.

A hiatus of quietness falls on us. It was past midnight. Then, a young, serious doctor with an undernourished goatee allows us into my mother's room. She has gained some lucidity. The doctor warns us clarity often occurs with patients before the final throes. Tubes and electronics of the analog type surround her, the blips and burps of the electronics getting louder, leaving ghostly traces of life on the CRT. With its ghost-like drops of electrons, it is more dramatic than today's soft digital interfaces representing our unhealthiness.

My mother squeezes my hand and smiles weakly. She turns her head and smiles at Annabelle. We stand next to her—no chairs in the emergency care cubicles. Eight or ten other curtain-drawn beds occupy the ward. All busy dying. I am aware of a man. He stands behind us—at first, I think he is one of the hospital staff. I turn to see a liver-spotted older man dressed in Holmesian garb: a heavy overcoat which the English call an Inverness cape, but with more buttons than a cape would have, made of a tight English tweed of brown and dark red. I hear rabid, frozen rain belts on the hospital's windows. He removes his deerstalker and uses both hands to hold it crotch-height. I am far from a believer, but I thought an executioner angel had come to hurry my mother.

He mumbles a Persian greeting like a Catholic priest who asks for a response from the congregation. I murmur a reply.

I then recognize our friend Davallou. He has aged irresponsibly. I estimate his age at the early seventies. He looks eighty. Gravity has forced the skin of his face to bunch and hang like a dishrag at the jaw lines. His eyes, in their deep sockets, carry the false wisdom-cum-sadness of an opium user. Opium dissipates flesh to the bone but keeps the addict alive. It guides him to a painless end. I can imagine worse deaths.

My mother falls asleep. Once again, the French doctor asks us to wait outside. He explains that the hospital only allows one or two families into the ward at a time. "*Une nuit bien remplie*," he says about the ward.

The three of us return to the neon-helium, yellow-lit waiting room. Davallou sits with us for another hour. He regales and amuses us with stories of our glory years, all cleansed for Annabelle's ears. Annabelle takes leave to stretch her legs. It's not a writer's convenient exeunt of a character. From the dribbling down of the stories and little silences, she senses men want to talk.

My detective-like curiosity takes over; I could have borrowed Davallou's hat. He answers, *sans gêne*, a few orbiting questions like he did when SAVAK agents questioned him. I then fall out of orbit and ask him about my uncle's visit to G. I had never revealed or volunteered any knowledge of or responsibility for needling SAVAK to question him in 1975.

He explains HIM knew about my uncle's visit. "*Magar batchehie,*" he says—don't be a child. "The Shah knew your uncle visited G. Your uncle told HIM about the memoir and his visit. It wasn't your uncle who asked me to go to her. Your uncle never liked me. After our Swiss adventure, he would never ask me to do anything for him. HIM asked me to act as the middleman. You know I am good as a go-between." I find a discrepancy between the story he told the agents and what he said to me. He told the Intelligence duo that my uncle asked him to deal with G. He lied. The addict showed remarkable loyalty. He didn't want HIM involved.

I surmise HIM and my uncle agreed to take the child away when Davallou returned to Court for further instructions. Politics is the art of fitting more hands on the dagger's handle.

He goes on to other anecdotes about his middle-manning prowesses. I don't listen. The Oscar-winning roles my uncle and HIM played the morning I presented G.'s death to them astonish me to this day. I would have sworn to any magistrate that HIM didn't know of G.'s death until we reported it. I would have sworn HIM didn't hatch the plan to take a child away from her mother. Conspiracies should have one rule: three people or less. In today's parlance, any more than three people, it is social media. It looked like my uncle, Davallou, and HIM followed the rule.

Davallou wishes my mother a recovery and good health. He leaves me with my thoughts.

Hadn't HIM said, "What's the emergency?" with a touch of irritation? The hint of irritation convinced me as I studied him. A life of keeping a poker face pays off. Quite a performance; it makes one question all past understandings.

I don't know how often Annabelle and I discussed my detective work to find those responsible for G.'s death. She returns trembling from the cold, her face and hair wet. I warm her up. She says she likes the cold. I rub both her hands now in a prayer gesture with my palms. I blurt out, "This fool Davallou told me the Shah knew all about G. Everywhere I turn, I see the same people in the know, everyone but me."

"You need to stop all this at once. Are you more concerned about being fooled or what happened to the poor girl?" she says, exasperated at my denseness. Her face flares with an anger I have never witnessed. She pulls her hands out sharply. "No one person killed her. We know who killed her. The evidence is in front of you. You all killed her: the Shah, Alam, Khatam, her mother, her father, Nassiri, SAVAK agents." With each name, she uses her left hand to grab a finger on her right hand to count. When she gets to the father, the fifth person on her verbal list, she knots one pinky over the other for emphasis. When the number of people she accuses exceeds her fingers on one hand, she switches hands and commissions the aid of her other fingers. She points to me, as the last murderer, with her index finger. "And you my darling husband. You are also responsible. You killed her. All of you passed a nineteen-year-old among one another like a chattel. You impregnate her. You introduce her to drugs. You threaten to take her baby away. What did you think? This Hercule Poirot detective work searching for a murderer is only a cover for your guilt. Poirot would point the finger at all the witnesses in the library." Annabelle stands up and looks down her nose in the terrible pose of a detective, red-faced. She is anything but comical; her tone is viciously sarcastic. "Poirot would say in his ghastly Belgian accent, 'You all killed her. Case solved.'"

She switches back to her Germanic self in an instant. "You don't need a Poirot, Sam. I could have told you the day you came home after the girl's death. I heard you cry. I don't dismiss your hurt. You cried with bitterness, with more sincerity than you have cried for your mother. You cared for her, but don't fool yourself; you aided in her murder. It's easy to say the system killed her, easy to say what you always tell me: You all played a Chinese whisper game. But you all designed this system for your pleasure." With her sturdy legs planted, she tapped her index finger three times on the armrest. Her fingernails went *tok tok tok tok* on the imperial blue plastic at the Salpêtrière Hospital. "Not for HIM's pleasure alone, but for your own."

I sit in the same position, head lowered in my hands, elbow to knee. Unsure for the first time of her love for me. Her words sting my soul. It reaches back to question the five years of our marriage. She wasn't finished. "Frankly, you and I should never talk about this again. And promise me you will never tell Marie any of it. She will hate you." I look up at her set face. The severe face doesn't flash back to her madcap face. My fabricated, maudlin emotions fizzle out to *eau plat*.

A terror of what was to come in our lives unfurled inside me. It chokes me. My wife sees me as a murderer. I never denied guilt but saw the district attorney of my brain charge me with manslaughter. She used the word "knowingly." She accused me of intentionality, the darling of all DAs. I could argue in front of the jury of one. I yearn to please, ache for power, and long for recognition. It is intentional but an unconscious intention.

A separate cold calculation grips my mind. I cannot lose Annabelle; it would be an intolerable life. My uncle's advice before his death—"Never lose her"—was an unnecessary reminder. I am "Sam & Belle." I cannot tell her Azar's fate. She will accuse me of double murder. I intended consciously, schemed, and, worst of all, I basked in the solution's elegance. There was nothing unknown about my deal with the devil. You know what, I would do it again and let it prick me, like it has, during all the moments of happiness, like a warning: "You don't deserve happiness," it says. There is nothing to argue, for at this point, it isn't about G., but about her cousin.

In the hospital, the stethoscope-decorated doctor approaches us at 4:00 a.m. to offer his condolences. I resolve never to tell Annabelle about Azar. I promise her never to talk about any of it again. There and then, I vow to be a different person.

I stop job hunting. It connects me to an old mode of life (imagine the number of creamy resume pages thrown out). I will live a quiet life, I decide. We will take Annabelle's job offer at the Boston consulate. I will learn new skills to lead an uncomplicated life.

I watch my adult daughter hear and learn it all. She looks at me with love and sympathy. A mature woman, older than her Maman when we moved to Boston. Thirty years older than her genetic mother. She begs me again to reconsider my stay at this urine-smelling charnel house. To live with Marianna and the baby girl lucky enough to have these two loving women as her mums. I refuse. Another year would force them to return me here. I will not saddle her with the decision. Three generations of adoptions. genetic bits and pieces don't need to resemble. Deep in our psyche, we want to belong to an identified sperm and egg. It is an ignorant belief system. See, it is all about the lifestyle.

AFTERWARD
1943: AN EMBARRASSING NAKEDNESS

What do I remember first? I recall an insignificant moment. I can say it makes up my first sustained memory. It rushed in like the photograph of Mount Everest next to all the other Himalayan peaks, which deserve better. But what can a photographer do but focus on the magnificent rise and let the other worthy mountains serve as the fuzzy support?

I stood, three or early four years old, in front of my paternal grandmother, the fecund mother of nine. She must have been sixty, but to me, she was an ancient crone; a witty, loud-laughing woman who saw life's humorous side. I know I had asked her to accompany me to or at least direct me toward the bathroom. I couldn't have been long out of diaperdom. I recall my conceit. I remember I lived a life drenched by a deep, baseless pride. To my core I believed myself to be the prince of some undefined realm.

Nature's call must have exerted significant pressure for me to plea to my grandmother. She sat in her dining room.

She looked down at me, with love and affection, through her crinkly turtle's eyes. She bent down and swiped my elastic wasted shorts and underpants to my ankles with surprising rapidity and agility. Her hands, on the way up, ended under my armpits. She lifted me in a quick hop and placed me sideways, clear of my clothing. Disheveled, my shirt half unbuttoned, I looked down past my convoluted, outie navel. It sat on my distended belly. Below it, I saw my tiny penis made up of mainly a puckered foreskin; its worm-like head looked sadly down, not yet circumcised. This rosebud memory was my first awareness of a penis. That it belonged to me. I saw it, throughout my childhood, not like a familiar limb, but some otherness connected to me as an afterthought. I lifted my head to hear my grandmother giving directions, and her arm and henna-coated extended finger pointed me toward the bathroom right next to the entrance to the house.

I swiveled my head upward. I saw, materializing out of nothingness, my grandmother's guests having lunch around the table. They must have smiled with understanding for my plight and respect for my grandmother's motherly efficiency, but I saw only stretched necks. Many faces smirked down at me. They guffawed at my naked state. Like in a silent movie, the tac-tac sound of a projector accompanies my memory, probably the later editing job of some part of my brain connected to the representation of silent film in modern movies. Otherwise, the memory remains mute. Deep shame spread through my body. It made mincemeat of my earlier haughty self-importance. I don't recall the walk of shame toward the stinking privy with its squat Islamic toilet where I locked myself. I am told it took a locksmith to rescue me.

The shame and the self-importance must have dissolved like a spoon of milk in a glass of tea. It left a milky, nebulous self-consciousness. I didn't recall it as an adult. I end my account with the last two lines in my uncle's 1977 diary. It took me more than two lines to tell my story. Our favorite Persian poet, Hafez, puts it all in perspective:

Darius, Alexander, their great hullabaloo.
Can be summed up simply in a line or two.

A PERSONA'S NOTE
J'ADOUBE

"By the end of the book, we realize that the figure which has been most completely and most subtly displayed is that of the author."

Virginia Woolf

Elmore Leonard's second rule for writers says, "Avoid prologues." He probably would include all logues in his rules. Why should you read an epilogue, an afterword? Inherently, they threaten the world of fiction. The Logue can represent a larger story, and admittedly, it borders closer to "reality." However, I have followed Nabokov's advice and added the quotation marks.

This is a political story whose history is close enough that readers might be interested in the characters' roots. When I finish a historical novel, inevitably, questions of accuracy arise, and questions of the characters' origins pop into my mind. What can I say? I have questions. Many authors answer these questions openly during readings in bookshops or when interviewed. Yet the same writers find a reader presumptuous to want the non-fiction details between the same covers as the novel. Supposedly, it mars the experience.

I held the same view until I read William Maxwell's *So Long, See You Tomorrow*. Before he begins the yarning, he details what he witnessed from far away: a crime of passion. As a kid, he cold-shouldered the murderer's son, his friend. He lived with guilt. He wrote the novel as an apology.

I mirror his construct, though I add my thoughts at the end. I thought it would damage my story if I revealed everything, as William Maxwell does in his prologue.

I found a few grainy black-and-white newspaper pictures from 1975 *Sepid-o-Siyah Magazine*. They attested to Gilda's beauty.

My first stirring for her history came about because of her name, which I associated with the movie *Gilda*.

Two scenes of beautiful women have dried my throat—one, the first glance of Grace Kelly in *Rear Window*. Fifteen minutes late for the film, I walked along the aisle with a bucket of popcorn when Grace Kelly's shadow, followed by her full technicolor face, filled the screen. Jimmy Stewart slept in his chair with a broken leg. I stopped dead while my companion plowed into my back, spilling a load of popcorn.

Gilda, the movie, had a more visceral effect. The posters had Rita Hayworth as the lead.

We are twenty minutes into the film without a shot of her. "Gilda, are you decent?" asks the character Ballin, played by George Macready, as he enters her room. We can hear her humming the movie's theme song, *Put the Blame on Mame*. Johnny Farrow, Glenn Ford's character, follows Ballen up the stairs to her room and recognizes her voice.

Then, the silver sprayed on the screen does the rest. I can't imagine it in color. You see her bent head and wavy hair for an instant. She throws back her head in one smooth motion. Her perfect face smiles and says, "Me?" The camera's still shot includes her beautiful naked shoulders. Then, the smile fades as she also recognizes Glenn Ford. She pulls the right strap of her off-the-shoulder dress for a semaphore of modesty. "Sure. I am decent?"

The scene had my youthful self enraptured.

In this novel, you can trace something of the movie: the theme of an older man's beautiful wife, Rita Hayworth, finding her old, much younger flame in Glenn Ford (miscast, for who would fall for that sap? But then who would fall for *my* sap?)

The more I researched, the happier I got. The absence of facts allowed me to invent. Julian Barnes says, "History is that certainty produced at the point where the imperfections of memory meet the inadequacies of documentation." Fiction writers frolic in the intersection.

Historical fiction has rules. I suppose you can imagine a Waterloo in which Napoleon wins. Philip Roth wrote *The Plot Against America*. In it, Lindbergh, in cahoots with Hitler, wins the American presidency. The plots cross into fantasy. Most historical fiction dramatizes but keeps on the side of the factual. Witnesses still alive make it even more challenging to dramatize. Facts must dissolve in scenes. Like a sugar cube in tea, the reader shouldn't observe the color of fact.

Writers of historical fiction may invent characters, but those characters cannot alter history. The protagonist must tiptoe. They can't leave a trace of reality laid out by history on the rice paper. My narrator, a cousinly branch to the court minister of the Shah, Assadolah Alam, increases the already large Alam family.

We, writers of historical fiction, consider ourselves historians but in the narrow sense of the profession. Obsessed with a thin slice of history, we delve into the nooks and crannies of the subject. As a wannabe historians, we instead develop malicious intentions. Fiction writers look to find space in those well-known nooks and crannies where we can expand unfettered. The trick is not to get caught by the professional historian as we make whole-cloth narratives.

The other intention goes to the vanity of writers who have read so much material on a subject. We form opinions, theories and then inject them into the narrative without the burden of proof asked of a professional historian. It needs to be plausible. I could go on about plausibility. Informed readers must judge the Shah or the Court Minister. Would they have matched the actions of the invented Shah and the invented Court Minister? Alam and HIM were born in 1919, three months apart. I see poetry in their relationship.

Alam and his father both loved their shahs. They served both kings unquestioningly all their lives. The elder Alam once wrote, "I fell in love on the day the sun rose on the Pahlavi dynasty." The old Shah loved him back. The two elder men's closeness served as the model their sons followed for the rest of their lives.

The younger Alam wrote, "When I go to Court in the morning and bow to HIM, I bow to Iran. When I kiss his hand, I kiss the owner of Iran." He believed a monarch transforms a nation, and a country changes the monarch with love. He saw himself, through his ancestors, as a servant to the kings of Iran.

Contrary to most of the aristocracy, the Shah and Alam obtained their higher education in Iran—one in the military academy, the other in the school of agriculture in Karaj. They had wives imposed on them by Reza Shah. Both men proved dutiful to a fault. Alam asked his father if he could say no. No was the answer. By midweek, he played tennis with his soon-to-be bride, witnessed by the Crown Prince and his Egyptian Princess Fawzia Fuad of Egypt. By Friday of the same week, he had married.

The two men often swam in parallel lanes. They ran into and out of the way of real and political bullets. They bore the young Shah's humiliations together. They celebrated his victories. They died of similar diseases a few years apart.

Gilda's presence in the summer of 1973 interested me because I wanted to create a milieu, or in modern parlance, a vibe; undeniably, it existed in Iran. A few other generations have experienced it. Shanghai, Singapore, Dubai in the past thirty years, or America in the fifties, Japan in the sixties, and Korea in the seventies—a period in which a generation experiences growth and a visual, tactile improvement in wealth beyond anything their parents could have imagined. The up-and-up betterment of economic life formed a bubble of goodwill around a generation, my generation, which had little experience of other, more difficult eras in our history. It makes the conclusion harder to bear.

As a population, we committed mass suicide. I remember Majid Majidi, a minister of the Shah. He said he could write, in ten minutes, forty reasons why what happened happened. Causes have a multitude of founts, someone said. None of it explains the hysteria. The injection of emotional motifs is the work of the fiction writer. We attempt to mainline directly to the amygdala and not get involved with the left hemisphere of logic. We try to move the reader's heart without explaining the causes.

Iran was far from isolated from the sexual revolution of the sixties in the West. We brought it back with us. I can't think of a more different lens applied to sexuality in the Shah's seventies than today's Islamic Republic. One lens was concave, the other convex in its focus. If we strip down the sexual act to a human biological need, like eating, all cultural lenses distort.

The story of our revolution is about lifestyle. I promise you: It all comes down to lifestyle. You don't have to read the screeds of Islamic psycho-babble to understand the religious filter. I once read a well-researched account of why the Pahlavi dynasty crumbled. An honest Muslim scholar had gathered evidence with well-pedicured footnotes and sincere quotations from the mouths of the Pahlavi family. It described the courtiers.

The poor author observes his subjects through documents filtered through a prism of Islam—a unique Islam brought about by his Imam, Khomeini. Scandalized, he reports the Queen-mother drank Cognac; like any good scholar, he mentions her preference for Hennessy. He sees women in bikinis as a naked challenge to Islam's commitment to women. He describes the Shah as a thousand-and-one-night potentiate: rolling in cushions and bedding with houris, drinking to excess while he gambles millions. The author drifts in his imagination to fill in the blanks of his ignorance with fantastical harem stories that couldn't be further from the truth. HIM ate and drank sparingly. He played cards with a few friends for small stakes. He might watch a movie at night. His sex life had a ritualistic cycle—a few hours away, a couple of times a week; varied but not twisted. He lived a mechanical, planned life. None of the women complained of lousy behavior or violence. He worked hard. He worked really hard.

When he used his religious microscope to observe life in Court, I allowed my Islamic scholar the excuse of applying a filter; like a Vaseline-smeared glass, this filter transformed his reality into a thousand- and one-night atmosphere. While he researched the paperwork of the Pahlavi dynasty with meticulous verve, his fellow mullahs played nasty outside his ivory mosque.

Before they beat the fifty-eight-year-old Mrs. Farrokhrou Parsa, minister for national education, to death, the Revolutionary Republic placed her in a sack. Why? To prevent the guards' sexual arousal. Horny little men raped virgins before execution to null and void the free pass to heaven. But our Islamic scholar judges the Queen-mother's weakness for Hennessy?

Genetics cannot explain it. We all grow up in a cocoon of our culture. It allows Indonesian people to wrap the dead person in special clothes and keep them safe in the house for months. In Thailand's Karen tribe, they bear the painful process of wearing brass coils, placed during childhood, to elongate their necks. Foot binding in China, circumcision of women in Africa, and luxury cemeteries for pets in the US are all deemed normal to those who grow up with them. We must wait for judgment day to reconcile these worldviews, but I don't believe in judgment days. The Shah did, of course.

The optimistic Mary Ruefle says, "Ignorance can be eradicated but in the way of a weed." She recognizes the everlasting Sisyphean work of educating humans but underestimates weed production. Edith Sitwell says we must be "patient with stupidity but not with those who are proud of it." Patience wears thin underclothes for good reason.

The Shah was the most religious person in the Pahlavi Court. The whole kit and caboodle were about the difference alone. The fifth element of the White Revolution, which, among other things, fostered women's independence, was perhaps a step too many. Both sides agreed it was central; both sides disagreed with its continuation. In 1979, we of the West lost the battle, but I don't believe we have lost the war.

The Shah's peccadillos were moral questions between him and his wife. I compare this to the lens used to view Kennedy's weaknesses; enablers saw no problems. However, those with another lens view the Shah as possessing the moral flows of a Muslim monarch who deserved death. The Shah's sexual adventurism didn't stop his monumental liberal policies for women's rights. Compare this with Khomeini, whose dutiful love letters to his wife belie the disaster he wrought on Iranian women.

The depiction of the Shah might ruffle a few plumes. Please don't confuse me with my character or hurl reactionary labels at me. I tried to distance myself. I attempted to abandon the I-narrator and vacillated twice. I rewrote the early chapters in the free indirect third person, i.e., the closest I could get to the character's consciousness without embodying him. Each time, the slightest distance made me return to my I-narrator, who is not I. I have in common with my narrator (let's call it the hatched area in the Venn diagram) only my unshaken conviction of the Islamic Republic's disastrous forty-year rule.

There is a history of comparing the thirty-seven years of the country under the Shah to the forty years under the rule of the Islamic Republic. There are plenty of metrics. I have a rule not to compare atrocities committed by humans or governments. Each stands on its own. Facts of deeds committed should suffice for rational people. Don't compare one massacre to another. Don't compare one individual's vile actions to another's. In retrospect, I ask myself if the Shah gets a free pass because the present regime's forty years have had an atrocious record. I won't compare.

When a novel covers people still alive, people associate the writer with the protagonist. Let me disassociate myself from the protagonist, Sam (Sum), who does not possess a family name. He displays a mix of reactionary and liberal sentiments. I, the author me, never bought into the hereditary forms of government, even when I lived it as a young man. I am no monarchist. How do you say it without equivocation? Monarchy as a system of government borders on the incredible. It is a bullshit system. I excuse the UK's monarchy because I deem it a profitable Disneyland venture. People with any form of power should not contemplate their job lasting for more than the digits on two hands, let alone for the generations born to them. As a dictator of words, I grant parents authority for eighteen years over their kids. That is all.

The Shah's reign, a complex series of eventful decades, had remarkable successes. We can compare successes comfortably. The ship of state had plenty of barnacles, however. They gradually clung to its hull during the reign, piling on and disabling the rudder. The character of the Shah needed revision. Two excellent historians have given it a good go. Abbas Milani wrote a more psychological portrait called *The Shah*. Gholam Reza Afkhami wrote *The Life and Times of the Shah*, a more statistical and fact-based review of those decades. I couldn't believe any book so full of statistical detail and facts could bring me to tears. The waste of so much promise does that to me.

My character treats the Shah reverently. He doesn't consider the Shah a dictator. He considers the Shah a monarch with historical rights. He sees him as a monarch with constitutional powers no other constitutional monarchy had in the twentieth century. The Shah controlled the armed forces. According to the 1905 constitution, he chose half of the Senate. In my character, the young man's reverence gives way to a more measured view in old age. The hatched area of the Venn diagram grows between us as we both age.

SAVAK's actions follow the Shah to the grave. No excuse

for the suffering of the innocent. It also has to be factual. In his book *The Fall of Heaven: The Pahlavis and the Final Days of Imperial Iran*, Andrew Scott Cooper quotes Emad al-Din Baghi, a former seminary student who researched the crimes committed by SAVAK after the revolution. "He could not match the victims' names to the official numbers: instead of 100,000 deaths, Baghi could confirm 3,164. The number was inflated. It included all 2,781 fatalities from the 1978–1979 revolution. The actual death toll was lowered to 383, of whom 197 were guerrilla fighters and terrorists killed in skirmishes with the security forces. That meant 183 political prisoners and dissidents were executed, committed suicide in detention, or died under torture. Political prisoners were also sharply reduced, from 100,000 to about 3,200."

The Shah, a highly nuanced and chameleon-like man, had fair intelligence and all the goodwill in the world for his country. It is unfair to compare him to Saddam or Idi Amin (remember, no comparisons). But with all the goodwill, my character and I came to a joint conclusion: No one should be in power for thirty-seven years, not over a nation, a business, or even as head of a family.

The press often called him paranoid. The dictionary defines paranoia as the unjustified suspicion and mistrust of other people or their actions. Let me grind down history into a litany of justification. During World War II, the Allies humiliated his powerful father and summarily exiled all of his family. They considered replacing him with a man who couldn't even speak Farsi. The old aristocracy referred to him as "the boy." English and American ambassadors belittled him at official meetings early in his reign. He survived several planned assassination attempts, including the time the Russians planted a bomb to detonate a VW on the way to the parliament and when a remote-control bomb destroyed his limo in West Berlin. Several of his ministers stabbed him in the back, including Ghavam, the old, operator opportunist; Razmara, his brother-in-law with crown fantasies; Zahedi, the militarist who wanted to rule and not reign; Saaed, the British sympathizer; Amini, the garrulous America's boy; and Mosaddegh the sheenaniganist who succeeded for a time. Islamists and the sleeper cells killed and injured his prime ministers. There were coups d'état in Syria, Turkey, Afghanistan, and Pakistan. Army colonels had sent the Egyptian and Iraqi monarchs scurrying to the south of France. The communist Tudeh party's military network conspired endlessly with the Soviet apparatchiks. If all this wasn't enough, he suffered childhood diphtheria, fell of a horse head first, and survived a crash that flipped his private plane end to end. Let me take a breath. And all this happened during the innocent years before 1965. One can wonder if he ever had PTSD. Victims of one gunshot have sought psychiatric help for years.

F. Scott Fitzgerald wrote, "Premature success gives one an almost mystical conception of destiny." The opposite may also be true. Close calls may have the same effect. Yes, I treat him more gingerly than I should. Despite his sexual activities, he evolved into a workaholic who ate and drank abstemiously. Resilient, flexible, nimble, and masterful, he dodged bullets, real and, no less dangerous, figurative. His ability to manage detail astonished those around him. For months, he met weekly for a few hours with his atomic energy planner to understand nuclear technology. He read the brochures of advanced armament bought by the government.

I found the critiques never allowed Mohammad Reza to evolve through life. He could never shake the image of the callow playboy he acquired in the fifties. Historical analyses of his early life superimpose the powers the Shah had accumulated toward the end of his reign. With the same breath, we judge the monarch of the seventies as callow and give the young boy of twenty powers he didn't yet possess. When young, he struggled like a fish out of water. It could have been different if Mosaddegh or Qavam, those old curmudgeons of the Qajar era, had acted as mentors. Without their support chose the life of an autodidact. He became the architect of his own wisdom. It isolated his mind. It created a super confident pedant.

He showed sang-froid when bullets rained on him during assassination attempts. He showed plenty of cowardice when he needed to decide to save his threatened crown. In the end, he faced a no-win situation. Iranians will forever argue whether he should or should not have dealt with the street demonstrators—all years too late. The narrator identifies the Shah's superstitious religious belief system as the true Trojan Horse of his reign. He sees the world in a harsher monochromatic color than I do. The Shah forgave his enemies readily when his wife, prime ministers, or friends intermediated. All of it is human; I would have preferred to see him replaced miraculously in 1973.

I introduced the Earth-walking Gilda at the start of the novel. I have just confessed that I invented the narrator from fluff. Behind the fluff, there's a bit more fluff, and then some concreteness. I met Sam, an Iranian man, in the eighties. We still pronounce it as Sum, but Americans call him Sam. I worked as a young software manager; he moonlighted as a technical writer. He didn't belong to the Alam clan. We both emigrated to the US after the revolution. Twenty years older than me, the Islamic Revolution had a more significant impact on his generation than mine. I moved smoothly from graduate school into the labor force. He could not package his work experience in Iran into a meaningful bullet in his resume. He spoke English with a French accent. He took night classes at the Harvard Extension, mostly to perfect his English. He built a clientele of a few companies to give him regular work. He wrote technical manuals. I learned much later that he attended the Free University of Brussels, which I duly had my character attend and graduate. The actual Sum graduated as an engineer.

I describe him in the novel. He had a pleasantly ugly face and the dark skin of the Khorasanis. The occasional gummy smile spread through his face like an earthquake. It made him instantly likable. He had a powerful upper body, his two shoulders curved forward, and he walked with a strange, simian gait. Both arms bent, and his elbows curved out from the body; you could put a basketball through the space. A quiet man with a charming, sophisticated conversation, he surpassed a naïve engineer's outlook. I had my head into the fast-shifting computer technology of the eighties. He meditated on the cud of the sixties and seventies. He had a talent for extended similes and metaphors. "We don't win the audience with logic. We win them with mere charm," he said once.

At the time, the company I worked for had developed complex software to test metals' fatigue characteristics. We used dangerous hydraulic instruments. I needed someone with a technical understanding to write the manual. The source for the science of fatigue crack propagation came from the sudden destruction of bridges, ship hulls, and later airplanes. Under the synchronized march of soldiers or the constant metronome of waves in the sea, small, harmless, microscopic cracks grow in the metal. When a crack reaches a specific size, it becomes unstable and grows at the speed of sound. In seconds, it destroys the bridge or cleaves the ship's hull in two. If the loads and stresses don't cross the boundary for a prolonged time, cracks live, like harmless viruses, inside the structure. The fatigue crack propagation begins when the stresses exceed the design parameters. Then look out. Soldiers get ordered to break their syncopated march over bridges. Designers let the manufacturers of airplane wings know the forces a plane can withstand.

As a courtesy from one countryman to another, I invited him and his wife to our apartment in the South End of Boston. His wife, a trim Belgian lady with a thin, old, wrinkled face, had suspicious eyes. She questioned, "Why invite us?" She had a yellow sweater over her shoulders. The sleeves flopped over her breasts like a French gamine in the 16th arrondissement. In the novel, I changed her nationality to the less neutral Switzerland. I never allowed her to walk with the sweater in the story. I liked her name, Annabelle. Another victim of fiction, I gave her a terminal disease. It proved terminal.

The evening in our loft, we talked over wine. I, all excited, had come from a talk at MIT by a young Bill Gates. In awe, I described how the MIT professors questioned Gates, who was not yet thirty. He listened with interest. Later, while the wives chatted elsewhere, I asked him if he was comfortable with the assignment.

He said yes. He said, "You know, revolutions behave similarly to cracks. Nations can withstand cracks for generations if the stresses don't surpass the limits of the people for extended times.

When they occur, and it takes one crack to grow like the equivalent of the crack in your science, the uprising becomes irreversible."

To my relief, I immediately knew he understood the science; I was not so sure of the politics. My character in the novel sees the rise of women in society as the scientific crack. It recently went supersonic. We met on and off for a few years. Then, my career took off, and I lost touch.

Later, I took a greater interest in the history of modern Iran (I better call it a tad obsessive), and I often thought about his observation. We all look for the cause of significant social upheavals. When variables or cracks multiply, the outcomes become random and unpredictable. I wrote a historical novel. It met with a tepid reception. He wrote me a kind letter, not praise but encouragement. I wrote back.

Thirty years later, a fiction-like device landed on my doorstep. I received a note from Annabelle, Sam's wife. Sam had passed in a home. Could I come and see her in Lexington? I lived in Wellesley. I motored up Route 128. I found a small house up a steep hill in a sparse neighborhood. An old lady with a rod-like carriage opened the door. Large green eyes, not at all suspicious. She welcomed me with a smile and asked me in. The sweater drooping from her shoulder was the familiar element in this tableau.

We drank chamomile around the kitchen table. From the table, I could see into the living room. A shiny grand piano contrasted with the shabby couch and armchairs. She talked to me about her husband. He had developed Alzheimer's five years before and had spent the last year of his life in care. "He died from Covid, thank God," she said. I heard some commotion above me from the second floor. A forty-something woman came downstairs. Out popped the suspicious eyes of a younger woman, a copy of her mother thirty years ago, chunkier and sans sweater. Her mother introduced her as Azar. "Cheri, can you fetch the envelope Papa left for the gentleman?" She went back up and came down. She handed me a manila envelope. I know it all feels concocted, but it is not so dramatic, as I will disclose.

We talked about the early days. "You gave Sam his first job as a technical writer. At first, we had a difficult time in the US. He liked you. He re-educated himself as if he had started from elementary school. All his life, he studied. He studied in the intelligence service like a maniac and later in the US. *Il s'est transformé en homme technique*, a technical man," she emphasized. " When I inquired about his strange career choice in SAVAK, she said, "Ah, well, it is because he had General Pakravan as a mentor. He loved my Sam like a son." She started with "Ah well," all sentences that required an explanation. She saw my overreaction and quickly repaired it. "Sam worked for SAVAK but for the seventh bureau. He analyzed the foreign division. You must understand that under General Pakravan, SAVAK was a proper intelligence-gathering department. Not like what General Nassiri turned it into."

I knew this to be true. The brightest worked at the seventh bureau. Pakravan saved Khomeini's life in 1963. A courteous man, he lunched with Khomeini weekly. I would have liked to be a fly on the wall. Pakravan was one of the first executed without a trial for all his troubles to save Khomeini's neck. I asked her how she and Sam had met.

"Ah well, my parents had opened a small restaurant near the university. I waitressed. My father cooked. My mother minded the till. Sam came to eat there whenever he could. Later, I found out he hated the food." She laughed with pleasure. She showed no bitterness. "He took me to Iran. We lived well until 1979. He had a colonel's rank. He wore civilian clothes. We had a five-year stint in Ankara," she recalled. Unlike MI5 and MI6, or CIA and FBI, SAVAK had both intelligence services under one organization, as Turkey's model did.

I didn't pursue Sam's SAVAK days in the seventies. I should have. We talked. She reminisced about *thé-dansants* in Hotel Ramsar on the Caspian Sea. She told me how they danced at Cheminée and La bohème in the seventies. "I also met the Shah, don't you know? *Mon dieu, il était beau cet homme.*" I have yet to find a foreigner who lived in pre-revolution Tehran and does not remember it with rose-colored irises. "Sam spent a year at Court. It was 1973."

I left but promised to return. "Let me know what he wrote to you," she requested. "I never opened the envelope, you know. *Bon chance.*" Azar had joined her at the door. You could see she disagreed with her mother's strict ethics.

"He wrote small notes to himself throughout his time in the home," Azar said. "I saw some of it. All loopy stuff." I thanked them and drove home to dinner with my wife and daughters.

I didn't open the envelope until the next day. Let me drain the novelistic tension right away. Azar called it—all loopy stuff. The envelope had hundreds of Post-it notes, all yellow and medium size. All of them had a time written in the middle in a shaky hand in Arabic script. Then dozens of notes said "notes to myself," but nothing followed the statement. Dozens of others had the sad comment, "Don't forget," with no follow-up. A note said, "I have been erect for hours." Another note: "I need to be cleaned." Another said, "Statements of fact." Three post-it notes had: "Gilda, mano bebaksh." "Gilda, Mazerat mikham." "Gilda, bitakhsir nistam." They translate to: "Gilda, forgive me." "Gilda, I am sorry." "Gilda, I am responsible." It sounds dramatic now after the novel. It had zero effect on me then. I had never heard of Gilda. I had no intention of writing another historical book after the flop of the first.

Sam interested me. The beauty of the Iranian diaspora is its flat organization. If they are still alive, you can reach the who's who of the ancient regime through two introductions: one or two degrees of separation. I spoke to my darling uncle, who once headed the Central Bank and the Plan Organization. He didn't remember anybody with the name or physical traits. I sent a note to Ardeshir Zahedi, the US ambassador to the Shah, and his brother-in-law. He sent back an acerbic message on the unimportance of a lieutenant. He also underscored that no SAVAK member would be at Court daily. HIM received reports from Nassiri, the head of SAVAK, and sometimes from Fardoust. I wrote to the two writers who knew and wrote the most about the Shah. One answered in the negative. The other didn't respond.

I connected with a college buddy whose father worked for SAVAK during the revolution. We had heated arguments with another college friend who had a religious family. The father had worked in Ankara at some point. The father, an older man, remembered Sam. "My father says he worked for the third bureau responsible for internal security. Did some wet work." My Sam had blood on his hands. No amount of calls or research gave me a clearer picture.

I called Annabelle back. She received me with as much grace

as the last time. Azar also sat with us around the table. A square squat woman, both feet arched on top of her flip-flops. She displayed filthy soles. I took with me the envelope full of sticky notes. I had scanned them with my iPhone. "I thought I would return these notes to you," I said. "Your daughter was correct. The notes have little flow, nor do they say anything to help me understand why he wanted me to have them." I piled the sticky notes in five or six stacks. At the top, I used my note to show the thickest "Time" column. It showed the random hours of the day.

"Ah well," Annabelle said, "I remember. He recorded the time before he napped." When she read "Don't forget," she had tears. She rummaged through the notes, which I had titled miscellaneous. At "Erect for two hours," she laughed uncontrollably. "Oh, Sam," she said to herself. Then, she looked at me and winked. "He didn't kid, you know. He had some condition." Azar flushed with mortification. Even at forty, a parent's sexual allusion embarrasses children. Annabelle then knotted her eyebrows and showed a flash of anger at "I need to be cleaned."

"It was all we could afford. The staff didn't pay attention. Sam was meticulous in his grooming."

I innocently asked her if she knew who Gilda was. She looked at me as if I had been born yesterday. "Of course," she said. "We all knew her; I mean knew of her. She was one of the whores who thought she could displace Her Majesty the Queen as the Shah's wife. She didn't last three months." I then placed the three notes from the bottom of the miscellaneous in front of her. "Can you make heads or tails of why Sam needed forgiveness?"

"No, I can't. But Sam escorted Gilda to Paris and then Germany for one summer. He came back angry. A few months later, they transferred him back to the seventh bureau. General Nassiri gave him a cushy desk job." I couldn't bring myself to press Sam's wife about his time in the third bureau. I asked her one more question: "Where did Sam work in 1973?" He worked directly with the office of Mr. Alam, the court minister.

I began my research into Gilda. I researched Gilda with a zeal characteristic of a historical fiction writer. I paid people who worked for my heroic mother-in-law, a historian and a publisher of note in Tehran, to scour the newspapers, books, and memoirs to gather information about her.

After one of her home visits, my wife brought me an impressive stack of paper clippings and Xeroxed pages. I worked through and discarded repetitions of the same story. The commentary reflected political times before or after the revolution. Before the Islamic Revolution, the stuff of gossip, with a tinge of malice, kept a polite and careful distance. All commentary after the revolution depicted the Shah as a wastrel.

After I eliminated most of the pile, a few scant facts remained. A few reports stretched credibility. At a party, Gilda mimicked the Queen's dress. The Queen slapped the impertinent nineteen-year-old girl. I couldn't use an overdramatic scene when the real Queen never showed the potential for the act; she was a woman of integrity and pathos. More credible material did pop up. In her memoir, the Shah's mother writes that she dissuaded the Shah from marrying the Earth-walking Gilda as a second wife. She writes, "A man should pick a flower from a field and continue his journey." She had experienced an unpleasant life with the old Shah's other wives.

I can't include coincidences in fiction that happen in life. Coincidence in fiction acts like superstition in life. In life, on the

23rd of June 2023, a Friday, I worked hard all week. I wanted to finish the first draft. I hung up my keyboard for the weekend. My wife returned from her studio, telephone glued to her ear. She looked at me and put a common friend on speakerphone. My wife had mentioned my niece, Tala, which led their conversation to Gilda, known as Tala. "Yes," our common friend said, "we know her sister well. I just talked to her. We knew the Azadeh family, who had to change their name after the affair." I, incredulous, asked how Gilda died. "Gilda isn't dead," she said. "She lives in Tehran. She lost her only son and is not doing well."

"The articles found by my mother-in-law discuss her suicide in detail," I said. I felt like someone had shot a friend—my novel, which had kept me company for the year. How unkind and selfish of me, but I needed Gilda dead. Our friend called Gilda's sister in LA. Five minutes later, she confirmed the facts. I didn't sleep well. I worked through the scenes to see if I could fix what I thought was a dead-on-arrival manuscript. Historical fiction meets this pitfall. I introduced a historical character. I betted on the blur of time to give me coverage.

The next day, calmer, I surveyed my emotions in tranquility. I realized I had fallen for facts when my métier was fiction. I needed to double down. My G. had to die. To kill is an action. One sentence does it. Killing is a process that takes a whole novel. I couldn't change my character's fate more than I could bring the Shah back to life. I doubled down. I moved her death scene from the end to the novel's start.

From what I understand, the Gilda of real life lives in Tehran. She mourns her adult son's tragic death in Texas. If she reads these words, my word to her is that at nineteen, any girl, factual or fictional, is a victim when she becomes a plaything of the powerful. I am sorry.

Material on the Shah and Alam and other note worthies exists. When Alinaqhi Alikhani published the volumes of Alam's diaries, hidden in a Swiss bank, the excitement was justified. Our grandees understood that tell-all books don't have happy endings for them or their families.

Our nation does not shine like the British and Americans, with detailed records, memoirs, and biographies. To our shame, we find more information from declassified documents in UK or US libraries than from our archives. My pile of junk on Gilda attests to the dearth of historical records. My mother-in-law has dedicated her life to righting the situation. She also gifted me hundreds of CDs. They contained past copies of the daily newspaper *Ettelaat*. Good coverage of foreign affairs probably borrowed from other papers; thin gruel if you look for internal news. The adverts tell the story of the sixties and seventies. You can watch the spread of the sexual revolution in the ads.

I never doubted the superiority of Western liberal philosophy over the seventh-century Islamic mode of governance. The former evolved in the last five hundred years and continues its sinewy, often close-to-the-line development. It is a work in progress replete with hypocrisy, wars, and crooked and racist biases, but it is undoubtedly alive. The latter, like the Neanderthals' genes in all of us, peppers small genetic material into our modern world of ideas. It arrived at an evolutionary dead end by the end of the twelfth century.

These technocrats, all solid, intelligent, and, yes, patriotic, reinforced each other's narrative of a vibrant country. The country pull itself up by the bootstraps to compete with places like South Korea. All failed to see or understand the cracks. That destroyed the promise of a nation.

ABOUT THE AUTHOR

Born in Iran, the author earned an MFA from the University of New Hampshire. He has published short stories in *The Kenyon* and *Massachusetts Review*. The novel *1001: Persiranian Stories of Love and Revenge* was a critical success, earning reviews such as this:

> *It is rare — truly rare — to find the perfect blend of brilliant writing and great story telling. These books are the ones that settle into our souls, the characters become a part of our extended family, their travails and adventures influence us in unspoken ways, and they make us just a little better as people. Marquez, Allende, Khaled Hossein, Harper Lee... to this list I add Yahya Gharagozlou.*

He currently resides in Wellesley, Massachusetts.